A GLANCING LIGHT

A GLANCING LIGHT

NG LIGHT

AARON ELKINS

CHARLES SCRIBNER'S SONS
NEW YORK

MAXWELL MACMILLAN CANADA
TORONTO

MAXWELL MACMILLAN INTERNATIONAL
NEW YORK OXFORD SINGAPORE SYDNEY

Charles Scribner's Sons
Macmillan Publishing Company
866 Third Avenue
New York, NY 10022

Maxwell Macmillan Canada, Inc.
1200 Eglinton Avenue East, Suite 200
Don Mills, Ontario M3C 3N1

Macmillan Publishing Company is part of
the Maxwell Communication Group of Companies.

This is a work of fiction. Names, characters, places, and incidents either are the product of the author's imagination or are used fictitiously. Any resemblance to events or persons, living or dead, is entirely coincidental.

Library of Congress Cataloging-in-Publication Data
Elkins, Aaron J.
  A glancing light / Aaron Elkins.
    p. cm.
  ISBN 0-684-19278-0
PS3555.L48G5 1991
813'.54—dc20   90-25885

Design by Glen M. Edelstein

10 9 8 7 6 5 4 3 2 1

Printed in the United States of America

With sincere thanks to Jay Gates, the real director of the real Seattle Art Museum, who has all the virtues and none of the faults of his fictional counterpart, Tony Whitehead

A GLANCING LIGHT

A GLANCING LIGHT

CHAPTER 1

"It's perfectly safe," Tony said with his most engaging *would-I-lie?* grin. "There's nothing to worry about, believe me."

Well, of course, that was when the alarm bells began jingling. It wasn't that I didn't trust Tony; it was just that he tended to have his eyes on the end results (or "systemic organizational objectives," as he called them)—so much so that he sometimes failed to perceive the trifling little problems that might lie along the way. And even when he did perceive them, he had been known to gloss them conveniently over. To the eventual sorrow of those who, like me, worked for him.

But the day was not conducive to misgivings. We were on Pier 56, in our shirtsleeves, sitting beneath a table umbrella under a rare Seattle sky of glorious blue, watching the ferries glide sedately out of Elliott Bay and into a sparkling Puget Sound. The good smells of salt water and creosote were in our nostrils, the dry, groaning creak of tied-up ships in our ears. On the round, enameled metal table in front of us were big cardboard buckets of steamed clams and glasses of white wine that we'd carried over from Steamer's take-out counter a few yards away. It was no time for presentiments of gloom.

Not that it didn't occur to me that it wasn't beyond Tony to have orchestrated this: to have waited for just such a bright and blameless day, and to have suggested just such a cheerful lunch spot, in order to spring his rash and risky ideas on me.

"And what about the Mafia?" I asked. "They're bound to be involved in this."

"The Mafia," he said contemptuously, "is a thing of the past. Don't you read the newspapers? Besides, do you think I'd consider it for a moment if there were any danger to you?" When I remained pointedly silent he smiled reprovingly. "Chris, would I?"

"Only if it was for the greater good of the Seattle Art Museum," I said.

I think I ought to explain at this point that Tony Whitehead is one of my favorite people. Almost everything useful that I know about the museum world I learned from Tony. For almost five years I had worked for him at the San Francisco County Museum of Art, and when he accepted the directorship of the Seattle Art Museum five months ago, he asked me along as his curator of Renaissance and Baroque art. I jumped at the chance. One reason was that my long and messy divorce had just concluded, requiring me to sell my Victorian house on Divisadero Street whether I wanted to or not, and I wanted to put that entire part of my life—the San Francisco years—behind me.

The other reason was Tony. He was a first-rate administrator, he gave me breathing room, he trusted my judgment, and hardly a day passed when I didn't learn something from him. But he was a born con man (no small attribute in an art museum director), with a style that was somewhat freewheeling, to put it mildly, and it was equally true that not too many days passed when he didn't have me grinding my teeth over something.

I wasn't grinding my teeth now, but I was worried. "It's not the danger," I said, more or less honestly. "I just don't like the feel of the whole thing. It sounds . . . sleazy. You're asking me to be an informer, to spy on the people I'm dealing with."

"Absolutely not. Far from it. The people you're dealing with aren't crooks. At least let's hope not." He put down a stubbornly closed clam he had been unable to pry open and used a paper napkin to wipe butter from sleek, round fingers. "Look, you're going to be in Bologna anyway, right? You're going to see everybody who's anybody. You're bound to hear things. All they want you to do is meet with their people a few times and pass along anything you hear that might be pertinent. That's all. Is that so terrible? This is a natural for you, Chris. Besides, if I know you, you'd tell them anyway, even without being asked."

"Maybe."

"Of course you would," Tony said comfortably. "You're the most law-abiding person I know. You're ethical. You stop at stop signs when there's nobody around. I've *seen* you."

I knew it was meant as a compliment, and it was true enough, but it annoyed me all the same; coming from Tony it sounded like a character flaw. Besides, who wants to be the most law-abiding person someone knows?

"Maybe, maybe not," I said more defiantly, and swigged at the cold wine.

The "they" Tony had mentioned were the Italian carabinieri, who had contacted the FBI for help. The FBI had in turn gotten hold of Tony, who was always ready to do anything that might bring the museum some favorable publicity. Or just about any publicity. And what we were talking about was a trio of sensational art thefts in Italy twenty-two months earlier. In one, thieves had gotten into the prestigious Pinacoteca Museum in Bologna, making off with a carload of precious paintings: two Tintorettos, a famous Perugino Madonna, and fifteen other highly valuable pictures.

The second break-in had been at the neo-Gothic townhouse of Clara Gozzi in nearby Ferrara. Signora Gozzi, a well-known collector, had been robbed of two portraits by Bronzino and a handsome Correggio nude, along with two other paintings. Her best-known picture, a portrait by Rubens, had been undergoing cleaning at a Bologna restorer's studio at the time, and the discriminating thieves had demonstrated that they knew exactly what they were after by their third burglary, the theft of her Rubens from the restorer's workshop. In accomplishing this, they had apparently been surprised by an elderly night watchman who had paid for his interference with his life.

All three burglaries had taken place on the same night, apparently within four hours of each other. This was not unusual in the highly evolved arena of art thievery. A major theft in a particular area is always followed by an explosion of security precautions on the part of shaken museums and collectors, so that stealing anything else becomes a very risky proposition until things become lax again with the passage of many years. Say, two.

But professional thieves are not patient people. They don't like to wait two years, so they get around the problem by robbing two collections—sometimes three—at virtually the same moment. By the time the first is discovered, the last is already a fact. When brought off successfully, this is always a sign of a highly sophisticated gang. (*Raffles* to the contrary, professional art thieves are never loners. They are always gangs.)

In any event, nothing was heard of the paintings for a year and a half. Then a month ago relatively reliable reports began to trickle in; the Perugino from the Pinacoteca had wound up in Dresden; a Saudi had bought one of signora Gozzi's Bronzinos on the black market for $180,000. And now the art world was boiling with the rumor that the rest of them were about to surface; that is, become available to buyers with ready cash and not too many questions.

The prevailing assumption was that they were still hidden away somewhere in Bologna, and that was how I came into it. For, as it happened, I was scheduled to leave for Bologna the following Sunday anyway, to make the final arrangements for an exhibition that would travel from Italy to museums in Seattle, San Francisco, Dallas, New York, and Washington, D.C. Northerners in Italy, it was to be called; a collection of thirty-two sixteenth- and seventeenth-century pictures that had been painted by Dutch, Flemish, French, and German masters while studying in Italy.

Since it had been my idea in the first place, it had fallen to me to make most of the preparations, and on the following Sunday evening, I would be boarding United 157 to Chicago, there to catch TWA 746 to Rome, and then an Alitalia flight to Bologna's Borgo Panigale Airport. The whole trip would take nineteen hours and I wasn't looking forward to it.

Among the people I would be talking to once I got there would be signora Clara Gozzi herself, who was lending the show a Fragonard, a Van Dyck, and two other paintings from her still-considerable collection; and Amedeo Di Vecchio, director of the Pinacoteca Museum, who was supplying most of the other pictures. And, as Tony said, there was little doubt that I would encounter everybody else who was anybody on the gossipy and rumor-laden Bolognese art scene. (All art scenes are gossipy and rumor-laden.) That, I supposed, was why it was a natural for me. But that didn't make me comfortable with it.

"What about Calvin?" I asked Tony hopefully. Calvin Boyer, the museum's marketing director, would join me in Bologna after I got there, to gather material for press releases or to perform whatever other arcane functions Tony was entrusting him with. "This is more his line, isn't it?"

Not that I had ever been completely clear on what Calvin's line was. But Calvin didn't have friends in Italy who would never trust him again when they learned he'd been passing tidbits of their conversation on to the FBI, or the carabinieri, or wherever they eventually wound up.

"Wouldn't work," Tony said. He ate economically, the way he did everything—spearing a clam, pulling it from its shell with a deft twist, and neatly flicking it into his mouth. "Calvin's going to be there only a few days, and his Italian isn't good enough. Besides, you're already involved."

CHAPTER 2

I was involved, all right. In fact, as my friend Louis, who happens to be a psychotherapist, informed me afterward, I brought the whole thing on myself in the classic mode of the Nietzschean Tragedy. Except, he said, it was more thriller than tragedy.

I don't know about that. It seems to me I may have forged the way for a new art form: the Nietzschean Farce.

It had started the previous Wednesday at a little after five. The museum had just closed, but I was in my office on the fifth floor, working on the catalogue for a Meissen porcelain exhibition that we would be mounting later in the year. Decorative arts are not exactly in my line, but Tony had found out about a summer internship I'd once put in at the Victoria and

Albert Museum in London, and now I was reaping the benefits. It was tedious work. As a curator, I admire Meissen porcelain enormously; who wouldn't? But looking at a roomful of it makes me glassy-eyed after ten minutes, and writing about it makes me positively catatonic.

"Knock-knock." Calvin's voice, from the doorway. I looked up. An interruption was not unwelcome.

Calvin Boyer is a small, nimble man in his late twenties with an interesting face; a little plump, a little bug-eyed, and just a little weasely around the mouth and chin. He always puts me in mind of a shifty rabbit, right down to an upper lip that quivers when he gets excited.

He is bright, hard-working, and upbeat, but there is something oily about him, at least to my eyes; a kind of smug cunning. Like Tony, he's a pitchman, but he lacks Tony's formidable credentials as a scholar. Calvin is the only member of the senior staff who is not expert in some aspect of art. His degrees are in journalism and marketing, and when I work with him I sometimes feel as if I'm on the other end of a salesman's spiel.

Nevertheless, I like him too, quite a lot. My friend Louis implies that this indiscriminate liking of people may signal a problem area. He wonders if it represents a displaced hunger for affection resulting from a failure on my mother's part to breast-feed me. This is something we will never know, because I'm too embarrassed to ask my mother whether she breast-fed me or not. When I tell him this, Louis looks at me darkly, shakes his head, and mutters about infantile repression and the anaclitic redefinition of love objects.

Everybody should have a Freudian psychotherapist for a friend. One's life is simplified tremendously.

I like Louis, too, by the way.

"Chris," Calvin said, "I just got a call from a guy named Mike Blusher. He imports old paintings from Italy, and he says he's pretty sure he's got a couple of genuine Old Masters that got included in his latest shipment somehow. He doesn't have any idea how they got there. He says he never ordered them. He wants somebody to check them out, and they're in your ball park."

This was not as exciting as you might think. Museums get agitated calls about Old Masters found in attics or cellars or furniture warehouses, all the time. In my six years as a curator, only one has turned out to be the real thing, and that was when a garbage collector called the museum in San Francisco to say that he'd found a pair of sculptured wooden hands, clasped as if in prayer, in a trash can, and they looked kind of old.

They were: They were from the workshop of Donatello and they had been part of a wooden altar shrine in Fiesole from 1425 to 1944, when they had been "liberated" by an overly enthusiastic GI who had whacked them off with a rifle butt. After that, they had remained in a cardboard box in his garage for another forty years, until he threw them out. They are now back in Fiesole; one of my more satisfying coups.

The only one like it in six years. "Fine," I said. "If he wants to bring them in tomorrow after three, I'll have a look."

"Well, I told him you'd go on out to his warehouse to look at them."

I laughed. "Are we making house calls now?"

"Look, you can't blame him for not wanting to drive them around in his car. And the guy's a steady patron of the museum, good for twenty thousand a year. I really think you ought to go. I don't suppose you could do it now?"

"No car," I said. I was living in an apartment in Winslow, across the Sound. I took the ferry to the city every morning and walked to work.

"I'll drive you. I'll even spring for dinner when we're done. We could be at Mike's warehouse by about 6:10, and I could have you back for the—" He consulted his watch and pressed some tiny buttons on it. "—for the—mm . . ."

When Calvin consults his watch, it is always something of a production. Calvin is the only person I know who actually sends away for those items you see advertised in airline magazines, and that's where his watch came from; a rectangular, sinister, dull-black thing with two faces. A navigator watch, he once explained to me, outfitted with chronograph, dual LCD display, luminous analog dial, and ratcheted safety bezel. Plus more buttons than I have on my stereo system.

8

"—for the 9:50 ferry!" he said triumphantly. "How's that?"

I nodded. It sounded better than the Meissen. And I certainly didn't have anything else waiting for me that evening, at my apartment or anywhere else. The fact is, I hadn't made the world's greatest adjustment to bachelorhood after ten years of marriage. I guess I hadn't made the greatest adjustment to marriage either, or I wouldn't be divorced.

I locked up the office and we walked to the covered garage at the Four Seasons, where Calvin insisted on parking his car. The rest of the staff parked in the slots behind the museum. Calvin was the sort of person you'd expect to drive a Porsche, and he did, although he claimed with a straight face that it was for reasons of economy. He had owned four, he said, and had sold each of the previous three for more than he'd paid for it. We pulled out onto Fifth Avenue, slowly made our way through the sluggish traffic to Madison, and turned right to jerk and grind our way down the steep incline to Alaskan Way.

"God," Calvin said, "this traffic gets worse every day. It's all you goddam newcomers. It's really hard on my Porsche." To Calvin, it was never his car or his automobile. Only his Porsche.

"I'm from San Francisco," I said. "This seems like a Sunday drive in the country to me. Calvin, what did you mean, this guy imports old paintings from Italy? That's illegal. You can't get an old painting out of Italy without special government permission."

"Well, they're not really old. They're just doctored to look old. He runs a firm called Venezia and he imports bushels of them. The Italian government doesn't give a damn about them."

I looked at him in amazement. "He imports *forgeries?*"

"No, high-class fakes that are baked in an oven or whatever they do to make them look old. They're only forgeries if you try to pass them off as the real thing, right? As long as you label something a copy, it's perfectly legal."

True, but nobody in the legitimate art world is made any happier by knowing that bushels of high-class Old Master copies are floating around. Paintings change hands often and unexpectedly, and what is sold as a replica today has a funny

9

way of turning up on the auction block next year as an original.

"What does he do with bushels of fakes?" I asked.

"He calls them 'authenticated simulated masterpieces,' and he sells them to motels and restaurants who want something classy on the wall for three hundred bucks or under. He also supplies fake antique ashtrays, lamps, mirrors, that kind of thing. From what I understand, he's the main supplier on the West Coast."

"And you can make enough from that to give $20,000 a year to the museum?"

"Are you kidding?" Calvin said with a laugh. "Jeez, Chris, you don't know beans about business, do you?"

I suppose I don't. I'm frequently amazed by the profitability of businesses I didn't even know existed. Who would have thought there was a lucrative market for fake antique ashtrays?

Traffic slowed predictably when we hit the industrial area south of the Kingdome, and we crawled along, avoiding the barriers and piles of broken pavement that mark the city's everlasting waterfront renewal projects. At one point Calvin sneered audibly, and I looked up, startled, but quickly realized it was merely an instinctive comment as we passed the Hyundai terminal.

A little beyond the Spokane Street viaduct Calvin turned left, following an arrow on a rather unpromising traffic sign for "vehicles hauling explosives and flammable liquids." We were now behind the Union Pacific yards, in an area of dusty warehouses and plumbing suppliers.

"You said he had two pictures he thinks are originals?" I said.

"Yup, a Rubens—"

I laughed.

He glanced at me. "What's funny about Rubens?"

"Jeez, Calvin, you don't know beans about art, do you?" I said. "In the long history of art forgery, there have probably been more fake Rubenses than anything else. Half the *real* ones are fakes."

"What's that supposed to mean?"

"Rubens produced a zillion pictures," I explained. "He

invented mass production two centuries before the Industrial Revolution. Two hundred assistants in his workshop, with all kinds of specialties; some did skies, some did walls. The advanced ones did textiles or animals."

"What did *he* do?" Calvin asked with a marketing man's transparent approval. "Besides charge for the finished product, I mean."

"It depended. He had a sliding price scale. So much for the ones he painted all by himself, so much for the ones his assistants did some of the work on, so much for the ones he simply approved. Of course, when you have people like Van Dyck and Jordaens in your workshop, your quality isn't going to be too awful."

"I love it. So you're telling me Rubens wasn't one of those poor bastards who died penniless."

"Not by a long shot. Anyhow, nowadays it's next to impossible to prove beyond doubt which is which, since most of them have his signature. I'd say two-thirds of the 'genuine' Rubenses—even the ones in museums—are arguable."

"But that still doesn't make them forgeries, does it? Not technically."

"No, but it makes it awfully easy for other people to fake them. You see, the most convincing Rubens forgery—or any other Old Master forgery—isn't something that was baked in an oven last week. It's . . . I'm not telling you something you already know, am I?"

"No, this is news to me. So what's the most convincing Rubens forgery?"

"A painting by a reasonably competent but unknown artist from Rubens' time and place. There are plenty of them that have been lying around in basements or hanging in little churches somewhere in Europe for three hundred years. The age would be right, the type of pigments, the kind of canvas, the varnish, the frame, even the style—all perfectly valid Flemish Baroque. All that's needed is a fake Rubens signature, and a five-thousand-dollar painting is suddenly worth five hundred thousand, with any luck."

We had pulled to a stop just off First Avenue South. Behind us was a huge shed of corrugated steel with "Pacific Sheet

Metaling" painted boldly on it. On the building across the street was a mystifying sign saying BUFFALO SANITARY WIPERS. But the one we'd stopped in front of said nothing at all; just a grimy, plain, brown brick warehouse. No, on second glance there was a faded message on the small steel door next to the rolled-down freight entrance: VENEZIA.

"What's the other painting?" I asked Calvin as we climbed out of the car.

"A portrait by Jan van Eyck."

My eyebrows rose. Van Eyck, often but inaccurately called the inventor of oil painting, lived 200 years before Rembrandt and Vermeer, and his technique was so forbiddingly accomplished that few forgers have had the nerve to palm off their own paintings, or anybody else's, as van Eycks. Why bother, when forging Rubens, or Hals, or El Greco, or Corot is so much easier and brings just as much profit?

The upper half of the steel door swung open as we walked toward it. A cool-eyed black man in an olive uniform with AETNA SECURITY on the sleeve impassively watched us approach. I could see the butt of a holstered pistol on his hip. Michael Blusher was taking his Rubens and van Eyck seriously.

"Can I help you gentlemen?"

"I'm Calvin Boyer and this is Dr. Norgren. We're from the art museum. Mr. Blusher is expecting us."

He nodded and unhooked the lower portion of the door, then carefully barred both sections again once we were inside the dreary little vestibule: no furniture; concrete floor with a worn, narrow carpet runner the original color of which was impossible to tell; nothing on the walls but a couple of fly-blown certificates from the building department or the health department, or some such. There was a dank, depressing smell of raw concrete and mold.

"If you gentlemen will follow me." He led us through a door and onto the runner, where it continued along the wall of a cavernous unloading area. The big room was filled with open crates, their contents scattered about the place: not the usual little *Davids* on pedestals, but eighteenth-century gilt inkstands and candelabra, Regency *torchères*, Sheffield urns. And paintings, perhaps three hundred of them: Titians,

Michelangelos, Raphaels, Rembrandts, Watteaus, Fragonards, most of them crackled and darkened and burnished with bogus age. Some of the pieces had a certain slapdash flair to them, but they were far from the first-class fakes I'd been led to expect. I was relieved; nobody with any kind of eye would ever confuse them with the real thing.

We followed the guard up a narrow flight of steps at the end of the corridor.

"Off-duty PD?" Calvin asked him casually.

"You got it."

"Cops call everybody 'gentlemen,' " Calvin explained to me knowledgeably. "I was once in this bar when there was a drug bust. It was great: 'Which of you gentlemen does this little plastic bag of white powder belong to?' 'Charlie, will you take this gentleman's gun?' 'Does anybody here happen to know the name of this gentleman on the floor that I've just had to subdue?' "

The guard was laughing as he tapped on the door at the top of the stairs. OFFICE had once been on it in press-on letters, but they had long ago fallen or been pulled off, leaving pale outlines on the dingy wood.

"The people from the museum, Mr. Blusher," the guard called.

"Send 'em right in, Ned." The answering voice was loud, robust; well matched by the man it belonged to.

Michael Blusher was a broad-beamed, big-boned man in his early forties. Sturdy as he was, he had the puffy, bloated look of someone who had once weighed a great deal more. He jumped up from a wooden swivel chair and came out from behind his cluttered desk, his hand outstretched. I recognized him now. I had seen him once or twice at preview receptions, but we'd never spoken.

"Thanks for coming, guys," he said, pumping my hand, and then grabbed Calvin's. "Great of you to come, Boyer. Believe me, I'll make my appreciation known the next time I write a check to the museum. And next time I have lunch with Tony, I'll be sure and tell him you two came out on your own time as a special favor to me. You guys are the greatest."

"That's wonderful, Mike," said Calvin, who did not seem

13

to find any of this offensive. "Chris, I'm sure you remember Mike Blusher. He's one of our most eminent patrons of the arts."

Blusher shook my hand again and beamed. Then he turned to Calvin with an expression of mock disappointment.

"Hey, I was hoping you'd bring that li'l gal that sits out front in your office with the skirt split up to the gazoo," said the eminent patron of the arts. "The one with the knockers."

Calvin tipped back his head and laughed appreciatively. This was part of his job and he was good at it; a lot better than I would have been. "Debbie's an eight-to-fiver, Mike. She gets paid time-and-a-half for overtime."

"Yeah, what does she get paid for undertime, if you know what I mean?"

Blusher had an interesting style. When he was saying something crass, which seemed to be most of the time, he underlined it with a husky, ho-ho-ho delivery, like Art Carney's old "Norton" character on *The Honeymooners*. "This is just a put-on," he seemed to be saying. "You don't think I'd *really* be this vulgar, do you?"

As you can probably tell, I did not take an immediate, indiscriminate liking to Mike Blusher. Louis, my friend-*cum*-therapist, would have been pleased.

"Well," he said, "let me show you guys what I have. This'll blow you away." He led us to a gray steel cabinet at the side of the room. The impression of a grossly overweight man slimmed down was reinforced; Blusher walked with the flat-footed waddle of a much fatter man.

The cabinet had large, shelflike sliding drawers; the kind of thing that libraries use to store big atlases and some dealers use to store pictures horizontally. Blusher wasted no time. He pulled out the top drawer, and there was the van Eyck; a small, wooden panel no more than twelve inches by ten, with a portrait head of a thin, dour man in a great black hat. The signature written carefully across the entire width of the bottom said *Joannes de Eyck fecit Anno MCCCCXXI. 30 Octobris.* October 30, 1421.

I was impressed. This was an extraordinary piece, a world

away from the monstrosities in Blusher's chamber of horrors downstairs. The man's hat was a soft deep velvet you could almost feel. The background was shadowed and indistinct, but rich with a sense of depth, and the whole was done with something very close to that remarkable combination of darkness and luminosity characteristic of the early Flemish work in oils.

Very close, but not quite on the mark. For it was a fake, as I'd supposed. Brilliantly, painstakingly executed, but fake. In the huge, under-the-table market of rich, gullible buyers, even buyers who knew their van Eyck, it would be worth a fortune. For without the aid of the cumbersome, expensive, and infrequently used technology of science—mass spectrometers, computerized thermographic sensors, multistratal X-ray photography—almost anybody would accept it as genuine. And wealthy private buyers lusting for genuine Old Masters of their own rarely had the nerve to bring in the mass spectrometers. For the same reason people with toothaches don't go to the dentist: If there's a problem, they'd rather not know.

I suppose that all this just might raise a question in your mind. I didn't have a mass spectrometer at hand and wouldn't have known what to do with it if I did. So how did I know after a fifteen-second examination that this was spurious? All I can say is, I knew. I have a friend in Italy, an art professor, who was once pressed as to how he could be sure a certain Titian was genuine. His memorable answer: "I know because when I see a Titian I swoon." I wouldn't go as far as that on the van Eyck, but I knew. After you've lovingly submerged yourself in a field long enough, the judgments that at first had to be carefully reasoned become intuitive. It's no different than an experienced breeder's ability to size up a horse instantaneously, or a master cabinetmaker's way of telling at a glance how good a piece of furniture is.

It's also the reason art authorities often differ so loudly and so publicly over whether such and such a painting is a genuine Degas or Manet or Duccio. But I had no doubts at all on this one.

"This is a forgery," I said. "An extremely good one."

Blusher's heavy face sagged. "But—I mean, *look* at it. I mean . . ." His expression changed from shock to resentment. "How the hell do *you* know? How does he know, Boyer?"

Calvin spread his hands. "He's the expert, Mike."

Blusher turned again to me. The flesh around his lips was a dull, mean purple. "I had Jake Panofsky in here looking at these"—Panofsky was the owner of a reputable gallery near Pioneer Square—"and he said they looked like the real thing, that I should call the museum. And now you—I mean, shit, how do you *know*?"

When you're dealing with eminent patrons of the arts, especially big, hostile ones, you can't be too careful. I was pretty sure that I wasn't going to get by with "I just knew."

Fortunately, beneath that first intuitive response there is always a foundation of solid perception, or there ought to be. And by now I'd been peering at the painting long enough to know what bothered me about it.

"There are several things," I said. "First, the *craquelure*." Foreign art terms, I have found, usually help establish credibility and cow skeptics.

Not Blusher. He made a disgusted face. "The *which*?"

"This crackling in the paint," explained Calvin, who was beginning to pick up a few things about art in spite of himself. "That's what makes it look so old."

"One of the things," I said. "It's hard to make *craquelure* look authentic, and most forgers fall down right there. This is beautifully done, though."

Blusher glowered at me. "Then how do you come off—"

"It's the wrong *kind* of crackling," I said. "Whoever did this served his apprenticeship on canvases, not wooden panels. Take a look at the cracks on this one. Look at a light area— his cheek. Do you see any kind of pattern?"

"No," Blusher grunted after a pause. "Well, a little. It's sort of in circles, like a spider web."

"Exactly. And that's just the way old paint and varnish cracks on canvas. But this is wood, and it's wrong for wood. The surface of a painted wooden panel cracks mainly along the wood fibers, in relatively straight lines, not like this. These cracks are artificially done, Mr. Blusher; I'm sorry."

16

He expelled a long, noisy breath through his nose. "Ah, what the hell. It's not your fault, Norgren." Was he mellowing? I hoped so.

There was more: The picture wasn't painted in van Eyck's style, it was painted to look like his style, and there is a very big difference between the two. Van Eyck's technique was still medieval; each area of a painting was treated like a separate little picture, with no overlapping. And there was no mixing of pigments; each color was applied in a thin, careful coat, one on top of the other, increasing in transparency and saturation. But this panel had been done with easier, quicker techniques that hadn't been invented in the fifteenth century. It was a mark of its excellence that I couldn't be sure whether it had been painted a year ago or a century ago. But definitely not in 1421.

By now I realized what paintings it had been adapted from, for a convincing forgery is seldom hatched full-blown in the forger's mind; it is borrowed from authentic works of the artist. The face was from *A Man in a Red Turban*, but turned to the right instead of the left; the hat was from the great *Giovanni Arnolfini and His Bride*.

Although I tried explaining all this, I don't think I got through to either of them. But Blusher understood enough to walk a few steps away and drop disconsolately onto a frayed sofa, then lower his head and massage his brow with both hands, as if he'd just heard the end of the world was due tomorrow morning.

There was something going on that I didn't understand. "Mr. Blusher—"

"Mike, Mike," he corrected absently, continuing to rub his temples.

"Mike, why is this so important to you? This isn't yours anyway, is it? From what Calvin told me, it's not part of your order. It got included by accident."

"Of course it got included by accident. You saw the crap downstairs. That's what I order. I already called my shippers about this three times, in Bologna. They don't know how it got included, they don't know where it came from, they don't want anything to do with it."

"What's the name of the shipping company?" I asked.

17

"Salvatoro, Salvatori, something like that."

"Salvatorelli?"

Blusher looked surprised. "Yeah, you know them?"

I nodded, not too pleased that I'd guessed right. "We're arranging a show, Northerners in Italy. Salvatorelli's handling the shipping."

"Nice move, Chris," Calvin said out of the side of his mouth.

"They're an old firm," I said unhappily. "They have a good reputation. The Pinacoteca uses them."

"Yeah, well, you better count your Brueghels all the same."

"Anyway," Blusher continued, "they said to go ahead and keep the paintings, as far as they're concerned. They didn't want to be bothered. I got that in writing." His head came up with a sudden shrewd glance. "Of course, I didn't tell them exactly what we got here." Down went his head again, into his hands. "Ah, what difference does it make, if they're fakes?"

"But even if they were real, you couldn't keep them. You'd have to return them to the owner. And even if nobody knew who the owner was, the Italian government would never sit still and let you have them."

"Yeah, sure," he said impatiently. "I was thinking of the publicity."

"Publicity?"

His head came up again to regard me with dull wonder, as if he couldn't comprehend how anyone could be this dense. "Look. I'm in the art business, right? I sell pictures, right? If I really turned up a genuine van Eyck it'd be news all over the country, right?" This time, apparently, he expected a response. He waited.

"Right," I said.

"Sure, right. And that's what we call publicity. If you were buying art from somebody, wouldn't you want to buy it from the guy that discovered the lost van Eyck?"

"I suppose so," I said doubtfully.

He sighed. "You explain it to him, Boyer."

"It's all a matter of marketing," Calvin said soberly to me. "Very important."

Blusher nodded, satisfied.

"Do you mind if I touch this?" I asked.

Blusher shrugged.

I lifted the panel, turned it over, and put it carefully back on the padded shelf, facedown, so the back was visible.

"Just what I thought," I said after a second. "This is real."

Blusher leaped up. "It's re—"

"Not the painting," I said hurriedly. "The panel."

"The panel? You mean the *wood*?" He gave a croak of laughter. "Who gives a shit about the wood?"

"It's not going to get you much in the way of big-time publicity," I said with a smile, "but it's interesting all the same."

I gestured at the back of the panel; it was made of two broad oak planks joined together, then enclosed in the groove of a sturdy, simple frame. "This black marking—like a V with a wreath around it—that's the logo of the Guild of St. Luke in Utrecht, the painter's guild. These cuts in the wood—they're from the way they sawed oak in those days in Holland. It was cut by a water-driven frame saw. Quarter-sawn, you'll notice. Early seventeenth-century, I'm pretty sure."

Calvin looked at me, gratifyingly impressed. "You really know your stuff."

"So?" Blusher said. "What difference does it make?"

"Well, it proves we've got a first-rate forger here; somebody who takes his work seriously. Somehow he's gotten hold of one of the genuine old panels that the guild gave to its members." I smiled. "Wrong century, though. Van Eyck painted in the 1400s. And he did most of his work in The Hague and Bruges, not Utrecht."

"Hey," Blusher said with a slow awakening of interest, "could there be a real painting underneath the damn van Eyck? You know, that got covered up, painted over?"

"Could be," I said. "Somebody probably did paint something on it in the seventeenth century, and the chances are good it's still there. If you're going to forge an old picture you get better results painting over an old one than scraping it off and starting fresh."

"Yeah?" He came closer to peer at the panel. "Is that right?"

"If you're thinking there might be a Rembrandt under there, forget it. That doesn't happen. Nobody paints over Rembrandt. Or Rubens, or van Gogh, or—"

"So sue me," Blusher said. "Excuse me for living. I just asked a question, that's all."

"You could always take it in to have it X-rayed," I volunteered. "We don't do that at the museum, but if you talk to Eleanor Freeman in the radiography department at UW, she'd be able to do it for you."

"Yeah," Blusher said. "Sure. Maybe I'll do that." He smiled good-naturedly, quite mellow now, shook hands with us, and started walking us back across the room. "Well, thanks for coming, big guys. Sorry I dragged you down here for nothing."

He laid his heavy arm around Calvin's slim shoulders. "What I said about that check still goes, buddy. It's not your fault."

"Thanks a lot, Mike. We really appreciate that. Hey, can I ask you something?"

"Shoot."

"If your goods come from Bologna, how come your firm is called Venezia?"

"It's all a matter of marketing," Blusher said with a grin. "If you were selling quality art products would you name your outfit Bologna?"

We all laughed.

"Hey," said Calvin, "we forgot about the other painting, the Rubens."

Blusher clapped his hand to his forehead. "You're right. What do you say, Norgren, you want to take a look as long as you're here?"

"Sure." If the "Rubens" was as well-done as the "van Eyck," I wanted to see it. And after that authentic old panel, I was curious about what this one was painted on.

We went back to the cabinet. Blusher slid in the drawer with the "van Eyck" and pulled out the one below it. In it was a slightly larger painting, not on wood but canvas, in an ornate, gilded Renaissance frame.

I leaned over to have a closer look at the painting itself. I looked hard, just to be sure, but it took me less time to reach a conclusion on this one than on the other. No more than five seconds.

I looked up from it, first at Calvin, then at Blusher.

"It's real," I said. "It's a Rubens."

Not only that, but I knew just which Rubens it was; a loving, exuberant portrait of his second wife, Hélène Fourment, painted in 1630. The pink and pretty Hélène had been sixteen when she'd married the gout-ridden but hearty fifty-three-year-old artist, and some of his most joyous and personal works—no question of student participation here—were portraits of her. This was one of the most charming—all flirty eyes, rosy flesh, and scaffolded bosom.

More important, it was without a doubt the Rubens that had been stolen from Clara Gozzi's neo-Gothic Ferrara townhouse twenty-two months earlier.

CHAPTER 3

So that was how I'd gotten myself involved in the Bologna thefts, at least from Tony Whitehead's perspective, and I suppose he had a point. I thought about it while he went back to Steamer's counter to get us some more wine, and when he came back I had an answer for him.

"I'll make a deal with you."

He brightened. This was the kind of talk he understood.

"I'll brave the Mafia and act as a conduit to the carabinieri, or whatever I'm supposed to do," I said, "if you put that sixty thousand dollars back in the Renaissance and Baroque budget to buy that Boursse."

"No way, Chris. Can't be done. It's too late to reallocate

the budget. Absolutely impossible. I couldn't shake loose a dime."

I was familiar with Tony's style. I waited.

"Maybe twenty thousand," he allowed after a few seconds.

I waited. I sipped my wine and watched the sea gulls. What we were negotiating for was enough money to buy a small domestic painting by Esaias Boursse, a nearly unknown seventeenth-century Dutch painter. Most of his work deserves its obscurity, but occasionally he created paintings of stunning beauty. Some of them were believed for decades to be by Vermeer, which gives you some idea.

The one I had in mind was owned by Ugo Scoccimarro, who was on my list of people to see in Italy, inasmuch as he was lending us four paintings for the exhibition. I had seen the Boursse several years before—an interior domestic scene, exquisitely done—and asked Scoccimarro if he would consider selling it. To my surprise he had said yes, as long as it was to a museum. The price was a nominal $60,000.

This year I had finally gotten Tony to include it in our acquisitions budget, only to have the money snatched away for something else a few weeks later. It was a common enough occurrence; I had merely sighed and put it out of my thoughts. But I was reminded of it when I went to Michael Blusher's warehouse. The panel on which the fake van Eyck had been painted was much like the panel on Scoccimarro's Boursse, which I had previously examined and researched thoroughly. (That was how I happened to know all about the marks made by seventeenth-century water-driven frame saws, etc., not that I'd tell Blusher. Or Calvin, for that matter.)

So the Boursse was on my mind again, and it had belatedly occurred to me that there might be a way to get it after all.

"All right," Tony said, "all right. Maybe I could get you thirty."

"Thirty's no help. It has to be sixty."

Tony examined me over the rim of his wine glass, his eyes narrowed against the sun. "You used to be such a nice kid," he mused. "When did you get to be such a wheeler-dealer?"

I grinned. "Been taking lessons from the best of them, boss."

He smiled back. "Okay," he said. "It's a deal."

U*n cappuccino doppio, per piacere,"* I called to the white-jacketed barman who stood leaning against the wall and looking, if possible, sleepier than I was.

"Va bene, signore, subito."

Like a mechanical toy that had just had a coin inserted into it, he jerked to life at his espresso machine, an imposing rococo apparatus of chrome tubes, levers, and spouts that sat in gleaming splendor on the marble countertop. He placed a cup the size of a bucket under a spout and slowly, with fierce, firm-jawed concentration, pulled down one of the long levers. With a faint, drawn-out hiss of steam the velvety aroma of good coffee suffused the cafe, and the big cup was half-filled with espresso as black as ink. A generous dollop of milk was tossed, not poured, into a metal pitcher and held up to another spout, thin and snaky, and still another lever was depressed. There was another hiss while the pitcher was rotated and jiggled, and in a few seconds the milk was a steaming froth. The barman topped off the cup with it, then lifted a shaker of shaved chocolate and glanced keenly at me for further instructions. At my nod the chocolate was sprinkled over the milk with a showman's flourish and the completed production was borne to the table.

"Grazie," I said.

"Prego, signore."

He went back to station himself behind the bar and, with a sigh, leaned against the wall once more, exhausted by his efforts. The internal mechanism switched off to await the next customer. All was still.

Ah, Italia. It was nice to be back. Not that there was any shortage of espresso bars in Seattle these days, but for the real drama, the true spectacle, of cappuccino-making, you had to come to the mother country.

It was Monday, a little after 4:00 P.M. Italian time; seven in the morning by my biological clock, and I hadn't slept the night before, what with long, gritty layovers in Chicago and

Rome. (Is it my imagination, or was there a time in the remote past, a time without "hubs," when you could actually fly directly from one place to another?) There was going to be a "small, informal" reception and dinner for me in three hours, and I was trying to perk up my sluggish nervous system with a fix of caffeine. I was also concentrating on an article in the *International Herald Tribune*, which I'd picked up at the airport and skimmed during the taxi ride to Bologna.

The piece began on an inside column on page four, and I'd overlooked it in the taxi, but it had my total attention now.

STOLEN RUBENS ON WAY BACK TO ITALY

Seattle—Peter Paul Rubens' *Portrait of Hélène Fourment*, conservatively valued at $1,500,000, will soon be back in the hands of its Italian owner, Clara Gozzi, almost two years after its disappearance from a Bologna restorer's workshop.

The theft of the Rubens, one of a trio of art burglaries in and around Bologna in the early morning hours of June 22, 1987, resulted in the murder of Ruggero Giampietro, 71, a night guard at the workshop. Along with five other paintings stolen from Mrs. Gozzi's palatial Ferrara home and some eighteen from Bologna's Pinacoteca Nazionale, the picture had been the object of a frustrating international search effort.

The seventeenth-century masterpiece was discovered unharmed by Michael Blusher, 46, a Seattle importer of objets d'art.

I paused. Just how reliable was this article? Could a reporter who referred to the stuff that Blusher imported as "objets d'art" be trusted? I took my first long, grateful swallow of coffee and continued reading.

Mr. Blusher, president of Venezia Trading Company, found the painting last week in a large shipment from Bologna.

Attempts to determine how it got into the shipment have met with defeat.

"I knew right away I had something special," Mr. Blusher said. "The first thing I did was get a guard, which I paid for out of my own pocket. Then I yelled for help."

The help arrived in the form of Christopher Norgren, 34, Curator of Renaissance and Baroque Art at the Seattle Art Museum. Mr. Norgren immediately identified the two-by-three-foot picture as the stolen Rubens, a determination subsequently verified by other art authorities. American and Italian customs agencies have worked together to minimize bureaucratic delay, and Mrs. Gozzi's agents have already arrived in Seattle for the purpose of bringing the painting back. Mr. Blusher will receive a substantial reward, according to a spokesman from Assicurazioni Generali of Milan, which insures Mrs. Gozzi's collection.

A second object unexplainably included in the shipment was a panel bearing the purported signature of the fifteenth-century Dutch artist Jan van Eyck. This was denounced by Mr. Norgren as a forgery, although he identified the wood on which it was painted as an authentic Dutch art panel several hundred years old.

None of the twenty-four other paintings from the three thefts has been reliably located, although rumors abound. The total value of the missing objects is in the vicinity of $100,000,000.

Thoughtfully I put down the paper. I am not by nature distrustful of others. I may not be as gullible as I used to be (a good no-holds-barred divorce has a way of curing that), but I'm far from a suspicious person. All the same, I began to wonder, in an unfocused way, about Blusher. During the time that Calvin and I had been in his warehouse, I had had the uncomfortable feeling that we were being used, that he wasn't being quite honest with us. Was it the reward he'd been after, and not the publicity? We were by no means dealing with peanuts: The standard insurance reward in art-theft cases was ten percent of the value of the object. So if the Rubens was really valued at $1,500,000, which did indeed seem conservative, Blusher would come away from this richer by $150,000.

I swallowed the last of the cappuccino and sat a while longer, pondering. Then I went to my room in the Hotel Europa to shower, and to try to nap for an hour before the reception.

But sleep wouldn't come. I couldn't stop thinking about Blusher's $150,000 reward. I tossed irritably on the bed. Well, what about it? He deserved it, didn't he? Who knew where the Rubens would be by now if not for him? He'd found it, he'd had the perception to recognize it as something important, and he'd immediately contacted the museum. If Gozzi's insurance company wanted to give him a fraction of the money he'd saved them, what was wrong with that? Nothing at all. It happened all the time.

Just what did I think I suspected him of anyway?

Bologna la Grassa—Bologna the Fat—they called it in the fourteenth century, and Bologna la Grassa they call it still. The words refer to the richness of the fare, but they might just as well apply to the richness of life in general, or to the people, who are so much more robust and hearty than their dark, lean cousins in the south that they seem to be from a different country. (Talk to the Bolognese and you get the impression that they are. Africa begins just below Rome, the northerners like to say.)

In the surrounding countryside are some of the aristocrats of Italian capitalism: Ferrari, Maserati, Lamborghini. Riunite, too. And in Bologna itself the boutiques tucked away among the arcaded, medieval streets display fashions that rival Rome's, and the cuisine in the grand old restaurants is the finest (and among the most expensive) in Italy, which is saying something. What makes it all so peculiar is that Bologna is Italy's center of leftist politics, and has been for forty-five years. It is a rare tourist here who realizes that he is doing his shopping and gourmandizing in the largest Communist-run city in the Western world.

Certainly you could never tell from looking at the decor, the menu prices or the flashy crowds in the Ristorante Notai, currently the foremost restaurant in Bologna and therefore, arguably, in Italy. It was here, in a private room, that the "small, informal" reception and dinner in my honor was held, courtesy of the Pinacoteca Nazionale, Bologna's most prestigious art museum, and co-sponsor of Northerners in Italy.

My experience with receptions in my honor is pretty limited, but I have to admit I don't seem to have any moral or constitutional aversion to them; as a matter of fact, I haven't been to a bum one yet. This one was no exception, although I found myself wishing I'd had a chance to catch up on my sleep first, and maybe my Italian too; I was having a hard time following the volatile conversation (a couple of Camparis to start with hadn't helped any). In any case, I was relieved when dinnertime came and I was seated at a small table with three old acquaintances who took pity on me and spoke English.

The topic of discussion was the one everybody had been talking about all evening: the finding of Clara Gozzi's Rubens. Of course, I had telephoned her the previous week, as soon as I'd left Blusher, but to my surprise the news hadn't gotten around to anyone else here until its appearance in today's papers, perhaps because Clara was something of a recluse. She lived in Ferrara, some thirty miles away, and didn't often mingle in the Bolognese mainstream.

"What do you think, Christopher? You've met this Blusher." Amedeo Di Vecchio, Cinquecento scholar and eminent director of the Pinacoteca Nazionale, looked up from his *tortellini di erbetta* and squinted penetratingly at me through rectangular, gold-rimmed glasses that sat crookedly on a long, pinched nose. "Is he involved in some way? Is he a crook?"

"I don't know, Amedeo," I said, as if the question hadn't been nibbling at my mind too. "I only met him once. I wouldn't say I'd trust him with my life, but as to his having any part in the thefts . . ."

Max Cabot's rolling chuckle drowned me out. "Mike Blusher? Impossible. Don't give it another thought. I've met the man too. Sold him a few things, as a matter of fact."

That surprised me. He and Blusher were unlikely business associates. Max was an expatriate American who had lived in Bologna for over a decade, and had made a niche for himself as a respected art dealer and restorer. He was good too, a former conservator at the Boston Museum of Fine Arts. His work was sought-after and correspondingly expensive. So were the pictures he sold.

"I would have thought your stuff wasn't quite his style," I said.

"This was two or three years ago, Chris. Blusher was just starting out in the art world. No shortage of money, though. He bought a few lots of eighteenth-century Venetian pictures at one of my auctions. Second-rate *vedutisti*, mostly, but expensive. I got the distinct impression he didn't have any idea what he was doing." He laughed. "I understand he's into a somewhat different level of quality now."

I thought about the two dozen or so identical "Rembrandts" in the warehouse in Seattle, each one lathered with a quarter-inch of gluey, caramel-colored, guaranteed-to-crackle-within-two-days varnish. "You could say that," I said.

"Two or three years ago?" Di Vecchio said sharply. "He was here when the Rubens was stolen? His sinewy neck tilted eagerly forward. This was not mere curiosity on his part. The Pinacoteca had lost eighteen of its most precious paintings that night.

Max frowned. "Well, let's see.... The Venetian paintings were knocked down, oh, some time in April 1987. Or maybe May? The thefts weren't until June twenty-second and as far as I know he was long gone."

Max's certainty about the latter date was understandable. It had been from his workshop, where it had been undergoing restoration, that Clara Gozzi's Rubens had been stolen.

"But he *could* have been here," Di Vecchio persisted.

"No, you can forget it, believe me. Whoever took those paintings knew what they were doing. They were selective. Only the best. They didn't take any junk, either from me or Gozzi or the Pinacoteca. Nothing but the best."

"The Pinacoteca Nazionale," Di Vecchio said severely, "does not have 'junk.' "

Max laughed appreciatively. "Well, I do, or did at the time. I had four eighteenth-century canvases of very dubious provenance in the basement for cleaning. You know, 'School of

Somebody' kinds of things. They were sitting about five feet from the Rubens, and to an uninformed eye they would have looked every bit as good. But only the one painting was taken. That kind of discrimination would have been beyond Blusher, I'm afraid."

Di Vecchio made a tight, irritated little movement with his mouth. "I'm not suggesting he carried it out personally, my dear Massimiliano. But he might have had something to do with it."

Max shrugged amicably. "Could be, Amedeo." Behind his soup-strainer of a mustache he chewed contentedly on a mouthful of tortellini.

Amedeo Di Vecchio and Max Cabot made an interesting study in contrasts. If someone asked you to guess by looking at them which was a son of Emilia-Romagna and which of Durham, New Hampshire, you'd answer without hesitation, but you'd be wrong. Di Vecchio was a bony six-two, a pallid, Yankeeish-looking man with a short, carroty Abraham Lincoln beard beginning to show some grizzling at its none-too-carefully groomed edges. Max was three or four inches shorter and thirty pounds heavier, graying and running comfortably to fat these days, with a smooth, padded complexion that made him look as if he'd been reared on tagliatelle and olive oil.

They were opposites in temperament, too. Max was easygoing and easy to be around, radiating satisfaction with his life. Di Vecchio was dour, itchy, critical, with a febrile glitter to his eyes like an Old Testament prophet's, at least if you can believe Bellini or El Greco.

"Well," our other tablemate said in his rich baritone, "at least we can be grateful that the painting's safe, what do you say?"

The speaker was Benedetto Luca, Regional Superintendent of the National Ministry of Fine Arts. Despite his imposing title, I had never gotten his precise function quite straight. But he had been extremely helpful in tunneling through the bureaucratic maze—sometimes terrifying, sometimes slapstick— that had to be negotiated in getting the thirty-two paintings in Northerners in Italy out of the country for a year. He was, therefore, a man of power and fortitude, and he was made for the part: white, leonine mane; patrician nose; craggy, lined face; voice as mellow and subtly colored as a bassoon.

The impression he made was so commanding, so mesmerizing, in fact, that I had known him for a year before I realized I had never heard him say anything intelligent, let alone profound. It was one banality after another—but, ah, what style.

"God willing," his resonant voice continued with conviction, "we'll get the others back, too."

"I hope so, *dottore*," Di Vecchio said absently. As host, he topped off our glasses with delicate, fruity red wine; Zuffa Sangiovese, locally made, and as pleasant and relaxing a wine as Italy produces.

By now the pasta course had been removed and the main dish brought: *cuscinetti di vitello*, veal scallops stuffed with prosciutto and cheese. The reverence with which the waiter and his assistant set it down made it clear that we were to give it our full attention, at least for a while, and we complied willingly. We concentrated on our plates and made discreetly appreciative noises.

That is, most of us did. Di Vecchio wasn't the type to murmur agreeably over food. For him, eating was a necessity, and from the looks of it, a grim one. He chewed in silence, slowly and methodically, sweating slightly, his mind somewhere else, his jaw ligaments shifting and cracking. Periodically, the fork was forced between closed lips, carrying one morsel of food at a time, at an unvarying rate; swallow one piece, shove in another, chewing rhythmically all the time, on the principle of the revolving garbage crusher.

Max, expectably, had a different approach. He was a man who enjoyed the pleasures of the table, and he made no bones about it. There were lip-smackings, eye-rollings, sighs of pleasure, exclamations. The food was tossed into his mouth with quick, happy little flips of the fork, which he held upside down in his left hand, European style (less time wasted that way). And all the while he managed a stream of cheerful chatter.

Dr. Luca had his own modus operandi, too, masticating slowly and weighing each mouthful with grave, head-tilted deliberation. The stock in which the veal was simmered—a trifle too salty? No, on second thought, quite good. The wine stirred into the drippings—is it not too, er, austere? No, no, on second thought, quite fine. Perfect, in fact. He seemed to be doing more cogitating than eating, but somehow the food was disappearing as fast as Max's.

Have I stumbled on a new psychological principle? Are people's eating styles extensions of their personalities? I'll have to ask Louis what he thinks. I know he enjoys my theories of psychology every bit as much as I enjoy his on-the-house counseling sessions.

After a few minutes the conversation came back to the theft of the Rubens. "You know what I keep thinking about?" Max asked. "I keep thinking about all the inside knowledge they needed. Somebody had to know the picture was in my shop at the time; somebody had to know exactly how to get by my door and window sensors, how to dismantle both security systems—"

"Who would know such things?" Di Vecchio asked. He looked uncomfortable. Somebody had known such things about his museum, too.

"I wasn't very smart about it," Max said with some bitterness. "A lot of people knew. Well, a few. Five, to be exact. I've gone over it a thousand times in my mind. Five people. The only thing they didn't know was that poor Ruggero would be there." Ruggero Giampietro was his longtime night watchman, an old friend hired whenever there was something particularly valuable in the shop. "So they killed him." He chewed steadily. "Or maybe they did know."

"A terrible thing, terrible." This from Dr. Luca, of course.

"*I* was familiar with your security arrangements," a prickly Di Vecchio pointed out. "I helped you plan them. Am I one of your five?"

"Sure," Max replied equably, "but I doubt if you did it." He followed this with a happy chuckle.

Di Vecchio was amused, but just barely. "I'm extremely happy to hear it."

I made my first contribution in a while. "Max, this list of suspects . . . Surely the police followed up on it?"

The look that passed between the three of them was hard

to describe but impossible to misinterpret. A swift glance that managed to combine amusement, derision, awareness of secret knowledge, and cognizance of the venality of mankind—especially official mankind. All very Italian; done with the merest flick of an eyebrow, the faintest of shrugs, the most minute contraction of the lips. Even Max did it as if he were born to it.

"The police were bought off?" I said to show them it hadn't gotten by me.

"Who can say for sure?" Luca asked rhetorically. "Let us simply say that Captain Cala strutted furiously upon the stage, producing sound and fury, but in the end signifying nothing."

Despite the garbled paraphrasing, it was the meatiest thing he'd said all evening. And beautifully delivered.

"Captain Cala," Di Vecchio muttered with a snort of contempt. "Well, he's been removed now, and it's about time. I hope this Colonel Antuono who's coming is better, but I have no high hopes."

"I do," Max said, "I have an appointment with him the day after tomorrow."

Me too, I almost blurted out. Colonel Cesare Antuono was the man I was supposed to contact on Wednesday, according to Tony's instructions. I caught myself in time and kept it to myself. Not because I didn't trust them, but because Antuono would no doubt expect a report on the conversation we were having at that very moment. And I would no doubt give him one. Ratting on people, I thought miserably, would be easier if they didn't know about it.

"I think we'll find him a different sort, Amedeo," Max continued. "He's a big wheel, you know; a deputy director of the carabinieri's art theft unit. He's the one who got back those Pisanellos from Verona."

"Certainly, he has a fine reputation," Luca agreed wisely. "They call him the Eagle of Lombardy."

Di Vecchio gulped some wine, and snorted again. "And how much of the ransom from the Pisanellos found its way into the Eagle's own pockets, do you suppose?"

"Well," Max said with warmth, "I'm sure going to give him a chance." He swallowed the last of the wine, wiped his lush mustache with the back of a finger, and refilled his glass. Max could tipple with the best when it came to good wine, and he had already put away quite a bit of the Sangiovese. While he wasn't exactly smashed, his gestures had grown more expansive, his voice louder. A thin sheen of sweat glistened on his forehead.

"I'm really going to give him an earful," he declared, loosening his belt a notch. "There's a lot I can tell him."

The look that passed between Di Vecchio and Luca was a dark one this time. Di Vecchio glanced warily around at the other tables. Luca slowly licked his lips, frowning.

Di Vecchio laid a slim, cautionary hand on Max's forearm. "Massimiliano, you have to be careful. You can't go around shouting things like that."

"Someone might overhear," Luca said.

"I'm not shouting," Max said, and promptly lowered his voice. "Well, maybe a little. Anyway, what do I care if people overhear? I haven't made a secret of it." He made an impatient gesture. "Am I the only one who wants the rest of those pictures found?"

Di Vecchio made soothing noises. "Of course not. We don't say you shouldn't cooperate with the police. Don't you think I'm going to cooperate? But do you see me going around advertising it?"

"Think," Luca said somberly. "Think about what happened to Paolo Salvatorelli, God rest his soul."

"Paolo Salvatorelli?" I repeated. "Is he connected with Trasporti Salvatorelli?"

"Of course," Luca said. "The two brothers founded it; Paolo and Bruno."

At this point I got what is commonly, and accurately, referred to as a sinking sensation. Trasporti Salvatorelli was the firm I was counting on to ship thirty-two paintings worth over $40,000,000 from Italy to the United States. I had an appointment with them on Friday to confirm the arrangements and sign the papers. They had been recommended unreservedly by Max, who did most of his shipping through them, and by the Pinacoteca and the Ministry of Fine Arts—that is to say, Di Vecchio and Luca—both of whom had a lot more to lose than I did, since most of the paintings belonged to the state. Luca had, in fact, generously assigned one of his deputies to the onerous chore of grinding through the preliminary paperwork with Salvatorelli, which would have otherwise fallen to me. For this, I probably owed him my sanity.

So far, I had no cause for complaint, but lately the Salvatorelli name seemed to be cropping up in ways that did nothing for my confidence. Accidentally shipping Clara Gozzi's Rubens to Blusher without even knowing they had it, for example. And now, if I was understanding Luca, one of the two brothers who ran the firm had been done in by the Mob. You will understand when I say that I was starting to get just the least little bit apprehensive.

"What *did* happen to Paolo?" I asked woodenly.

They explained. It was a matter of common supposition that the Salvatorelli brothers had some knowledge of the art thefts of two years earlier—

I came halfway out of my chair. "*What?* We're trusting those paintings to—"

Luca's sonorous, calming laughter bathed me. "*Knowledge* of," he said. "That is not to imply any *connection* with. They are simply in a position to hear things, you understand."

"They're wholly reliable," Di Vecchio said. "We've used them many times. "We've trusted our Guido Renis to them, and our Raphael. There's no cause for concern, believe me."

I settled back, not entirely pacified, while Luca, with some help from Di Vecchio, filled in the pieces: Despite these suppositions of "knowledge," the notorious Captain Cala, for all his sound and fury, had been no more inclined to seriously pursue the subject with the Salvatorellis than with anyone else. But Colonel Antuono was a different matter, and expectations had risen that the brothers would be subjected to painstaking interrogation when he took over. There were even rumors that Paolo had set up a secret contact with Colonel Antuono on his own. At that point the underworld had taken matters into its own hands.

Max brought this lengthy story to its point. "He was shot," he said to me with a shrug.

"Killed," Luca emended gravely.

"Not merely killed," Di Vecchio said, his small mouth twisted by a grimace of repugnance. "He was found in the Margherita Gardens with a cork stuffed between his lips. There were one hundred and sixteen bullets in his body."

"My God," I said.

"I have a friend," Luca said, his creased face grim, "the physician in charge of the mortuary. He told me that the bullets fell out of his body and rattled on the table like beads from a rosary." He let the unsettling image sink in a moment. "And now, of course, his brother, Bruno, will say nothing. Who can blame him?"

But even this wasn't enough to subdue Max entirely. "Look," he said, "nobody would hurt me. Paolo Salvatorelli was *one* of them. Everybody knows that. He could tell secrets, inform on them, break the code—"

Di Vecchio stiffened in the way that many Italians do when the Mafia comes into the conversation, even indirectly. "The code?" he repeated coolly. A long time before, he had made a point of telling me that the long arm of the Mafia no longer reached to Bologna. "The spirit and collective solidarity of the cooperative movement have eliminated it here," he had informed me. Amedeo Di Vecchio frequently sounded like the dedicated Communist he was.

"Hell, forget it," Max mumbled, a little bellicose now. "Don't worry about me, I can take care of myself just fine." He got up to head for the restroom with the doggedly straight, precise stride of a man who's had too much to drink and is therefore bent on showing how steady he is on his feet.

"Ah, but can he take care of himself?" Luca asked doubtfully, watching him go. "Massimiliano has many virtues, but is prudence one of them?"

"Oh, I think Max is pretty prudent," I said. "He's had a little wine tonight, but—"

"When the theft at the Pinacoteca occurred," Di Vecchio interrupted, "the first thing I did was to telephone the other local museum directors and some of the more prominent gallery owners to tell them to be on their guard. These things often occur in clusters, you know."

"I know."

"I awoke Massimiliano from sleep. When I warned him he could be next, his response was to laugh." Di Vecchio allowed himself a thin, retributive smile of his own. "The only painting of value in his shop, he informed me, was Clara's Rubens, and it was unlikely that the thieves would know about that or even bother with it, given the riches they had already helped themselves to at the museum. No, they were probably already on their way to Rome. What did he do? Nothing. He went back to sleep, simply leaving the useless Giampietro to his task." He twirled his wine glass irritably by the stem. "Do you call that prudence?"

"No, indeed," Luca answered for me.

"What about Clara Gozzi?" I asked. "Did you warn her?"

"No," Di Vecchio said defensively. "Why would it occur to me they would go to Ferrara?"

Max came back looking fresher. He'd washed his face and dampened and combed his hair, and I caught a whiff of the cologne the Notai stocked in its restroom.

He was more conciliatory, too. "Look," he said amicably, "all I meant was, what can I do that anyone would be so afraid of? I don't have any inside secrets. I can just tell what happened to me, that's all—the same as you. It's my duty. They're not going to go around killing ordinary citizens."

Luca waved a magisterial hand. "It makes no difference. These policemen are all the same, you'll see. One way or another this Colonel Antuono will line his pockets."

He let go a deep sigh. "*O tempera!*" he said. "*O mores!*" Understandably, he did better with Cicero than with Shakespeare.

CHAPTER 4

With Luca's Ciceronian world-weariness the evening's energy seemed to fizzle out. Conversation tapered off at the other tables as well, and people began coming up to wish me good night, to thank Di Vecchio for the dinner, and to pay their respects to Luca, who accepted them in kingly fashion.

Among them was Ugo Scoccimarro, one of the three contributors—along with the Pinacoteca and Clara Gozzi—to Northerners in Italy. He was also the owner of the Boursse I was hoping to get for Seattle. I was surprised to see him there at all. The thickset, balding Scoccimarro, a native Sicilian, had complicated things for me by moving from nearby Milan, where he'd lived for three years, back to Sicily several months before; I was planning to fly down there to settle things with him before I left Italy. But as it turned out, he was in Milan on business, and when word had gotten to him about the reception, he had taken the two-hour train trip to Bologna.

Scoccimarro was an extraordinary being in the world of art collectors; a peasant in the literal sense of the word. Like his father and grandfather, he had provided meager and toilsome sustenance for his family by making olive oil, growing almonds, and keeping a few sheep for the production of romano cheese, which he made himself twice a year. Then providence had smiled. The Aga Khan had decided to put up a condominium development on the Strait of Messina, and Ugo Scoccimarro's rocky eleven acres on the coast near Scaletta Zanclea just happened to be the perfect spot for it. Smooth-talking representatives in suits and ties had appeared at Scoccimarro's decrepit stone farmhouse one day in 1967 to ask him what he wanted for the land. The flabbergasted, twenty-three-year-old Ugo got up his nerve and stammered out a demand for fifty times what he thought it was worth, then almost fainted when it was accepted on the spot; no arguments, no bargaining.

He had slapped his forehead and grinned when he told me the story. "I could have asked for ten times more." But it had been enough to start him on a remarkable career.

Ugo had turned out to be a shrewd businessman, putting his money first into country land, then into commercial developments in Catania, and finally into the production of an aperitif called Jazz!. This was one of those awful medicinal concoctions the Italians seem actually to enjoy. Made from olives and almonds, and based on a family recipe, it was an immediate success. Reluctantly, Ugo had moved to Milan to build his new factory; it was the only place he could find the technical skills he needed.

Some years ago he had gone to an auction and bought himself a ready-made art collection of twenty-five paintings, mostly of the Utrecht School, a group of seventeenth-century Dutch artists who had come to Rome as students and been heavily influenced by Caravaggio. Ugo had bought them as an investment, he said, but although they had quadrupled in value in nine years, he had never tried to sell one, as far as I knew, although he'd bought a few more. The truth of the matter, I thought, was that Ugo Scoccimarro, former tiller of the soil, was thrilled at being a gentleman art connoisseur, and saw little need to make any changes. The day I had asked him if he would lend some of his pictures to the exhibition, he had swelled before my eyes and practically floated away like a helium-filled balloon.

The reason I hadn't seen him during the reception, he explained now, was that he had just arrived. His train had been delayed for two hours before it ever got out of Milan. Knowing he was going to be late, he had eaten en route in the dining car. He was lucky to have made it at all.

The others clucked at his misfortune; he had missed a fine dinner. But I thought I knew better. Ugo Scoccimarro, like many a self-made man before him, was of several minds about his social position. On the one hand, he was pugnaciously proud of his peasant background. On the other, he was often desperately insecure. I knew him, for example, to be uneasy about his table manners. He was happiest with a napkin tied around his neck, a tumbler of wine at his elbow, and a plate of pasta in front of him (which he preferred to eat with the help of a spoon), and he went to considerable lengths to avoid dining among the gentry. I didn't doubt that his missing dinner was premeditated.

He grinned warmly at me, his brown teeth as square and sturdy as the painted ones on a German nutcracker. "Ah, Cristoforo, I'm glad to see you." He spoke Italian with a broad Sicilian accent that I had seen lesser men sneer at behind their hands. "My train doesn't leave until after midnight. Let's go and drink a brandy somewhere."

I was ready for bed, not brandy, but what could I do? Ugo had made a four-hour round-trip just to see me. Besides, after an evening of Di Vecchio's acerbic opinions and the disembodied locutions of Doctor Luca, his robust, down-to-earth conversation would be a relief.

"Fine," I said. I gestured toward the upstairs bar, where some of the others were already heading. "Why don't—"

"No, no." He squeezed my arm and drew me aside. "Somewhere away from all the *gran signori*."

Max overheard. "I hope that doesn't exclude me," he said in Italian.

Ugo clapped him on the back. "No, no, certainly not. Would I accuse you of being a gentleman?" He bellowed with laughter and I realized he too had tossed down a few glasses. "Come on," he said, "I know a place on Via d'Azeglio. Just the three of us. Old friends."

We spent almost an hour in the Bar Nepentha, where the woman at the piano serenaded us with "Smoke Gets in Your Eyes," a Scott Joplin medley, and similar old Italian favorites. Most of what we talked about I don't recall (I'd had quite a bit myself by then), but I remember how happy Ugo was, telling us about the modern house he'd bought in Sicily on the slopes of Aci Castello, overlooking the Ionian Sea, a few miles from Catania. He was immensely relieved to have left Milan's genteel, cosmopolitan atmosphere, where he'd lived restlessly for seven years, a fish out of water.

"Ah, it's so beautiful there," he told us rapturously. *Bellissimo, meraviglioso*. "The air is clean, the people are real, a word means what it means. A man knows where he stands." He patted the back of my hand. "You have to come down and see. My pictures are in a wonderful room, all natural light from the north. You too, Massimiliano. Hey, why don't you open up a shop in Catania? Wide streets down there, not these little alleys. And no Communists around to look at you funny because you make a few lire."

Max laughed. "I know; just the Mafia. No, I'm glad for you, Ugo, but I like it right here."

He more than liked it. He had fallen in love with northern Italy on his first visit, and for fifteen years had dreamed and planned until he could move there. Now, as far as I knew, he never planned to leave, an Italianophile to the core. He had married a petite, black-haired woman from Faenza, but she had died of cancer about two years before. Max had been stunned with grief. I realized suddenly that this was the first time since then that he'd seemed anything like the old, jolly Max. "Come for a visit, then," Ugo persisted. "Next weekend! The two of you. You'll stay with me."

"Well, I can," I said. "I was going to come and see you

anyway. We have to work out the final arrangements on the pictures you're lending. And I want to take another good look at that Boursse. You're still willing to let it go for sixty thousand dollars?"

Max almost choked on his grappa. "Ugo, you don't mean you're selling your Boursse for sixty thousand? I'll give you—"

Ugo chortled. "Always the businessman. No, Massimiliano, this is a special favor to Cristoforo. For *you* . . ." He rolled up his eyes, pretending to calculate. "Maybe three hundred thousand?" He leaned back in his chair, shaking with laughter.

"Thanks a bunch," Max said in English, but he was smiling, too. Max had a big gap between his upper front teeth. When he grinned, which was often, he looked like a mustached, middle-aged Alfred E. Neuman, the *What, me worry?* kid on the cover of *Mad* magazine.

"You'll really come?" Ugo said to me. He looked delighted.

"Of course. I've already checked the schedule to Catania. There's an Alisarda flight that leaves at noon on Saturday and arrives about two. How would that be? Could you have someone meet me at the airport?"

Ugo beamed. "Sure, sure. Wait till you see my—my—" He was jiggling with excitement. "I have a surprise for you. Don't I, Massimiliano?"

"Surprise?" Max said, frowning. "Oh, Jesus, you don't mean—"

"Sh, sh!" Ugo's thick forefinger wagged in front of his lips. "Don't tell him."

"Ugo," Max said, with a sort of pained kindness, "I'm telling you. That picture isn't good enough—"

"Don't tell him!" Ugo was bouncing up and down. "It's a surprise!"

"But I already told you," Max said patiently. "Amedeo already told you—"

"I believe you, all right? But if Cristoforo's coming to Sicily, then I say what does it hurt if he looks at it? Let him make his own decision."

Max shrugged and raised his eyes to the ceiling.

Ugo looked at me suspiciously. "Hey, do you know what we're talking about?"

"Not a clue," I said honestly.

"Good!" He thumped his thick fist on the table. "Massimiliano, you come, too! Come with Cristoforo Saturday. I'll show you Sicily. We'll eat, we'll drink! We'll have a wonderful time, just like in the old days."

I wasn't sure of just which old days he was talking about, but at that point it sounded like a great idea to me. Ugo was like a breath of fresh, honest air after the rarefied conversation of art connoisseurs, and Max was good company, too.

"Come on, Max," I said. "Why not?"

He grinned. "Why not?" he echoed to my surprise. "All right, I'll come, I can use a little time off."

"Wonderful, wonderful!" boomed Ugo, and hammered his fist on the table some more.

The waiter thought he was calling for another round and hurried over with three more grappas, which we accepted. Then we proceeded to sink happily into a sentimental swill of good fellowship.

I'm afraid we were a little on the riotous side by the time we started for the train station. I blush to admit it, but I think we were bawling "Santa Lucia" as we crossed the deserted Piazza Maggiore, and I seem to remember a chorus of "O Sole Mio" in there, too, but I wouldn't swear to it.

"Guess what. I'm changing my name," Max announced somewhere on Via dell'Indipendenza. "I am soon to be signor Massimiliano Caboto."

Ugo frowned tipsily at him. "You were always signor Massimiliano Caboto."

"I mean legally. Max Cabot no longer exists. But *you*," he said, turning that gap-toothed grin on me, "may still call me Max. A special dispensation."

"A papal dispensation," Ugo said, choking with mirth and convulsing the rest of us, which gives you a pretty good idea of the state we were in.

"It's my way of righting an old wrong," Max said. "Did I never tell you that I am a direct descendant of John Cabot, the English explorer who discovered North America?"

"No, you never did," I said.

"Who's John Cabot?" Ugo asked.

"And did you know," Max went on, "that John Cabot, the English explorer who discovered the North American continent, wasn't born in England?"

"No," I said.

"Who's John Cabot?" Ugo asked.

"Well, it's true," Max said. "John Cabot was Italian, not English. Born in Genoa in about 1450, and his real name was Giovanni Caboto. You can look it up."

"Really?' I said.

"Oh," Ugo said. "Giovanni Caboto. Why didn't you say so?"

I don't remember too much more until we had seen a still-chortling Ugo off on the 1:04 and started back toward the center of town. Of the great old cities of Europe, Bologna is probably the most walkable. The pavement on the ancient downtown streets isn't cobblestones, or rough-hewn granite blocks, or even concrete, but a glassy terrazzo tile, easy on the feet and as smooth and level as an ice-skating rink. More than that, most of the sidewalks are arcaded, protected from the elements by the colonnaded porticos that were a standard feature of Bolognese architecture for five hundred years.

A misty rain had been drifting down for an hour and the city was almost deserted. The big Piazza Medaglia d'Oro fronting the railroad station, usually swarming with cars, was so empty we strolled across it without bothering to wait for the green AVANTI sign. Once back on Via dell'Indipendenza, the only sounds we heard were our own heels clicking on the tile and the occasional restrained hum of a small car in no particular hurry.

We walked slowly, shielded from the rain by the porticos, stopping now and then to look absently into a darkened shop window. I had passed from fatigue through hilarity, and was now in a state of mellow calm, content to let the still-exuberant Max carry the conversation. He was giving one of his glories-of-Italy lectures.

"Chris, just think for a moment where a city like Bologna fits in the great scheme of things! Guido Reni, Galvani, Marconi, the Gregorian calendar ... Look at this, look at this!" He gestured vaguely about him. "Some of these buildings date from the 1300s."

"True."

More vague arm movements. "This colonnade we're walking in, this building I can reach out and *touch*—" He demonstrated. "It was standing here when Columbus discovered America. Think about that!"

Well, not quite. The "imprisoned" columns of this particular building's facade, the finicky, corrugated texture of its walls, marked it as late Mannerist, somewhere around 1590. But why argue? It obviously made Max happy to think otherwise. Besides, what was a hundred years in the great scheme of things?

"Chris, I'd never go back to the Land of Round Doorknobs, never. Not to live. I've never regretted moving here, not for a minute."

"Mm." When he got like this, I was never sure which of us he was trying to convince.

"Do you realize it's practically midnight, and we're walking the streets in complete safety? Can you do that in America?"

"You can in Winslow," I couldn't help saying. I wasn't so sure about Seattle or New York. Or Bologna, when it came down to it, considering the stories at dinner. I glanced nervously around. Across the street a man and a woman, arms wrapped around each other, were quietly mooning along, walking the other way. Half a block behind us, in the darkness, a car coughed softly and started up. It couldn't have been more peaceful.

"Ah, Chris," Max raved on, "just think about it. How do you compare two and a half thousand years of history to—to Michael Jackson and—and McDonald's?"

In some deeply buried vault, patriotism stirred. "Now wait a minute, Max, you're comparing unlike things. Besides, I think the Italians would be happy to trade in some of that history if they could."

"Oh, you mean Mussolini? The Borgias?" He dismissed them with a wave. "Every culture has— What are we stopping for?"

I pointed to the street sign on the corner of a building. "Via Montegrappa. My hotel's down here."

"Oh." He was crestfallen. "You wouldn't want to have one more drink?"

"No, thanks." Overeating, overdrinking, and jet lag had finally, irrevocably, caught up with me. All I wanted to do was fall into bed. "You want to come in and call a cab?"

He shook his head contemptuously. "To go six blocks?"

Max lived on the other side of Via Marconi, in a section where big, blocklike, modern apartment houses had replaced buildings destroyed in World War II. "You going to have time to get together again for dinner in the next couple of days?"

"Sure, anytime."

"Day after tomorrow? Come by the gallery about six, and we'll go from there."

"You're on. See you then."

I turned onto the unlit Via Montegrappa, which was more medieval alley than Renaissance boulevard, while Max continued down Indipendenza. After a quarter of a block I stopped abruptly, listening hard. I wasn't sure what had alerted me. Something. I stood stock-still. What had I heard? No, nothing. Behind me, on Indipendenza, an automobile had driven slowly by, that was all. I'd heard the engine purring, the tires crackling on the pavement.

I started walking again, puzzled, replaying the sounds. Something wasn't right. The car had been going too slowly, cruising at a walker's pace. In the direction Max was going. The same car I'd heard before, the same quiet engine? Is that what had caught my attention? The hairs on the back of my neck prickled. I turned and made quickly for Indipendenza, thinking about all those bullets falling out of Paolo Salvatorelli. Via dell'Indipendenza was empty and silent. It was still raining, but the clouds had thinned, and moonlight glistened on the wet street. I stood still again for a moment, straining to hear. There was a scraping noise, sounds of scuffling, a muffled grunt. With my mouth suddenly dry I ran to the corner where Max would have turned to head home.

He was there, a few yards down Via Ugo Bassi, struggling awkwardly with two men, a tall, lean one in a leather jacket, and a fat, bald monster with a neck that was thicker than his head, and arms and shoulders like Conan the Barbarian. The tall one was roughly shoving Max backward a step at a time, his palms flat against Max's chest, the way a kid does when

46

he's daring another kid to do something about it. Max was stumbling back, trying to hold his ground, making small, outraged noises.

Just as I came in sight of them the fat, muscular one drew back his fist and punched Max in the face. If you have never heard the sound made when a powerful adult male hits someone in the face with all his might—and I guess I hadn't—it comes as a surprise. It isn't the crisp *krak* of old movies or the explosive *crump* of new ones. It's nothing at all like the clean slap of a boxing glove. It's a mushy, hollow sound, bare knuckles grinding against bone, and it makes your knees weak to hear it.

At least it made my knees weak. The man drew back his fist again.

"Hey," I said.

I know you will be amazed to learn that they were not paralyzed with fright. They didn't even jump. They just turned very slowly and looked coldly at me for a long time, which didn't do anything for my knees. Meanwhile, Max slid down the wall of the building, moaning softly. The two men glanced at each other. I think they nodded. The bull-necked one calmly turned back to Max. The tall, thin one walked toward me, not hurrying. Sauntering, in fact, with his hands held out a little from his hips, gunfighter-style.

Part of me wanted to run, of course. All right, *all* of me wanted to run. I'm fit enough, and I don't think I'm any more cowardly than the average man, but I'm an art curator, for God's sake, and these were professional thugs, as even I could tell. This was out of my line; I didn't go around getting into fights in bars. I couldn't even remember the last time I'd been out-and-out angry with anyone. Well, not unless you count the divorce proceedings, which hardly seems fair.

My legs were aching to turn and run. Believe me, all the ready-made rationalizations leaped to my mind: What was the point of getting Max *and* me killed or maimed? What did I think I could do against two bruisers? Wasn't running and shouting for the police, for any kind of help, the best thing I could do for Max?

But I didn't run. I can't claim I was being terrifically brave,

47

because I couldn't stop trembling, but I simply couldn't turn tail and leave him there, and I couldn't make myself start bawling for help, either. I stood my ground, my fists knotted. My stomach, too, if it comes to that.

He came up to me and stopped, examining me with his head tilted to one side. I saw that he wasn't really thin; he was hard, with flesh like weathered teak. He was bigger than I'd thought, two or three inches taller than me, and he'd taken a few punches in the face himself. His brow was spongy with scar tissue and his nose had been pounded into a flat, formless lump that sat like a codfish fillet on the middle of his face. The top half of his left ear was gone. He looked very, very tough, very seasoned.

"Back off, fuckface," I snarled. Not my usual m.o., I admit, but I'd heard somewhere that the best thing to do in situations like this was to establish your authority at the outset.

He didn't back off. Far from it. His right hand—I never saw it coming, but it must have been his right hand; the stiffly extended fingers of his right hand—dug upward into the left side of my abdomen, just beneath the rib cage. The pain was extraordinary. For a horrible instant I thought that I'd been stabbed, that he'd slipped a stiletto under my ribs and up into my lung. I gagged, momentarily unable to breathe, or even to gasp. He drew his hand swiftly back, diagonally over his shoulder, the fingers once again rigidly extended. This, I realized, was going to be a blow to the throat with the edge of his palm. Clutching my left side, incapable of doing much more than warding him off, somehow I had the presence of mind to tuck my chin into my shoulder and step into the blow, toward him rather than away.

As a result, it was his leather-clad upper arm, not his hand, that caught me in the temple, not the neck. Not an enjoyable experience, but a lot better than it might have been. I could draw breath again, and I realized thankfully that I hadn't been stabbed. While his left arm was caught in the crook of my neck and shoulder I punched him just under the armpit—a little gingerly, because I wasn't used to hitting people, and then again, harder. His torso jerked and a whoosh of warm air blew onto my cheek. I smelled something sweet on his breath; tarragon. I remember a moment of bemused surprise. Garlic, I might have expected, but tarragon?

We were locked together in a tangle of arms. One of his elbows was in my face, and I think one of mine was in his. He twisted suddenly, too quickly and complexly for me to follow, and broke away. He bobbed and spun, so that his back was to me, and then, seemingly from nowhere, his foot crashed into my face, heel first, just under the eye. I was knocked back, slamming noisily into the wooden side of a boarded-up flower stand at the curb's edge.

From off to the side, near Max, the bull-necked one called to him: "*Presto, Ettore, presto.*"

Come on, Ettore, hurry it up. It was not said urgently, but with a grousing kind of irritation, as if I were no more than an annoying bug to be squashed.

Until then, I had been by turns concerned, startled, scared, and combative. But such is the nature of the male ego that for the first time I was wholeheartedly hostile. Bug, indeed.

The kick had stung my cheek and knocked me off balance, but hadn't done any real harm. But for Ettore's benefit I sagged against the flower stand, my head nodding. I figured that I was entitled to some subterfuge to make the odds a little more even; Ettore was frighteningly fast, with a repertory of moves I had seen only in martial arts movies. And I hadn't seen many of those. He closed warily in, arms held up and out in front of him, crossed at the wrists.

There were some cardboard trays stacked hip-high at the side of the stand, and I had managed to get my fingers around the rim of one. As he took another step forward I swung it sharply at his head. It startled him, as it was meant to. His crossed hands flew a few inches higher, and as the cardboard bounced harmlessly off his wrists I drove in with a blow to his midsection. This one had everything I had behind it, and it landed just where I'd aimed it; in the center of his flat, hard abdomen. He doubled over instantly, and I managed to get in a second punch, this one not much more than a sloppy swipe at his head as he was going down.

But even when he was on the pavement in a heap, Ettore was formidable. As he hit the tile he twisted like a cat into a compact ball, catching my ankles between his arms and legs. "Pietro!" he shouted.

While I was struggling to get free something snaked around me from behind; an enormously thick, ironlike arm that pressed the breath out of me with a single squeeze, then kept on squeezing. Pietro had arrived. I panicked, beating with both fists at the gargantuan forearm. If he kept it up for one more second, my ribs would crack.

He didn't. He shifted his hold, plucked me easily from Ettore's grasp, and threw me—simply heaved me—a good eight or ten feet out into the street. On the fly. I didn't even hear him grunt with the effort. I managed to break my fall with my arms and jump quickly if unsteadily to my feet. I was muddled, though, facing in the wrong direction. I turned dizzily, almost losing my balance, until I found the two of them again. Ettore was up now. He and the monster were standing together, next to the flower stand, looking quietly at me again. Ettore had something in his hand that looked like a piece of metal pipe. Max was moaning softly on the ground behind them. The rain drifted lazily down onto my face.

There was a sudden roar to my right, only a dozen or so feet away. Startled, I spun around and found myself facing a small, dark car with its headlights off. I could see a figure behind the wheel.

The car . . . I'd forgotten the car—

Even now, it still seems to me as if the thing literally sprang at me, like a tiger at a deer. And even if I hadn't been as frozen as a terror-stricken deer, there wouldn't have been time to get out of the way. I put out my hands feebly in an absurd effort to keep it off.

And astonishingly I did, after a fashion. When my hands hit the front of it and I pushed, I was bumped upward, not downward, and an instant later I was doing a handstand, or at least a rolling shoulder stand, on the hood while it moved under me. I slid heavily into the windshield, or rather it slid into me—thank God, it didn't break—and then, somehow, I was flipped over and up, landing on the roof.

That was the most painful part, because I landed sharply on the base of my spine and also managed to bang the back of my head somewhere along the way. I felt the car speed up under me, and I skidded the length of the roof on my back, slithered down over the trunk without doing much additional damage, and landed back in the street, amazingly enough on my feet.

I hit hard on both heels, jarring every bone and joint in my body, and then juddered crazily over the pavement, my teeth rattling, until I tripped over the curb and fell onto the terrazzo. On instinct, I dragged myself between two columns, out of reach of the car, then sat shaking, not comprehending what had happened. I had been caught by surprise, after all, and the whole thing couldn't have taken even two seconds. And believe me, it was a lot less intelligible in the experiencing than in the telling. Besides, from the moment I'd seen the car, I'd expected to be killed. Sitting there, I wasn't sure I hadn't been.

A wave of nausea billowed over me, and I leaned sideways and put my forehead down against the smooth tile. My teeth ached appallingly. Something warm was flowing thickly by my ear and along my neck. I saw the column next to me tilt slowly and begin to revolve. I must have passed out then, for how long I'm not sure, but I remember jerking awake with a start at the sound of an approaching siren.

The thugs were gone. The car, too. But Max was still lying there; alive, thank God. He was painfully trying to haul himself to his elbows. His legs, flaccid and boneless-looking, seemed not to belong to him. For the first time, I noticed he was lying beneath the darkened windows of Bologna's newest restaurant, opened a few weeks before on the busy downtown corner of Indipendenza and Ugo Bassi, across from the venerable Piazza Nettuno.

McDonald's.

CHAPTER 5

The next time I was aware of anything at all I was drifting in and out of cottony, white clouds. I was quite comfortable. Happy, in fact. I was in the Ospedale Maggiore, so I'd been given to understand, and I was going to be just fine. I certainly felt fine. Solicitous, cheerful men and women in white hovered about me, making pleasant sounds and occasionally sticking needles in me with great gentleness. It was very pleasant to simply lie back and be fussed over.

At one indeterminate point I surfaced—or rather descended from somewhere around ceiling level—to find myself listening to someone speaking in Italian with quiet confidence.

"—was named Ettore. I remember because the other one, Pietro, called him that." The voice was pleasant and familiar.

I was lying peacefully on my back with my eyes closed, and I waited with interest to hear what would follow. Whoever it was, he was talking about the two thugs. Had there been a witness, then?

Another person spoke, also in Italian. "Thank you. Now I would like to ask another question. Tell me, why did you, signor Scoccimarro, and signor Caboto go out drinking?"

I waited. The question was a little complex. I yawned and settled myself farther into the bed. Time passed. I began to float off again.

"Signor Norgren?"

I started. "Yes?"

"Why did you, signor Scoccimarro, and signor Caboto go out drinking?"

I opened my eyes. I was in a cranked-up hospital bed. Through the lowered window blinds I could see daylight. Was it Tuesday morning already? To my side were two young, blue-uniformed policemen in chairs, one of them with a pad. On the bedside table, a couple of feet from my face, a tape recorder was whirring softly. I realized belatedly why the first voice had sounded so pleasant and familiar. It was mine.

"How long have we been talking?" I asked.

The two policemen looked at each other. "About twenty minutes," the one without the pad said. He seemed to be in charge; a long-limbed, athletic-looking man in his late twenties. "We won't keep you much longer. Will you answer the question, please?"

The question. I searched my mind for it. "Uh, out drinking?" I said lamely. Where was that quiet confidence now that I was awake?

"The three of you had several brandies at the Nepentha. I would like to know why."

"Why? Why did we have several brandies? Well, we were old friends, and it was the first time we'd seen each other in a while."

"Who suggested it?"

I thought back. My mind was beginning to clear. "Ugo. To celebrate old times."

"And are you all really such good friends as that?"

53

"As what?" I think a note of irritation must have crept into my voice. Even half-zonked on whatever the doctors had been sticking in my arm, I could see where he was leading: If Max had been set up, then wasn't it likely that it had been by one of the two people he'd left the restaurant with? And if it wasn't me, he was thinking, then it must have been Ugo.

I suppose I would have been in contention, too, had I not been fortunate enough to have nearly gotten killed in the melee myself. I shifted my shoulders with a grimace. The clear-headedness was coming at a price. I was starting to ache at every joint, and a few other places, too. I thought of asking the cops to get a nurse to give me something but decided I'd be better off undoped for the rest of the interview. It had already occurred to me that I couldn't be in a very serious condition. For one thing, there were no bandages, no tubes going in or out of me, no oxygen tent. For another, the hospital had permitted the police to interview me.

What I thought the young cop was thinking didn't make me happy. Ugo Scoccimarro was probably the most straightforward, aboveboard person I knew. Coarse sometimes, ignorant sometimes—how could he not be, with four years of schooling all told?—but unfailingly honest and openhearted.

"Yes," I said, "we're good friends." We had, in fact, met perhaps half a dozen times.

"Did you ever go out drinking together before, or was this the first time?"

I didn't like this "go out drinking" business either. I began to object, but caught myself as a chorus of "O Sole Mio" in the Piazza Maggiore flashed before my eyes. Maybe the guy had a point.

"Well, this is the first time that it was just the three of us, as I recall, but—"

"Tell me, did you actually see signor Scoccimarro leave Bologna?"

"We walked him right to the train station."

"But did you actually see him leave?"

I tried to recall. Things had been pretty muddled by then. "Yes," I said, finally remembering. "He was on the 1:04."

We had gone to the wrong platform first, and Ugo had

almost boarded a train heading toward Rome. Then we had found the train to Milan, helped him up the steps of the first-class car, and seen him fall happily into a seat. His next breath had been a snore, and Max and I had left.

"Then you didn't actually watch the train leave?" the officer persisted.

I thought it over. "No, I guess not, but the man was sound asleep when we left." What was he suggesting? That Ugo, soused as he was, had hired the two thugs and crept back to town to mastermind the attack? Perhaps even that he had been behind the wheel of the car? What for? Surely Ugo wasn't on Max's list of five.

"I don't understand why you're concentrating on Ugo. Fifty other people could have overheard Max talking about going to the police. Max was practically shouting—"

The other policeman, older and softer, held up his pencil and shook his head. He looked tired. "You have told us already."

Gingerly I readjusted myself on the pillow. I was tired, too. And I was beginning to hurt quite a lot. My joints were like wood when I moved them, and my teeth felt as if they'd all gone through root canal explorations. Maybe another shot wouldn't be a bad idea after all.

Even as I was thinking it the curtains around my bed parted and a nurse came in with a broad smile and a hypodermic at the ready. The staff was all very happy here. I was ready enough for her, but I hesitated. "Maybe I'd better finish answering these gentlemen's questions," I said.

But at a nod from the younger man the soft one had closed up his pad and was reaching for the STOP button on the tape recorder. "We have everything we need, signore. You've been very helpful. We'll bring a transcript of this for you to see, and if you can think of something else you can tell us at the time."

By then it didn't matter very much. The needle had been eased in and I was already four feet above the bed, on my way to those soft, white clouds. I felt my chin touch my chest.

It's really not so amazing," Dr. Tolomeo explained pleasantly. "Generally speaking, an adult pedestrian hit by an automobile is not run *over*; not unless he is struck by a tall vehicle such as a truck—or he is lying down at the time." He chuckled benignly. "No, generally speaking, a pedestrian hit by an automobile is run *under*." The easily amused physician chuckled some more. "It's a simple matter of centers of gravity."

"Oh," I said, not very graciously. By this time—it was one o'clock in the afternoon—I had convinced myself that my escape from certain death by vaulting over an onrushing automobile had been a feat of iron nerves, extraordinary coordination, and lightning-quick reactions. In an inspired moment I had just described it to him as having been something like the remarkable bull-vaulting paintings that have come down to us from the Cretans. And here he was telling me it had nothing to do with me at all; it was merely an example of the inalterable laws of physics. The same thing would have happened to me if I'd been a sack of potatoes, given a high enough center of gravity.

Dr. Tolomeo was a man highly sensitive to the needs of his patients. "Of course," he added quickly, "it was miraculous that you were able to land on your feet and escape with no more than a mild concussion and a few strains. Usually, it is the other end that hits the road. There are terrible spinal injuries, and scalp and facial skin is often shredded from road friction. And often, from being thrown onto the hood, there is tearing of the fatty tissue, with perforations of—"

With a grimace I held up my hand. That kind of solace I could do without. I was still in my hospital room. Dr. Tolomeo had come in a few minutes before to tell me that the prodding of my bodily parts and the analysis of my bodily functions had revealed no serious injury. I was free to get out of bed, get dressed, and go. There might be a little lingering achiness, but he had prescribed something for that. And he would advise bed rest for at least a day. My body needed time to compose itself.

"I don't suppose you know if they caught the two men? Three men, rather," I added, thinking of the car's driver.

"No," he said, then added with some eagerness, "but I know that there was a terrific chase across Bologna, with two police cars in pursuit, guns blazing. You heard none of it?"

I shook my head. "Just a siren. How is Max . . . Massimiliano Caboto doing?"

The doctor's round, sunny face darkened. "Your friend will be all right in time. He will adjust."

"Adjust?" I stared at him with a sudden, sick twisting in my abdomen. I'd asked some of the other staff about him earlier, but they had just shrugged and gone on with their work. I'd taken it to mean that he was all right, that he'd already been sent home. "What's the matter with him?"

"His legs," Dr. Tolomeo said softly. "They—"

"Legs—!" All I'd seen was the one punch to his face. I hadn't known there'd been anything else. But now I remembered that boneless, flaccid look below his hips. I also remembered the piece of pipe in Franco's hand. "They . . . smashed them with that pipe?" I asked. My chest was tight and empty.

"Apparently so. The abraded margins of the wounds, the compacted underlying tissue, the smashed bones, all suggest such a weapon."

"My God," I said to Dr. Tolomeo, "I've got to see him. Where is he?"

The physician shook his head. "Not today. He just came from surgery, and it was a difficult procedure. Perhaps tomorrow. Better yet, the day after."

"When you say 'smashed,' " I said slowly to Dr. Tolomeo, "how bad . . . ?"

"The knee is an extremely delicate joint," Dr. Tolomeo said gently. "Even under the normal stresses of life it often fails. In a case like this—" He spread his hands. "Each leg was brutally struck several times. The fractures are multiple and complex, and there was much damage to the cartilages and soft tissue. The patellas themselves . . ." He shrugged.

"Will he be able to walk?"

Dr. Tolomeo looked uncomfortable. "You must understand that a long, somewhat painful course of therapy will be required. More operations may be necessary." He sighed. "He will never walk as he did before."

Depressed, utterly washed out, I took a taxi from the hospital to the Hotel Europa and followed Dr. Tolomeo's advice; I slept away the rest of the day, waking up every few hours to grope for the bottle of pain capsules. At about 10:00 P.M.

I dragged myself out for a bowl of soup and a plate of spaghetti and clam sauce at the first trattoria I came to, then went back to my room, fell onto the bed again, and slept through until eight the next morning.

When I awakened I could tell the worst was over. My body had composed itself. The lingering aches that Dr. Tolomeo had promised were there, all right, but I was more stiff than hurting, as long as I didn't do anything silly such as stamping my foot on the floor or clamping my teeth together. It wasn't bad enough to endure the spaciness that went along with the painkillers, so I threw the bottle away, relying on aspirin instead. I showered for the first time since Monday, the day before yesterday, finding some bruises and contusions I hadn't realized were there, then called the hospital to see if I could talk to Max.

I couldn't. He had spent a restless night, I was told, and he was asleep. Try again in the afternoon.

Half an hour later, over *caffè latte*, rolls, and jam in the hotel breakfast room, I was trying to concentrate on my exhibition notes, but thinking about Max instead—worrying about him and also nursing a highly unaccustomed feeling: the desire for vengeance on his behalf. On mine, too, for that matter. The obvious connection between Max's announcement that he was about to tell the police everything he knew, and the attack on him just a few hours later, had not escaped me.

It had not escaped the two policemen who had interviewed me, either, and we had spent substantial time reconstructing the scene. Amedeo Di Vecchio and Benedetto Luca, who'd been Max's and my tablemates, had to be formally considered as suspects, unlikely as it seemed on the face of it. Beyond that, who could say? There had been about fifty people in the room and, given Max's pickled state and robust voice, none of them had been out of earshot. I had suggested that the policemen get a guest list from Di Vecchio, and they had said they would.

Thinking hard, I broke open the second crisp breakfast roll. Was there anything I was forgetting, anything I'd neglected to tell them, anything that might help find Max's attackers? I had described the thugs, told them their names, described the

car as well as I could, which was pitifully—"small, purple
or red, or dark anyway, no hood ornament." (According to
Dr. Tolomeo, it was the absence of a hood ornament that
had saved me from those nasty perforations.) What was I
forgetting—?

I sat up with a start, almost spilling my coffee. What I
was forgetting was my appointment with Colonel Antuono.
Yesterday's dreamy haze had constituted a sort of nonday,
and I'd forgotten this was Wednesday. I was due in less than
an hour. I gulped down the rest of the coffee, went upstairs
to grab a jacket, and ran—or as near to it as I could, given the
state of my joints—off to my meeting with Cesare Antuono.

If the Eagle of Lombardy couldn't help, who could?

Even at my creaky, halting pace, it was only a five-minute
walk. According to the instructions Tony had passed on to
me, Antuono's office was in the Palazzo d'Accursio, which
served as the city hall and was one of the old buildings border-
ing the Piazza Maggiore in the heart of town.

The attendant at the great main door, under a benevolent
bronze statue of Pope Gregory XIII, had never heard of
Colonel Antuono, so I went up the main staircase, an imposing
sweep of red-carpeted stone steps, on my own. It was slow
going for a man in my condition, not just because it rose three
flights at a single sweep, but because the extremely shallow
steps were slanted backward. This was an amenity of Italian
fifteenth-century public architecture that permitted the gentry
to mount to the upper floors without troubling to get off their
horses. But what suited noble status and equine anatomy
wasn't so easy for human ligaments that had taken a rude
beating a couple of days before.

On the upper floor were most of the city bureaus, but the
people there shook their heads when I asked about Antuono's
office. Not up there; that was all they could say. Back down
I went, stiff and grumbling, feeling a hundred years old, and
grateful that there was a railing to hang on to. Maybe I'd been
a little overhasty in tossing those pain pills after all.

The grimly handsome Palazzo d'Accursio is not only huge,
but confusing. Like many medieval buildings it was built

slowly, over several hundred years, and when that happened, plans tended to get lost, ideas to change, styles to evolve. The result, as in this case, could be an unpredictable hodgepodge. I wandered around until I finally found the office I was looking for, in a bleak little courtyard jammed with haphazardly parked cars. In a low annex, beside a plain door set into a colorless, much-patched stucco wall, was an unprepossessing sign:

CORPO VIGILI URBANI
SETTORE CENTRALE
COMMUNE DI BOLOGNA

A question occurred to me, not for the first time. Unless I had it wrong, the *vigili urbani* were little more than traffic police, but Antuono was with the prestigious carabinieri, the national police force, something like our FBI. Not just your everyday carabinieri either, but the elite art-theft unit, the *Comando Tutela Patrimonio Artistico*. And according to Max and the others, he was a figure of importance within it. Why would he be housed in this dismal place? Carabinieri headquarters were several blocks away on the Via del Piombo, in an imposing building befitting its status.

When I opened the dusty, glass-paned door, I found myself in a small room with a worn, linoleum-topped counter. Behind the counter a uniformed clerk was sitting in a wheeled wooden chair, with a wire basket full of envelopes in his lap. He was slowly—very slowly—inserting them into the wooden pigeon-holes that ran the length of one wall, wetting his finger with his tongue every time he picked one up.

I waited. I cleared my throat. He continued to insert envelopes.

"*Prego*," I said finally, "*dove si trove l'uffizio del signor Colonnello Antuono?*"

Without turning around to look at me, he jerked a thumb over his shoulder. I went down a short corridor crowded with gray file cabinets and stacked cardboard cartons lining both walls, but I must have read the thumb-jerk wrong, because no offices opened out of it. There was, however, a small table wedged between a couple of the cabinets, at which another clerk, this one in civilian clothes, fussed over the hopeless task of filing the dog-eared contents of a tableful of bruised and sagging cardboard cartons.

"*Prego, signore,*" I said, hoping for better luck this time. "*Dove si trove l'uffizio del signor Colonnello Antuono?*"

At least this one looked at me. He paused reluctantly (leaving his finger inserted in a folder for ease of later reference) and examined me with impassive gray eyes. He seemed surprised to have been addressed, and maybe a little annoyed; I wondered when the last time was anyone had spoken to him. Stooped, balding, narrow-shouldered, with old-fashioned green plastic cuffs protecting the sleeves of his white shirt, he might have lived his whole life alone in this windowless dungeon of a corridor, the quintessential clerk, filing and refiling his curling papers. And probably preferring it that way.

"*Colonnello Antuono?*" he repeated sourly. Yes, he was annoyed, all right. He jabbed a forefinger—the one that wasn't occupied in the files—against his thin chest.

"*Io sono Colonnello Antuono.*"

CHAPTER 6

I suppose my heart didn't really sink, but it didn't swell with confidence, either. Now I wouldn't want you to think that I go around stereotyping people based on their physical appearance. But I do admit to a slight tendency to forejudge, to generalize, to . . . okay, okay, to stereotype. And whatever vague image I had in mind for Colonel Cesare Antuono, this wasn't it.

Well, think about it. The Eagle of Lombardy—in green plastic cuffs?

But this was an unworthy reaction on my part, and I knew it. I smiled warmly and held out my hand. "*Colonnello Antuono, io sono Christopher Norgren. Sono felicissimo di conoscerla.*"

"*Dottor* Norgren?" he said, continuing to sound surprised. He pushed a plastic cuff up on his arm and out of the way and studied his wrist watch. "Eleven o'clock already," he said mournfully in English. "The time flies away." He gave a last, longing look to his folders, and finally removed his finger, first inserting a torn paper marker. He had, I gathered, abandoned all hope of working on his files for a while. He extended his hand without perceptible enthusiasm. "I'm happy to meet you also."

From under a couple of moldy cartons he produced an armless, wooden antique of a swivel chair. "Sit down, please."

He used a folder to brush the dust off the seat (no wonder they were dog-eared), and motioned me into it.

There was a somewhat strained silence. "I'll go and get another chair," he said.

I looked around at the cramped space. There were folders and cardboard file boxes everywhere. I didn't see how he could squeeze another chair in. "Maybe we ought to talk in your office," I said.

"My office?" He blinked at me. "But this *is* my office."

We looked at each other, embarrassed. I didn't know what to say. I said, "Ah."

"There was little space available," he explained stiffly. "This is in reality a storeroom, of course, but it will be perfectly acceptable once I have arranged things."

I still didn't know what to say. My confidence in Antuono's status was not rising. He could spend the next three months arranging things and the place would still be a hovel. Was this any way to treat a big wheel?

He left, returning in a few minutes with a ratty, cane-seated chair. Somehow he got it wedged at the table between the cartons piled on the floor. He pulled off his plastic cuffs, produced from somewhere a charcoal-black jacket with the faintest of narrow gray pinstripes, shrugged into it, and buttoned it. It was snug across his spare shoulders. He looked like a hungry, vaguely predatory undertaker.

He sat down, working bony knees between the cartons and facing me across the littered table.

"Well," he said.

"Well," I said. Then, when he didn't say anything further: "You're aware that Max Cabot and I were attacked a couple of nights ago?" I wasn't really sure. The policemen who had interrogated me had been in the municipal blue-and-gray uniforms, not the khakis of the carabinieri. Maybe Antuono hadn't heard. Maybe he hadn't been out of his storeroom yet.

"Yes, of course. I've read the transcripts of your interview. You're feeling all right now?"

"Much better, thanks."

"Very good. I was sorry to hear you were hurt."

I smiled politely and made an appropriate pooh-poohing gesture. Merely another day in the life of an art curator.

"It was quite brave of you to go back and help your friend."

"Thank you."

He was being courteous enough, but it was all form. Antuono had that petty official's knack of making you feel that he had a thousand pressing things on his mind, every one of which was infinitely more important than you were. But Antuono wasn't supposed to be a petty official.

Again the conversation lagged. If he was really anxious for my reports on gossip from the Bolognese art world, he was hiding it very well.

"Did they ever catch those thugs?" I asked.

"Oh." The question seemed to surprise him. "The ones who attacked signor Cabot?" He shrugged. "I'm afraid I don't know that, Dr. Norgren."

My concern deepened. How could he not know? It wasn't that I didn't believe him, but how could he not know? He'd responded as if it hadn't even occurred to him to wonder about it. Wasn't he supposed to be in charge of the whole thing? Who was this guy?

"It is something for the local police, the *polizia criminale,* to be concerned with," he said. "It's not a matter for the carabinieri."

It wasn't? Was he suggesting that the attack wasn't related to the thefts? If he had read the transcripts, he knew that it had come just hours after Max had prattled so loudly about coming to him, Antuono, with pertinent information. It had come, in fact, almost the very first second he had been alone.

I pointed this out to Antuono, rather persuasively, I thought, but the Eagle of Lombardy was not impressed. With a weary sigh he twisted to reach a black telephone on top of the metal cabinet behind him and placed it on the table.

"If you really want to know, I imagine I can find out for you."

If *I* wanted to know? Why didn't *he* want to know? I began to wonder if Di Vecchio and Luca had been right about him. Could he be another Captain Cala, more intent on lining his own pockets than on catching anybody? But I quickly dismissed the thought. Some local cop, maybe; not a carabiniere. And certainly not the deputy commander of their famous art theft squad. They were as close to the Untouchables as anything was nowadays. But something was awry.

"Colonel, to tell you the truth I don't understand what's going on. Here's Max. He announces that there are five people who knew about his security arrangements, and that he's going to come and tell you who they are. Two hours later he's savagely beaten up. And you don't even seem to—"

He had begun to punch some numbers into the telephone, but he stopped and made an irritated noise. I was repeating myself, apparently something one didn't do with Colonel Antuono. "Five names," he snapped. "Do you happen to know them?"

"Only one: Amedeo Di Vecchio."

"The director of the National Museum. Yes, a highly suspicious character. We'll certainly keep our eye on him. None of the others?"

"No," I said, getting annoyed myself, "but I don't think you'll have any trouble getting them from Max."

He had been toying with a pencil. Now he tossed it sourly onto the table. "But I did have trouble, Dr. Norgren. I've already seen him. He will say nothing. He has no list of five names, he has no idea of why he was attacked, he saw no faces, he has no enemies—nothing."

"But that's—" My surprise didn't last for long. They had broken—"shattered"—his legs with a metal pipe, after all. As admonitions went, it had to be considered highly persuasive. And the two gorillas involved weren't the type to have reservations about going further if the need arose. And if more guidance were needed, there was always the hortatory example of Paolo Salvatorelli with the cork in his mouth and the 116 bullets rattling out of whatever was left of his body.

So why be surprised, even for a moment, that Max had concluded that his best interests lay with refusing to tell Antuono anything? The Rubens taken from his shop had already been recovered undamaged. Clara Gozzi was satisfied. Even the insurance company was relieved. Was Max supposed to risk his life to get them back their money? Would I have done differently if I had been the one lying in the hospital with shattered legs?

Truthfully, I didn't know. And yet—unfairly, sanctimoniously—I was disappointed in my friend.

"In any case," Antuono said, "I think these names are also a matter for the local police, not for the carabinieri."

I laughed, more in frustration than anything else. "Colonel, is there anything that *is* a matter for the carabinieri?"

"The art," he said evenly. "And the people behind the thefts; the organizers, the receivers."

"Well, couldn't one of those five people be—"

"I don't think so."

"But how can you say that so certainly? It seems to—"

"Dr. Norgren," he said, cutting me off, "these thefts were not locally planned. We have very good reason to suspect the involvement of the Sicilian Mafia."

"The Mafia?" What was it that Tony had said about the Mafia being a thing of the past?

"The Sicilian Mafia. The *onorata società*." His voice dripped contempt. The honored society.

"But . . . why are you here, then? In Bologna?"

"You have a great many questions, *dottore*." He looked steadily at me for another few seconds, then picked up the telephone again and hit four or five buttons, muttered a few quick words in rapid Italian, and replaced the receiver. "They will call back. You understand, signore, that my concern is with the stolen art. I'm very sorry about this incident on the street, but you must see that it's not a matter of highest priority."

That, I said with commendable restraint, depended on who was setting priorities. It was high enough to me.

He stared at me without smiling; without anything to suggest that a human being might live somewhere beneath that dusty exterior at all. "Dr. Norgren," he said, "I am a deputy commander of the *Comando Carabinieri Tutela Patrimonio Artistico*. Your Italian is good enough to understand the words?"

"Of course. The command for the protection of Italy's artistic patrimony. Its heritage."

"Correct. Recovery of our stolen heritage. That is our first goal. We do not overly concern ourselves with the apprehension of criminals."

"I would have thought the two might be related." Sarcasm is not something I use often, particularly with public servants who are doing their jobs, and especially with policemen. But Antuono was giving me a pain. And I had my doubts about how well he was doing his job.

He looked at his watch; studied it, in fact, as if to determine just how much of his invaluable time could be squandered on me. Apparently, he decided there was a little more to spare. "I want to explain to you something of the way we work." He cleared a space on the table and leaned forward to rest his elbows on it, his hands steepled beneath his sharp chin. He pursed his small mouth pedantically.

"In many ways we are like narcotics agents. Most of our work is undercover. Our men use disguises—false mustaches, invented identities. We pretend to be buyers, and arrange false purchases. We make use of crooked dealers, petty criminals, and informers—they are much the same people—to help us, and when they do, we protect them. They may help us another day."

"They may also steal some more paintings another day."

"Let me ask you something. When a seller of narcotics hears the police pounding down the door to his apartment, what does he do with the kilo of cocaine in the closet?"

I shrugged. "Flushes it down the toilet, I guess. Or throws it out the window."

"Very good. He destroys the evidence. A criminal with sto-

67

len art does the same thing when the police are about to close in. He does not flush it down the toilet, of course; the circumstances are different. But he tries to destroy it. Now: If it is cocaine, the world is better off for its loss, no?" He leaned back and economically crossed one knee over the other in the cluttered space beneath the table. "But what if it is a Tiziano, a Raffaelo? Should I risk the destruction of an irreplaceable work of art for the satisfaction of seeing a thief in jail for a year? For two years, if the courts are feeling particularly stern?"

He knew how to hit an art curator where it hurt; talk about the destruction of Old Masters. "I guess you have a point," I said.

The telephone buzzed. Antuono picked it up. "*Prego.*" He sat there nodding impatiently into it. "*Sì, capisco. . . . Capisco. . . .*"

Most of what he had explained to me I had already known. The *Comando Carabinieri Tutela Patrimonio Artistico* was the most celebrated art-theft squad in the world, and rightly so. With a staff of less than a hundred, they had recovered a staggering 120,000 works of art in the twenty years they'd been in operation, and I couldn't really quarrel with their first-get-the-art-then-worry-about-the-bad-guys philosophy. But when it's your own body that's been battered by the bad guys, you tend to see things in a different light.

Antuono emitted a final "*capisco*" and hung up. "No," he told me dryly, "they were not caught." He rose. "If there is nothing else, Dr. Norgren, I have a great deal—"

I looked up at him, surprised. "Don't you want a report on what I've been hearing?"

"To reply with perfect frankness, no."

"But I thought—"

"May I speak directly? This matter of your running to me with tidbits of gossip—"

"Look, Colonel," I said hotly. I was feeling distinctly ill-used. "It wasn't my idea in the first place. If you—"

"Nor mine. It was a suggestion made by your FBI, and I have no doubt it was well-intentioned. I felt it was best to accept the offer of your services. But between us, signore, truly, it's not necessary. We are well able to gather our own information."

"The FBI?" I stood up too rapidly and winced, barely managing not to groan as my knees straightened out for the first time in fifteen minutes. "How could they offer my services? How could they know I was coming?"

"I believe the original idea came to them from a Mr. . . . Let me see . . ."

"Let me guess," I said. "Whitehead."

"Ah, yes, I think so. Whitehead. Exactly."

It figured. Tony Whitehead's belief in the virtues of publicity was every bit as unequivocal as Mike Blusher's, even if more sophisticated and of purer intention. If his curator of Renaissance and Baroque art could have some part in the recovery of the Bolognese art thefts, so Tony's reasoning would run, then publicity for the museum would result. And that would of necessity be good for the museum.

I wasn't so sure. I also wasn't so sure about my obligation to stay in touch with Antuono. Tony's agreement to fund the purchase of Ugo's Boursse was contingent on my continued reporting. But the Eagle himself had just made it amply clear that he had better things to do than listen to my "tidbits." Could I therefore consider my obligation fulfilled? Could I go ahead and buy the Boursse with a clear conscience? A moral dilemma.

I knew what I was going to do, of course, but how was I going to rationalize it? We ethical people are very fastidious about our rationalizations. It was going to take some thought.

After leaving Antuono's hodgepodge of an office, I stopped at a coffee bar for a lunch of cheese and tomato *panini*. Then I went back up to my room in hopes of getting there before the maid did so that I could recover my precipitately discarded codeine capsules. No luck. She had been there and done a thorough job. I took a couple of aspirin and, with a muffled groan or two, lay myself stiffly down on the freshly made bed.

Twenty minutes later I was roused by a telephone call from the *polizia criminale*. They understood that I was still recuperating, but would it be too much of an imposition if they came in a car and brought me to police headquarters to verify the transcript of my interview and perhaps look at a few photographs of local criminals? As miserable as I was feeling, it was still far from an imposition. It was, in fact, nice to know somebody cared.

When I looked at the transcript, I was astonished to find it lucid and complete, with the remarks I made while I was unconscious being, if anything, marginally more coherent than what I said after I woke up. I signed it, then leafed through a few thick looseleaf books of photographs, but was unable to find either of the thugs. The two policemen accepted this fatalistically, then shook my hand with expressions of gratitude. I was courteously taken back to the Hotel Europa, where I went back up to my room to try to sleep again. I napped for almost two hours, and woke up at 3:30, feeling better and worrying about Max. I caught a taxi at the stand in front of the hotel and headed for the hospital, this time without calling first.

CHAPTER 7

Among the many social skills in which I seem to be lacking is the knack of providing cheerful solace at hospital bedsides. My conversational charms atrophy, my sense of humor withers, my smile petrifies. My friend Louis, who experienced this firsthand after his double-hernia operation, has a ready explanation, of course: My relief that it is someone else and not me in the bed creates a powerful sense of guilt, which in turn effects an overcompensatory reaction that sharply suppresses any behavior approximating good cheer.

Maybe so—who am I to argue with Freud?—but if I felt any relief at seeing Max, then it was deeply suppressed indeed. I had run into Dr. Tolomeo in the hallway outside the room, and he had taken me aside for an ominous warning. "Your friend— It looks worse than it is. Don't be frightened when you see him."

It was a good thing he told me, because Max was a frightening sight. He was propped into a semi-sitting position by the mechanical bed, with his naked legs straight out in front of him. Instead of the casts I'd expected, there was a horror-movie contraption of bolted-together steel rods encasing each leg from just above the knee almost to the ankle. Heavy steel pins—six on each leg—skewered the limb, piercing it through and cruelly transfixing it between the rods. The flesh was ghastly; purple, red, and black, swollen and split open like a hot dog that had been on the grill too long.

"Sit down, will you?" he said. "I wouldn't want you to faint on me." He was trying to sound chipper, but his voice was feeble, the words blurry, as if he had something in his mouth. He seemed to have lost thirty pounds. Once-sleek skin sagged clammy and pale beneath his eyes. His mustache had been shaved off to allow for five or six gruesome stitches, and without that imposing landmark his face seemed featureless and indistinct, like an out-of-focus photograph.

He didn't look remotely like Alfred E. Neuman.

"I look like hell, don't I?" he said.

"Not too bad. How do you feel?"

"You have to be kidding."

I saw a sluggish movement of tongue where it wasn't supposed to be, and realized that under the wound on his lip some teeth had been knocked out. Why that should have shocked me more than the state of his legs I don't know, but it did. I remembered the mushy sound of that heavy fist hitting him in the face, and I felt a single cold drop of sweat trickle down between my shoulder blades.

"Do you want me to come back another time, Max?"

"No, no," he said quickly. "Stay, I'm glad you're here. And I don't really feel too bad. They keep me doped up."

A good thing, I thought.

"These things on my legs . . . They're not as bad as they look. They're supposed to be better than casts for my kind of fractures. They say I'll be able to start walking a little as soon as the swelling goes down and the cuts heal up. Next week, maybe."

"Really. That's great." I'd believe it when I saw it.

"Maybe sooner," he said. "They say I'm doing fine. They're amazed, in fact."

Well, there I was, doing my usual sterling bedside job. Poor Max was working like mad to cheer me up.

"Glad to hear it," I said heartily, finally sitting down. "Anything I can do for you?"

"Do? No." He shifted awkwardly on the bed. There were ropes strung from the metal rods on his legs to a simple pipe frame over the bed, keeping his feet a few inches off the mattress, and movement was difficult. At one point he twisted too far and gasped.

I flinched. "Do you want a nurse?"

"Uh-uh. Chris . . ." He shrugged awkwardly. His mouth moved like an old, old man's as he probed with his tongue in the gap between his teeth. "They told me you came back, that you actually tried to fight off those two goons. I heard you wound up in the hospital yourself."

"Just for observation. I wasn't hurt." My own pains and aches had shrunk to insignificance the second I'd seen Max.

"Well, I just wanted to say . . . I just wanted to tell you how much I—"

"That's okay, pal. You would have done the same for me."

"I hope so. I'd like to think so." He dropped his eyes. "I'm not sure, though."

"Sure you would have. Look, it wasn't anything that extraordinary. There wasn't really time to think about it. Believe me, all I—"

"Chris," Max said abruptly, "those guys really scared me."

"Of course they did. You'd have been crazy not to be scared. How do you think I felt?"

"I mean *really* scared. I'm still scared."

"Well, naturally. Anybody—"

He jerked his head with a listless kind of impatience, finally deciding to come out with what I knew he was driving at. "I'm not going to talk to Colonel Antuono. I can't, Chris.

73

This was just a warning. The next time they'll kill me. I know these people. They're animals."

"I know, Max, but are you just going to let those bastards—" I clamped my mouth shut. Who the hell was I to be giving lessons in moral duty to him? Nobody had issued a sadistic warning to me. My involvement was circumstantial and temporary, my own fault. And I was doing fine, walking around with a few lingering aches. Max was the one impaled on that orthopedic Iron Maiden, hoping, in Dr. Tolomeo's dark phrase, to adjust.

"Chris, you ought to be scared, too. You ought to get out of here and go back to Seattle."

"Me? What do I have to be scared about?"

"You saw their faces. You could identify them."

"If they were going to kill me over that, they'd have done it then," I said, none too confidently. If running you down with a car doesn't qualify as attempted murder, what does? "I'm not going anywhere. I have things to talk about with Clara and Amedeo. Then I'm going down and see about that Boursse of Ugo's before he changes his mind. *Then* I'm going home."

His eyes closed. "I'm too tired to argue with you. I just wish the hell you'd clear out."

A husky, gray-haired nurse came in with a tray of equipment. "I must examine the insertion sites," she announced brightly in Italian.

I stood up. "I'll go."

"No," Max said. "She does this every couple of hours. It just takes a few minutes. Don't go yet." But he looked terribly haggard now, and gray-faced with pain.

"I don't know . . ." I looked at the nurse.

"It's all right," she said. "He's fine. It isn't as bad as it looks." So everyone kept telling me. "Go outside, and then you can come back in ten minutes."

"Please," Max said.

"Sure," I said. "Of course I will."

Fifteen minutes later, she emerged, wafted on a pungent billow of antiseptic, and motioned me back in with a tilt of her head. "I gave him something for the pain," she whispered. I returned to find the bed straightened and Max neatened as well, even to having had his hair combed. His face looked tired but no longer drawn with pain; wistful and relaxed. "Hi there, buddy," he said. His hands, which had been gripping the sheets the whole time I'd been there, were loosely clasped on his abdomen.

"The thing is," he was murmuring pensively, mostly to himself, "the thing is, you don't really mean to stay, not forever."

The subject had apparently changed.

"You always mean to go back home someday," he went on dreamily. "And then one day you realize you stayed too long. You go home to America, but it isn't home anymore. You feel like a foreigner. So you run back to Italy, only that's not home either. It doesn't even exist, the Italy you thought you lived in. You made it up. You've never even seen the real Italy, let alone understood it. You've never been anything but a foreigner to them." He shook his head, sadly, slowly. "And they'll never let you be anything else. Can you even understand what I'm talking about?"

"Sure, I can," I said. "I'm hearing the Expatriate's Lament, as sung by the great Italian tenor Massimiliano Caboto."

You have to understand Max. When he was in his cups— or high on painkiller, apparently—he sometimes shifted from his natural ebullience to a tranquil but distinctly theatrical melancholy. Comedy to Tragedy, and often as not on this very subject. I had long ago learned that taking it at face value tended to make him genuinely downhearted, as if he began to believe what he was saying. And this didn't seem like the time to make Max downhearted. He had more than enough to be glum about as it was.

"You sting me," he said, hamming it up to show me he wasn't taking himself seriously. But a moment later he said: "I'm a man without roots, Chris. I'm alone now, ever since Giulia died. I'm going to die here, 5,000 miles from my native land. They're going to bury me in the corner of the cemetery they save for Englishmen and other crazy people."

"Max, believe me, you're not going to die," I said. "Dr. Tolomeo—"

"I don't mean now," he said, lifting an irritable eyebrow. I was spoiling his scene. "I mean eventually."

I smiled as reassuringly as I could. "You're just feeling down now. It's understandable. You'll be yourself again in a few days."

"Ah, what the hell," he said wearily. "What do you understand, a kid like you."

I was having my typical success at jollying the patient up, and I fidgeted in the uncomfortable visitor's chair, wondering if I ought to go before I depressed him even more. I was rescued by the return of the nurse.

"I think maybe now he should rest."

I leaped from the chair. "I'll go, then. I'll drop in again in a day or two, Max."

"Fine, fine." His eyelids were slipping down. "Chris?" he said as I got to the door.

"Yes?"

"When was it we were supposed to go see Ugo?"

"This weekend. Saturday."

"Oh." He sighed and settled himself back against the pillows, his eyes closed now. The structure of rods and pins on his legs was horrible, like a mechanical monster slowly ingesting him from the bottom up. "Well, I think I'm probably not going to make it."

By the time I got back downtown I was thoroughly depressed. Seeing Max had taken the spirit out of me, and, added to the morning's frustrating session with Colonel Antuono, it had been a tough day for a body that had not yet entirely composed itself, as Dr. Tolomeo might have said. My mind didn't feel all that composed, either. Too weary to cope with a real dinner, I stopped at a little bar on Via Ugo Bassi for a couple of stale *panini* with ham and cheese, willingly paying the extra lire charged for sitting down. Then I went up to my room in the Europa to make another early night of it.

I was starting to feel guilty, too. Here I was, concluding my third day in Bologna on a generous expense account, and what had I done to earn my keep so far? Not a thing. I grant you, it wasn't my fault, and it had hardly been what I'd call a pleasure trip. All the same, I hadn't gotten anything done and I was beginning to get fidgety. Achy joints or not, there was a major show to be organized. I picked up the telephone. No doubt Louis would have chirped gravely (yes, Louis can chirp gravely) about obsessive-compulsive work behavior, but Louis wasn't there to know. I telephoned Clara Gozzi, who would be contributing several pictures to the Northerners in Italy show, and made an appointment to visit her in Ferrara the next morning to discuss the arrangements.

My sense of responsibility pacified, I was virtuously, dreamlessly asleep by eight o'clock.

CHAPTER 8

It was half an hour to Ferrara by rail, over restful green countryside dotted with farms. The 10:10 A.M. train was clean and smooth-running, with good *caffè latte* available from a cart and big windows that let in the warm morning sunlight. I soaked up both gratefully and arrived relaxed and feeling almost whole again. My appointment was still forty minutes off, so I took a slow, lulling, roundabout walk to Clara's house. Lulling was just what I needed, and Ferrara was the right place for it, a sober Renaissance city of gardens, broad boulevards, and gracefully crumbling palaces, all of it bathed in the sweet, melancholy sheen of decaying grandeur.

Clara Gozzi, who was rich enough to live anywhere she liked, had chosen not to reside on the elegant, palazzo-lined

Corso Ercole d'Este with the rest of the gentry. "Who wants to live in a damned mausoleum?" she'd grumbled when I'd asked her about it on an earlier visit. "Besides, half those monstrosities are let out to technical institutes and government offices. Would *you* like to live next door to the traffic police?"

Instead, she had a house on the southern outskirts of the city; in a tree-lined, middle-class neighborhood picked because she thought it looked like Aix-en-Provence (it did), where she'd spent her summers as a girl. Here, there were solid blocks of modern, four-story apartment houses built in a not-displeasing neo-Venetian Gothic style, with modest loggias, balconies, and central patios. Clara had bought an entire four-family building, left the outside as it was, and had the inside redone to her specifications. Beyond installing an elevator, a track-lighting system to spotlight her collection, and a bank of security systems, there wasn't much to the redoing. Like many serious collectors, she made only one demand of interior decoration: that it not compete with what hung on the walls. The linoleum-tile floors had been replaced with oak; other than that, the inside of the house still looked like the four separate, identical apartments it had been before, and the furniture, if not quite shabby, was surely nondescript. She had, as a matter of fact, simply had her agent buy most of it from the departing tenants; less fuss that way.

Clara Gozzi had come into the world rich by birth, had been made considerably poorer by a short, disastrous marriage in the 1950s to a dashing, self-styled Luxembourgian count (subsequently done in by wife number three), and had recouped her original wealth and more by her hardheaded management of the Gozzi interests in publishing, kitchenware, and sporting equipment. She was richer even than Ugo Scoccimarro and, like him, scorned the pretensions and niceties of refined social behavior. But whereas Ugo did it from motives of pride and stiff-necked insecurity, Clara did it without giving it a thought. In other ways, she was altogether unlike Ugo: imperious, supercilious, peremptory in her dealings with others.

But underneath this spiky exterior there was—well, I wouldn't go so far as to call it a heart of gold, but certainly a strongly developed philanthropy. Clara was one of those people who had no use and little patience for other human beings as individuals, but who gave handsomely to charitable causes. Knock on her door and ask for a handout to buy your first meal in three days and you were out of luck; write her a letter and ask for $10,000 dollars for an international feed-the-hungry plan and you'd probably get it.

Most people thought of her as an essentially misanthropic woman burdened with a grudging and high-handed sense of noblesse oblige. I saw her differently: as a physically ill-favored woman who'd been taken advantage of in an early marriage (she'd been seventeen) and had thereafter erected a thorny, unscalable facade to protect herself. After a while she'd probably come to enjoy playing the Tartar, and she was rich and influential enough to get away with it.

I liked her. Naturally. More or less. And I was pretty sure she liked me. The one usually goes along with the other. In my dealings with her I'd found her to be intelligent, forthright, and without artifice; she knew what she wanted, what she said was exactly what she meant, and her mind was unlikely to change. In the flighty, volatile art world, traits like those made up for a lot of personality flaws.

It was signora Gozzi, you may remember, who had lost several paintings to thieves the same night the Pinacoteca was broken into two years earlier. Six had been taken from her home, and one—the Rubens that had eventually wound up in Blusher's warehouse and was now on its way back to her—had been stolen from Max's workshop. I had been in touch with her on the telephone about the Rubens several times in the last ten days, but we had yet to discuss the specifics involved in her loan of four other paintings to the exhibition.

Often these specifics are the trickiest part of putting together a show. Understandably enough, lenders can get picky about the security and transportation of their treasures. Some insist that paintings be hand-carried in airplanes, rather than crated up and shipped as baggage. This usually means a separate trip for every piece, with two seats paid for each time; one for you and one for the painting. First class, of course; Titians and

Holbeins don't travel economy class. Sometimes lenders demand extra insurance coverage. Sometimes they come up with finicky sets of demands that seem, to a curator at any rate, designed to make life difficult: *This* particular painting may be reproduced in the catalogue, but not on postcards; *that* particular painting may be shown in Cleveland and Chicago, but not in Baltimore. You just never know.

On the other hand, some lenders have little to tell you. From what I knew of Clara, I expected her to be one of these. Crusty, yes, but she wasn't a stickler. Or so I hoped.

My pressing of the buzzer was answered by a tall, annoyed-looking woman in a severely tailored suit. She peered distractedly and with impatience at me, as if I'd interrupted some terribly pressing task. This was the third time in a year I had come to see Clara, and the same woman had responded each time in the same way. By now I was beginning to understand that this was her normal manner. It was, I supposed, what came of working too long for Clara.

"I'm Christopher Norgren," I said in Italian. "I have an appointment with signora Gozzi."

"You're too early," she told me brusquely, remaining in character. "Your appointment is in fifteen minutes. You'll have to wait."

Clara's querulous voice rang out. "Who is that? Christopher? You're early, damn it. Come in, come in!"

Under the stern eye of the maid, or secretary, or whatever she was, I headed for the doorway from which the gruff voice had come, walking down a long, unfurnished hallway hung like a museum gallery with rows of contemporary paintings on both walls: Kiefer, Dine, Diebenkorn, others I didn't know. I didn't like any of them. Clara's tastes were quite eclectic, more so than mine, and her collection was arranged chronologically, with the most recent on the ground floor, the earliest (fifteenth and sixteenth centuries) at the top. The higher I climbed, the happier I usually was.

I entered an unfurnished room that had probably once been the dining room, and was treated to a restrained version of the full Mediterranean greeting: bear hug, back-pats, even a kiss on, or at least in the vicinity of, each cheek. This was uncharacteristically exuberant for Clara. I understood that I was being thanked for my part in recovering the Rubens.

"This is Christopher Norgren," she announced in Italian to a shiny-faced man with pale, plastered-down hair and a dandy's pencil-line mustache. "A scholar of note in his field, but lamentably narrow."

Had Clara delivered her many such remarks with a smile or even the mordant lifting of an eyebrow—anything to suggest irony—she would have been regarded as a witty woman. But she never did. Her pouchy, homely face rarely changed its indifferent expression.

"*Sono molto lieto*—" the man began, but Clara interrupted him.

"His Italian stinks. If you hope to be understood, Filippo, use English."

"Okay, sure, but, you know, my English stinks." He said this in English with a grin, a small man of fifty in a polka-dot bow tie and a checked, wasp-waisted sport coat. His accent reminded me of Ugo's speech, so I assumed he was Sicilian, too. He held out a manicured hand with bulky rings on two fingers. "I am Filippo Croce. And *you* are Christopher Norgren?"

I was used to the mild wonder with which this was asked. The trouble is, you see, I don't look like any kind of a museum curator, let alone a curator of Renaissance and Baroque art. At thirty-four, I'm a little young for the job, but more than that I don't look scholarly or even particularly intelligent; I don't look patrician; I don't look . . . well, consequential. I'm of average build, average height, with an average brown mustache, and I look, so I've been told, like your average, easygoing, nice guy who works in a computer store or maybe for the government. I mean, I look like a curator to *me*, but enough people have told me I don't so that I'm used to it by now.

"You two don't know each other?" Clara said, surprised. Her English was excellent, the slight accent not so much Italian than a sort of generic Continental, the result of having homes in four countries. "But no, of course you wouldn't. Filippo's been in Ferrara less than a year, haven't you, Filippo?"

"Five months," he said to me. "I was in the south before. I am a dealer in art." With a small flourish he produced an embossed card:

F. Croce
Galleria d'Arte Moderna
Corso della Giovecca, 16
Ferrara

"Christopher is the man who rescued Max Cabot the other night," Clara told him.

"I'm afraid I didn't do too good a job," I said.

Croce clucked sympathetically.

"It was Max's own fault, of course," Clara said crossly. "If he hadn't gone around shouting about going to the police, it wouldn't have happened at all. Stupid man." She hadn't been at the dinner the other night, but of course the story wouldn't have taken long to get to Ferrara.

"They smashed both his legs, you know," I said. "He won't ever walk normally again."

I suppose that what I had in mind was to stir up a little sympathy for poor Max, but it was wasted on Clara. "The man doesn't understand the meaning of discretion, of simple prudence," she said, going along with Di Vecchio and Luca. "Careless, thoughtless. He runs off at the mouth." This was accompanied by an illustrative twirling of fingers at her own mouth. "What about the other one, Scoccimarro? Wasn't he with you, too? Was he hurt?"

"No, we were on our way back from seeing him off at the station when it happened."

"Ugo's a good sort. If you ask him something he gives you the answer. You can tell him I said so."

"I will. I'm flying to Sicily on Saturday.'"

"You can also tell him he likes his grappa too much."

There was an awkward silence broken by Croce's clearing of his throat. "Well, signora, perhaps I go now. I can return—"

"Filippo is trying to convince me I can't live without some more pictures," Clara said, gesturing at three huge paintings propped along the walls, mounted but unframed. "What do you think, Christopher?"

I looked at them. Each was about seven feet by six and consisted of pallid, empty backgrounds on which a few lurid streaks of purple, orange, and bloody red had been whacked on with a trowel—thick and garish. Two of them were done on pegboard, with the holes clearly showing and even some hooks and brackets attached. They seemed to be examples of Comic Abstractionism, which Penny Hauck, Seattle's curator of contemporary painting, had once explained to me. It was, she said, an ironic Abstract Expressionist movement dedicated to demonstrating the absurdity of the Abstract Expressionist movement in today's image-ridden world.

I know, I don't understand it either. I'm just telling you what she said.

"Well?" Clara said.

If it were I, I thought, I could live without them. "They're not really the kind of thing I'm too informed about," I said delicately.

"Christopher's very discreet," Clara said. "He means he can't stand them."

I've been told (by Tony Whitehead, mainly) that I'm not catholic enough in my tastes, that I should strive to appreciate modern and postmodern art more and curb my anachronistic tendency to think in terms of better and worse.

"Taken in their own context," Tony once demanded, "can you stand there and say that the chipped urinals and rusty bottle racks of neo-Dadaism are any less valid, any less 'art' than the sculptures of Michelangelo, the paintings of Raphael? Can you?"

"You're damn r—" I'd begun.

"Of course you can't. You know damn well that art historians don't make that kind of culturally biased value judgment."

"But *I'm* an art historian and *I* make that kind of value judgment, so obviously they do," I'd said, which I'd thought was pretty good, but which didn't seem to strike him as much of an answer.

This is all by way of saying that Clara was right. I couldn't stand the stuff.

Croce tipped back his head and laughed indulgently. "You don't like these pictures so much?"

Not like them so much? I wasn't that keen on being in the same room with them. But I didn't want to offend him. "I work mostly in Renaissance and Baroque art," I said with what was intended as a self-deprecatory smile. "Pretty much representational stuff. The twentieth century's a little new for me."

"Ah!" Croce exclaimed, interpreting my response as one of ignorance and launching into a vigorous discourse on projective spaces and revolutionary perspectival structure. His English wasn't up to it, forcing him to slip in and out of Italian, which left me even further behind. Despite his enthusiasm, I couldn't help feeling there was something inauthentic about him, something a little off. Maybe he was selling too hard, which reputable dealers don't do. Maybe it was the checked coat, polka-dot tie, and glittery rings (and pointed, mirror-shined elevator shoes); he was foppish and raffish at the same time, like an old-time music-hall performer. Maybe it was the way he kept smoothing that plastered-down hair. He just didn't look like a trustworthy dealer to me.

But then I don't look like a bona fide art curator.

I wasn't worried about him putting anything over on Clara, who stood in a corner, impassively watching him go through his paces. "I don't think you're going to convert Christopher," she said dryly when he paused for breath.

He laughed, not very emphatically, and blotted his forehead with a handkerchief. "I think I don't convert you, either, signora. But that's all right. I leave them here for two, three days, and you decide, all right?"

"Fine. Call me Monday."

"*Molte grazie, signora. A lunedì prossimo. Arrivederci.*"

A bow to Clara, a tentative, quickly withdrawn motion as if to kiss her hand, a bow and a sweaty handshake for me, and he was gone.

"Are you really thinking of buying these?" I asked her.

"I am, and don't look so damned superior. Do you know what your problem is, Christopher? I'll tell you. You persist in seeing art solely in aesthetic terms; you refuse to consider it from the standpoint of capital investment."

I smiled. "That's my problem, all right."

"Tell me, does your pitifully limited knowledge of this century's art extend to the Italian Transavantguardia?"

"Mimmo Paladino, that bunch?"

"Yes, that bunch," she said sarcastically. "I have two Paladinos. Do you know what I paid for them in 1978? A thousand dollars each. Would you like to know what I sold *one* of them for this week?"

"I don't think so," I said.

"I don't think so, either." She laughed suddenly, and her eyes warmed. Her laugh, not a frequent phenomenon, was one of her few redeeming physical features. When I said that Clara was ill-favored, I was putting it mildly. She was a bulky, shapeless woman with pockmarked skin and bulging, red-rimmed eyes, one of them disconcertingly larger than the other. I had yet to see her dressed in anything but a capacious, dark dress of indeterminate style.

"Well," she said, "you're here to talk about the arrangements for your show, yes? So let's talk about them. Come."

She stumped out of the room. I followed. With Clara, that's what you did. We went to a room with a couple of armchairs and a settee, which was hung with canvases by some of the foremost artists of the Italian Transavantguardia, best left undescribed. As expected, Clara had no unrealistic demands about the security and showing of her pictures, and only a few questions about transportation. These were summarily and satisfactorily dealt with.

She terminated the discussion with a nod. "So, you want to go look at the paintings, I suppose?" She spoke gruffly, but the light shone again in her eyes.

I had already seen them more than once, but of course I said yes. To say no would have been unkind; every collector loves showing off her treasures. Besides, I really wanted to. What kind of art curator would I be if I didn't enjoy looking at paintings? Most important, I needed to look at some *real* art (forgive me, Tony) after having been trapped on Clara's ground floor for an hour.

The four pictures she was lending were two floors higher: one by Fragonard, one by Van Dyck, and two by a couple of lesser-known seventeenth-century Dutch painters; all had studied in Italy. To tell the truth, none of them were first-rate examples of the artists' work, but they were pretty enough (surpassingly so, after what I'd just been looking at), and historically instructive. The point of Northerners in Italy, after all, was to demonstrate Italian influences on northern European artists who had lived in Italy.

Those influences were most obvious in the two Dutch pieces, *A Village Fair* by Jan Baptist Weenix and an evocative *Shrimp-Catching by Moonlight* by his cousin Nicolaes Berchem, both painted in the 1640s, both set against classical Italianate landscapes complete with the romantic ruins of ancient buildings. Jan Baptist, in fact, had been so thoroughly Italianized he returned to Holland calling himself Giovanni Battista. An early soulmate of Max's.

The Van Dyck was a portrait of Maria dé Medici done in 1627, at the end of a six-year stay in Genoa and Venice. In it Van Dyck was not at his elegant best; it was almost as if the intense color borrowed from the Venetians had overwhelmed his own restrained good taste.

Finest of the lot was a mid-sized painting by the young Fragonard. Not one of the congenial, fluffy pieces that would briefly make him the toast of Paris later on, but a classical landscape obviously painted to please his master Tiepolo, airy and alight with clean, clear colors.

This we stood looking at for some time. "I love the sunlight in this picture," Clara said. "Not lush, like the *Caravaggisti*, but—what would you call it, Christopher?"

"A glancing light," I said after a moment, "like real sunlight on real water and trees. It's not *of* the objects; it's reflected off them. You feel as if it all depends on your own perspective. I'm not quite sure how he did it."

She nodded, smiling. "A glancing light. Well, come on, it's almost one. I owe you the best lunch in Ferrara."

"You owe me a lot more than that, but, okay, I'll settle for lunch."

She drove me herself, in an unpretentious blue Fiat, to La Provvidenza, a restaurant so exclusive there was no sign outside, nothing to indicate there was a restaurant behind the blank white wall. Inside, it was elegant-rustic, with used-brick walls and gleaming wooden floors. It was filled with dark-suited businessmen at the tables, and humming with lithe, sloe-eyed waiters in peach dinner jackets, any of whom might have served as the model for Donatello's svelte, young *David*. A bottle of Soave was opened and poured without our asking as we sat down.

"To the Rubens," Clara said, lifting her glass.

"To the Rubens."

She drank a third of the wine and put down the glass. Immediately a peach-sleeved arm reached between us to top it off. A few seconds later it returned to lay down menus.

Clara lifted hers without looking at it. "Will Max really never walk again?"

"Not well."

"Well, I'm sorry for him. It's a hard thing." This inadvertent moment of human kindness was quickly made up for. "But he has no one to blame but himself. He's a careless man, not discreet. He shouldn't be in the business he's in."

"Clara, Max said that there were five people who knew his security systems well enough to disengage them. Amedeo Di Vecchio was one. Do you know who any of the others were?"

The question surprised me almost as much as Clara. What was I doing, starting my own investigation?

"*Me?*" Clara exclaimed. "How should I know that?" A cigarette jiggled at the corner of her mouth while she spoke, her third since we'd left her house twenty minutes before. She had lit up greedily the moment the door had closed behind us. As a collector, she wouldn't smoke around her paintings, but she made up for it everywhere else.

"In any case," she said, "I don't believe for a minute that Max told only five people. I think everybody in Bologna knew. Max doesn't have secrets. Have you ever been around him when he's drinking?"

"I know what you mean."

"Talk, talk, talk," she said, which pretty well summed it up. "I should have sued him at the time, when the Rubens was first stolen."

"Why didn't you?"

"Why didn't I?" Clara peered at me with a sober, bleary look that I was beginning to recognize as her version of waggishness. "Christopher, how familiar are you with the Italian legal system?"

"Not very." And Colonel Antuono hadn't done much to edify me.

"You're fortunate. It is, should I say, a little tangled, and the results somewhat erratic. We have a saying here: Never sue when you're in the right. It's too risky."

I laughed, and we ordered from the young waiter who had been standing at the ready. Lunch began with antipasto from a self-service table against the far wall. I offered to get Clara's for her, but she shook her head and, with a movement of her chin, sent the waiter scurrying for her instead. A good thing, too, because I had all I could do to manage my own. It is not lasagna or fettuccine or tortellini that I dream hungrily about when I think of Italy's food, but the antipasto tables, and the one at La Provvidenza was as good as they come. I loaded my plate with mussels and shrimp, marinated octopus, prosciutto, smoked mackerel, oily roasted red peppers, two gleaming whole anchovies, and a thick wedge of artichoke frittata. Halfway back, I returned to get a roll, which had to be precariously set on top of the frittata.

This Smorgie-Bob's-all-you-can-eat approach is not the way they do things in Italy, but in my own defense I'll point out that I had had only coffee and a brioche for breakfast, a couple of stale little sandwiches for last night's dinner, and not much else since the attack three days before.

Clara was already eating when I came back. One of those large people who never seems to eat much, at least in public, she had on her plate only a slice of prosciutto and some cheese. She stopped chewing and studied my heaped plate intently. "I think you missed the squid," she said.

"I'll get some when I go back for seconds," I told her, and dug in.

"Christopher," she said after leaving me to it for a few minutes, "this matter of my Rubens. Tell me, what are your impressions of the way it resolved itself? How much do you believe this Blusher's account?" She had finished her hors d'oeuvres and pushed her plate away. A cigarette was back dancing at the side of her mouth.

I considered the question while I finished chewing a bony, crackling mouthful of anchovy. By now I'd given Mike Blusher a lot more thought, and I knew precisely what it was I suspected him of. In the last few decades the field of art thievery had developed well beyond the crude old days when paintings had usually been stolen and then held for ransom. Now, with the prodigious rewards offered by insurance companies, nasty ransom demands had become unnecessary. You could be more decorous. You merely stole the piece of art, waited awhile, and then turned it in for the insurance reward. All you had to do was come up with some reproachless way of "finding" the object in question and getting the word to the insurance company.

It was safer, less complicated, and more civilized than trying to collect ransom, less dangerous than trying to fence stolen art. The money was better, too. On the black market the going rate was only three or four percent of the value, as opposed to the ten percent most insurance companies would pay. And, as in Blusher's case, one could even wind up with some favorable publicity as a bonus.

After all, wouldn't you want to buy a fake antique ashtray from the guy who discovered the famous stolen Rubens?

But it took patience, ingenuity, and care, none of which had seemed to be Blusher's strong suits. Or had I underrated him? Was he more patient, ingenious, and careful than I'd thought? I was beginning to believe it was possible. And if ever an operation was made for processing stolen art, Venezia Trading Company was it. Remember Chesterton's famous question about the best place to hide a stolen Madonna? Well, apply it to a stolen painting and the answer was surely among five hundred look-alike paintings.

There was another possibility, too. It might be that Blusher wasn't in it alone. It might be that Trasporti Salvatorelli was more in the thick of things than Luca and Di Vecchio gave them credit for, and the whole affair had been concocted between them and Blusher. After Blusher collected his reward and the dust settled, the money would be split. Or maybe not split. Maybe the Salvatorellis had been behind it, and Blusher was only a hireling who would receive a small cut.

I told all this to Clara, almost beginning to believe it myself. She sat listening, fingers steepled against her upper lip. "Christopher, let me ask you this." She leaned forward, shaking another cigarette from her pack. Before she got it to her mouth the peach-sleeved arm shot forward with a lighter. She sucked in a deep lungful and wedged the cigarette in the corner of her mouth as before. "Assuming that something crooked is going on," she continued, "why do you think the Rubens is the only picture to surface in this way? Why none of my other paintings? Why none stolen from the Pinacoteca?"

"I suppose," I said doubtfully, "that the theft of the Rubens might have had nothing to do with the others, that it was a different gang. A coincidence."

She snorted. "On the same night? Within a few hours of the time my Correggio and my Bronzinos were being taken from my home?" She shut her eyes for a moment, mourning her Correggio and Bronzinos. "Don't be ridiculous."

I nodded, agreeing with her. "Why, then?"

"I'm asking you."

By now our second courses had come. I had a couple of mouthfuls of a fragrant *risotto con funghi* while I thought about it. "Clara, do you happen to know if all the paintings stolen that night were insured by the same company?"

"They were, yes: Assicurazioni Generali."

"Well, then, the Rubens could have been a feeler, to see if the insurance company would come through and be cooperative—you know, no hard questions, no investigation, no charges."

She cocked her head, evaluating the idea. "It's possible, yes."

"Now may I ask you something?"

She lifted her head warily.

"How did they manage to steal the paintings from your house? How did they get in?"

91

"What's the difference?" she said gruffly, poking away at her *spaghetti alla Bolognese*. "It's water under the bridge."

"Didn't you have security systems in place?"

"Of course I had security systems in place. What do you think?"

"Well, who knew about them?"

"Nobody knew. You think I'm your friend Max?"

"Do you think it was an inside job? Somebody on your staff?"

"No." She was mumbling into her food. I could hardly hear her.

"Well, then, what—"

The hand holding the fork thumped exasperatedly on the table. "They weren't turned on, all right? I forgot to turn the damn things on!"

"You—" I did manage to keep down a sudden burst of laughter, but something must have twitched somewhere, because she raised her fork menacingly.

"The merest hint of a smile and you'll be impaled, Christopher. I warn you."

I said: "I was startled, I wasn't amused," half of which was true.

It had been a fleeting moment of amusement, however. Clara had my sympathy. Comic Abstractionists and Trans-avantguardists may have represented so much capital investment for her, but her love for the Old Masters was as deep as mine. To lose a Correggio from carelessness . . .

"I take my paintings down fairly often," she said quietly. "Sometimes I would forget to reactivate the systems." She lifted her shoulders in a glum shrug. "Sometimes I would forget for days."

I nodded my commiseration. "It happens."

It does, too, unbelievable as it may seem. Clara's case was far from the first example. The most recent one, as far as I know, happened a few years ago on Christmas Eve when a priceless group of pre-Columbian artifacts was taken from the Great National Museum of Anthropology in Mexico City. How did the thieves get in? They got in because the alarm system was switched off. How did they know it would be switched off? They knew because it had been switched off ever since it had broken down three years earlier.

"I leave the alarms on all the time now," she said grimly.

I didn't doubt it. The National Museum of Anthropology does, too.

CHAPTER 9

I'd barely had time to put my feet up after getting back to my hotel room when the telephone rang.

"Hi," the familiar voice on the other end said. "I'm here. Where've you been?"

"Uh . . . Calvin?" It took me a second to remember that Calvin Boyer, the Seattle Art Museum's marketing director, the man who had hustled me off to Mike Blusher's warehouse, was coming to Bologna to take care of his end of the arrangements for the show. The plans we'd laid in Seattle only last week seemed from another lifetime.

"Right, sure," he said. "Let's get together. We ought to go over some stuff."

"Where are you, downtown?"

"Yeah, I'm staying at the Internazionale, a couple of blocks from you."

We agreed to meet in half an hour, at 6:00, at the Caffè Re Enzo, a café-bar in the arched stone colonnade of the Podesta Palace, the long, fifteenth-century building that forms the northern side of the Piazza Maggiore. It was a place we'd had drinks in when we'd been in Bologna on a preliminary visit six months earlier.

It was only a five-minute walk for me, but I headed right there, chose a good table looking out over the piazza, and ordered an espresso, which was quickly brought, along with the usual tall glass of water. Then I settled down, my head tipped back against a carved rosette on one of the ancient, peeling columns, to wait for Calvin and take in the scene.

Bologna's Piazza Maggiore is enormous, one of the world's great public squares. Offhand, the only open civic space I can think of in Italy that is larger is the one in front of St. Peter's, and this one is livelier if not quite as handsome. Directly across from me, some 500 feet away, was the hulking Basilica of San Petronio. To my right, making the piazza's western border, the Palazzo Communale (with Colonel Autuono no doubt in his stuffy little "office" at that very moment, happily ferreting away his dog-eared folders in his dog-eared cardboard boxes). On my left another long, porticoed building, the Pavaglione, completed the perimeter of the square. Five big tour buses stood next to one another at one corner of the basilica, hardly noticeable in the vast space.

And in the center, milling about on six acres of stone-block pavement, were the people. Ordinarily, I don't go in much for people-watching, but when I'm in Italy I make an exception. The scene before me was a bigger version of the one that can be found in the main plaza of any Italian town in the late afternoon of a fine day. At about five o'clock you can count on groups of talkative old men beginning to materialize. I've yet to make out where it is they all come from. The square just gradually fills up, like a swimming pool being fed through a hole in its bottom. After a while, women and younger people also appear and get into the act in smaller, marginally less voluble numbers.

It always gives me the feeling that the curtain's just gone up on a crowd scene in a Donizetti opera, that it's all being choreographed for my benefit, and that in another moment everyone will burst into glorious song. They never do, of course, but they gather into noisy clusters, talking, laughing, arguing, jabbing each other with their index fingers, eloquently smacking their own foreheads and lifting their hands to the sky. Every now and then—at least to the eyes (and ears) of a phlegmatic American observer—they give every appearance of being on the verge of physically attacking each other, only to have the crisis dissolve into laughter and good fellowship.

Add to this a few hundred kids chasing the whirring flocks of pigeons that inhabit the place, and a few hundred tired, overexcited tourists trying to keep up with tour guides who are brandishing red or yellow umbrellas and urging them on with exhortations in German, Japanese, and French, and you have a bracing spectacle that's worth a trip to Bologna in itself. Not something I'd want to do every evening, you understand, but once a visit anyway.

Calvin showed up as I was finishing my coffee. "Six hundred years working on that church, and they still can't get it right," he said, slipping into a chair across from me. He was looking at the Basilica of San Petronio, begun in 1390 and, as Calvin had pointed out, with its marble facade not yet completed.

I laughed. "You can't hurry these things." A profundity worthy of Benedetto Luca himself.

Calvin took his first good look at my face. "Jeez, what happened to *you*? What did you do, get run over by a train?"

"A car," I said, and explained.

He listened, his chubby, rabbity face gloomy and intent, then thought a long time before speaking. "If you work it right," he said, "our workmen's comp insurance ought to cover you."

That was why he was a marketing director and I was just a curator.

"It's okay, Calvin. My own policy'll pick up most of it."

He shrugged. "Suit yourself. Well, I'm glad you're okay."

The waiter appeared. Calvin ordered a Cynar, one of those peculiarly bitter European aperitifs along the order of Ugo's

Jazz! They claim it's made from artichokes, and I don't doubt it. Somewhere, somehow, Calvin had actually gotten to like it. I asked for a martini, which in Italy brings you a small glass of Martini-brand vermouth.

"So," Calvin said after his first sip. "Did you hear about Mike Blusher's reward?"

"I heard he's getting $150,000."

"Correction, *we're* getting $150,000."

"Come again?"

"Blusher's donating the money to the museum."

I was stunned. "To us? All of it?"

"Every bit. In appreciation."

"For what?"

Calvin grinned. "I'm not too clear on that part. For helping him get the publicity he wanted, I guess. And this is getting him even more. He actually made *Time* this week. Or, who knows, maybe he just felt guilty taking all that money for doing nothing. Tony said not to ask too many questions, just take it and say thank you."

"That I can believe. Well," I said with a sigh, "I guess Blusher's not pulling anything after all."

"Well, sure," Calvin said, blinking his surprise, "what did you think?"

For all his pitchman qualities, Calvin is at heart an innocent. It's one of the things I like about him.

"No matter," I said. Why harass Calvin with the complex and nefarious schemes Clara and I had been hatching in Blusher's behalf? None of them held water anymore anyway. A guy who gave away $150,000 to which he was legitimately entitled could hardly be accused of pulling a fast one.

So why didn't I trust him, even now?

A gusty wind had whipped up. A square of tissue paper, the kind local vendors used for making little cones to wrap fruit, blew up onto the table and caught on the stem of Calvin's glass. He brushed it away. "Blusher followed your advice on the other one, by the way."

"What advice?"

"You told him to take that van Eyck—"

"That fake van Eyck."

"—in to Dr. Freeman to have it X-rayed."

"Oh, yeah. But I didn't *tell* him to, I just said he could if he wanted to. What did she find?"

"I don't know. I haven't heard."

"Well, she's not going to come up with anything, or at least not what Blusher's hoping for. There's no Rembrandt or Titian under that van Eyck, Calvin. Nobody paints over a—"

"I know, I know. You told me. Hey, you want to go get some dinner?"

I nodded. The wind was beginning to make things unpleasant, not just because it was sucking little whirlpools of litter and grit up onto the table, but because it had driven many of the old men from the square into the protection of the long portico. They had not noticeably adjusted their volume, so that what had been a charmingly boisterous clamor now sounded like a war happening a few feet away.

I waved to the waiter. "*Il conto, per favore.*"

"Watch this, watch this," Calvin whispered to me. He pulled out a thin black calculator the size of a checkbook. It had what I had come to recognize as the look of one of his airline gift-catalogue toys.

"Automatic currency converter?" I said.

He shook his head.

"Expense analyzer and recorder?"

He shook his head again. He was punching keys and concentrating hard, his tongue sticking out.

When I'd paid the waiter, Calvin motioned for him to stay, punched another key, and held out the calculator to him. The waiter looked confused. Calvin kept sticking out the calculator. The waiter glanced at me for help. "*Prego . . . ?*"

I shrugged. I didn't know what Calvin was doing, either.

Finally, the waiter took the calculator from him and looked at the display. He smiled politely and looked at me again. This time it was he who shrugged.

Calvin took it back and showed it proudly to me. The display said "WHERE IS / DOV'È, DOVE C'È."

He went back to punching buttons while the waiter remained restively at the table. There were a lot of people waiting to be served. "Calvin," I said, "I can ask—"

"Sh, sh." He made a mistake, muttered, hit a few more buttons and grinned. This time he showed the display to me first: "A GOOD RESTAURANT / UN BUON RISTORANTE."

"Ah," said the waiter again, and began to reply.

"No," Calvin said, and tapped the calculator. "Here."

He handed it back to the waiter. "It works both ways," he told me proudly.

"Calvin," I said, "he's in a hurry. There are a million people here, and he's the only waiter. Why don't you just let him tell us?" According to Clara Gozzi's standards, my Italian might stink, but this I could handle.

Calvin did some grumbling about the calculator's costing $170, but pocketed it with reasonably good grace while the waiter told us about a restaurant a few blocks away on Via Nazario Sauro, then quickly made his getaway.

To get there we crossed the Piazza Nettuno, a small square named for the famous sixteenth-century fountain by Giovanni da Bologna in its center, a flamboyant, thirty-foot high wedding cake of bronze and stone topped by a nude, muscular, triumphantly male Neptune. At its base sirens riding dolphins squeezed their ample breasts, producing five jets of water from each nipple. Four sirens, forty streams. Michelin demurely describes the whole thing as having "a rather rough vigour."

Calvin paused, studying the sirens appreciatively. "Oh, Debbie said to say hi," he said absently, then flushed. Debbie was the young woman who handled incoming calls in the staff offices, the one Blusher had inquired about in his genteel way, "the one with the knockers." You didn't have to be Louis to figure out the association.

He fumbled in his pockets and came up with an envelope. "She gave me your messages, the personal ones anyway."

I opened the envelope and pulled out two telephone message slips. The first was from "Mr. Poulsen." The message was "Can't get to you till 5/1." I turned slightly away from Calvin, suddenly feeling naked. Five days gone, and only two personal calls, one of which was from the plumber who was supposed to repair my garbage disposal unit. It didn't say a lot for my life outside of work.

The other was more personal, but it didn't do anything to

raise my spirits, either. The caller was described as "Anne." Under MESSAGE Debbie had written: "No message. Just wanted to say hi."

Anne.

I stuffed the envelope into my pocket. "Come on," I said a little roughly, "let's go find this restaurant."

The meal with Calvin was not what you would call sparkling. He told me his plans for the next couple of days: meetings with Di Vecchio's staff at the Pinacoteca and with Luca. I told him about mine: a visit to Trasporti Salvatorelli in the morning, a meeting of my own at the Pinacoteca in the afternoon, and then, the following day, off to visit Ugo for the weekend.

Calvin was talkative, as always, but I had turned gloomy and uncommunicative, and after a while he tired of carrying on a conversation with himself. We parted company early, and Calvin went off to to whatever Calvin does at night in unfamiliar cities. I went back to my room at the Europa and moped.

You will have noticed by now that there's no woman in this story. Well, sure, there's Clara Gozzi, but you know what I mean. This absence of a Significant Female Other in my life was not the result of personal persuasion. It was just that things hadn't been going well for me in that regard lately.

My divorce, only eight months old, had come after ten years of a marriage that I thought was going just fine. I loved Bev, I was happily faithful to her, I enjoyed her company. We laughed a lot, our lovemaking was terrific, we liked the same music, the same food, the same sports, the same people.

And then one Saturday, when I got back from looking over a Mantegna *Head of St. Paul* that the museum had just gotten from Geneva, she wasn't there. No note on the refrigerator door, no clothes cleaned out of the closet, no nothing. She was just gone. This, mind you, after we'd casually agreed that morning on the Chinese restaurant we were going to for dinner. Two horrible days followed; repeated telephone calls to the police, the highway patrol, the hospitals. There was even one awful visit to the morgue. In the end I found out she'd moved in with a stockbroker, a guy I'd never even heard of. Moreover—worse, in a way—she'd been having an affair with him for a year and a half completely without my knowledge or even my suspicion.

Which shows you what can happen when you're dumb enough to leave your beautiful wife home alone while you spend your weekends blissfully buried in the fifteenth century. Oh, later on, when I thought about it, I could see that we'd been drifting apart a little over the previous year or so, but the truth is, at the time, I just didn't have a clue.

The long divorce negotiations, miserable as they were, at least had the virtue of killing the feelings I still had for Bev. But they went on so long, and I got so tired of our carping at each other through our lawyers, and niggling over every piece of furniture, every book, every tape, that in the end I gave almost everything to her, and was relieved to be done with it. The only thing that was important to me that I wound up keeping was our dog, Murphy, which, in effect, I traded for our new $8,000 car.

Impossible, you think? I'm exaggerating, you say? The system doesn't work that way? Well, think twice before you get divorced is all I can say.

The worst of it was, Murph got killed by a car a month later, so I came out of it with nothing at all that was worth anything.

And I loved that damn dog.

Now, while all this was going on, I took on a temporary European assignment, working with the Department of Defense to help put together a traveling exhibition of Old Masters paintings that had been looted by the Nazis in World War II, and later recovered for their owners by the American military. Anne Greene was an Air Force captain, a community liaison officer, assigned to the exhibition, to do whatever community liaison officers do. We met at the U.S. Air Force installation in Berlin, where the show was administratively headquartered.

This was fourteen months after Bev had left; fourteen months during which I'd been joltingly reintroduced to a singles scene that had changed so much I never did get my bearings in it—or wanted to get them, for that matter. At thirty-four I felt like a dinosaur from another planet, let alone another era. I even started to think that maybe I didn't like women anymore; modern women anyway. Anne changed that. Intelligent, self-sufficient, career-oriented, she was as modern as they come, yet I loved being with her, being anywhere near her. I started thinking that maybe I was healing, becoming whole again. I started thinking that maybe I loved her.

My European assignment lasted six weeks. Then I had to go back to San Francisco to resume my regular job at the museum. Anne and I stayed in touch, of course, and when the final divorce proceedings came up, she offered to take a week's vacation to be with me during what she figured would be a rocky time. I told her it wasn't going to be rocky at all—in my own mind it was already over and done—but it would be wonderful to see her. And when the whole business was finished, I would show her San Francisco. If she could afford to take two weeks, I'd show her the whole West Coast.

It turned out to be a mistake. I just wasn't able to keep my two worlds straight. The court appearances were bad enough, but I was ready for them. What I wasn't ready for were the out-of-court negotiating sessions in which Bev and I bitterly carved up and appropriated the rubble from a decade's shared history while our lawyers nodded sagely and dispassionately to each other: "That seems fair to me, Bernie, what do you think?" "Oh, I think we can live with that, Rita. We're not trying to be vengeful here."

Like hell we weren't. One thing you learn in a divorce is that you have reserves of vengefulness you never dreamed were there.

It had been far worse than I'd expected. In the afternoons I would slouch home to a waiting Anne, drained and dispirited, sullen and combative. And unable to make love.

Which, on top of everything else, made me defensive and quick to take offense. At one point, following a particularly humiliating nonperformance in bed, I remember ranting and going around kicking chairs and wallowing in noisy self-recrimination. Anne, after four or five days of unbelievable tolerance, finally blew up.

"Goddammit!" she yelled, suddenly sitting bolt upright in bed, "I didn't come 6,000 miles to get laid, so just shut up, will you!"

It was so unlike her, it stunned me into silence.

"You jerk!" she added after a moment, and whacked me with a pillow. It was the sort of thing that should have ended in teary laughter, but it turned into an ugly, heart-searing fight instead. Early the next morning, after lying all night with our backs turned stiffly to each other, we patched it up. But not really, not satisfactorily. It was never the way it had been before. Anne stayed another two gingerly days, then told me she really had to get back to her job in Germany. My heart was like lead, but I didn't argue. And so she left, looking tense and pale. God knows what I looked like.

In her place I would have left, too, only sooner. She had come to offer comfort, and I wasn't having any. I just wasn't ready for it.

That had been five months ago. Since then we'd exchanged two or three guarded letters. I didn't know if she was seeing anyone else, and she didn't know if I was. (I wasn't; the divorce, and then the miserable hassling with Anne had scraped me raw, worn me down. I gave it a try, but I just couldn't face the modern premating ritual, not yet.) I'd wanted to call her a hundred times, but never got myself to do it. The thing was, I felt like such a twit. What would I say? Apologize? I'd already done that. So, afraid to bring things to a head, I had let them drift unresolved. In five months we hadn't spoken to each other.

And then this call. "No message. Just called to say hi." Surely it was time to see if we could work things through, and here was Anne—blameless, openhearted Anne—making the first move. And here was I, in Europe—as Debbie had probably told her—only a few hundred miles away from her base at Berchtesgaden. All I had to do was call her, tell her where I was, arrange to meet . . .

I looked at the telephone a long time, unmoving. After a while I undressed and went to bed.

CHAPTER 10

Trasporti Salvatorelli was located on the city's western outskirts, beyond the Florence-bound railroad tracks, in the
Quartiere Mazzini. It was one of several low buildings in a
sterile, modern industrial park near the intersection of Viale
Vladimir Ilic Lenin and Via Carlo Marx. And for that matter,
not all that far from Via Stalingrado and Via Yuri Gagarin.
As I mentioned earlier, despite its overlay of luxury hotels,
great restaurants, and glittering boutiques, Bologna was not
exactly a hotbed of capitalist ideology. To give credit where
due, however, you couldn't really accuse it of being parochial,
either, at least when it came to names. Not far from where I
stood Viale Lenin crossed underneath Tangenziale JFK. There

was a Piazza Franklin Delano Roosevelt too, and a Via Abramo Lincoln. No Via Adam Smith, however, and as far as I knew no Piazza Ronald Reagan was being contemplated.

You may be wondering, with some justification, what I was doing at Trasporti Salvatorelli. That is, why were we entrusting Northerners in Italy to a firm that had proven itself inept at best (the accidental shipment of Clara's Rubens), or "bent" at worst (Paolo's assassination and presumed connections with the underworld)? The answer is that we had no choice. Their unsettling recent history aside, they were simply the best there was in Bologna, and the most experienced by far; not only when it came to the handling, crating, and shipping of valuable artwork—which is a demanding field in itself, and one requiring considerable expertise—but in coping with the Byzantine complexities of getting anything officially deemed an art treasure out of Italy, even temporarily and for the most virtuous of purposes.

The Pinacoteca had been using them satisfactorily for years. The nearest shipper of comparable reputation was in Milan, but to use them we would have had to ship the paintings *to* Milan in the first place, which would have put us back where we started. So we were stuck with Trasporti Salvatorelli. Not that I'd given them much thought until the last hectic week or so. Several months ago Benedetto Luca had volunteered the service of Ofelia Nervi, one of his deputies, to make the necessary arrangements with Salvatorelli. This was fine with me. Having someone on the spot was more efficient than my trying to conduct business from Seattle. Instead, I had simply chatted every couple of weeks with Ofelia to head off any potential problems, few of which had arisen. As far as I knew, everything was in order.

Still, I had to visit Trasporti Salvatorelli myself. For one thing, I was nominally responsible for the whole affair, so I had to sign the ton or so of paperwork that had no doubt accumulated by now. Besides, by this time I'd gotten more than a little uneasy about the firm. I wanted to see the place, get some idea of how it was run, meet Bruno Salvatorelli himself. So at ten o'clock on Friday morning I found myself stepping out of a taxi in front of a long, gray, windowless building, featureless except for an unobtrusive sign over the entrance: "Trasporti Salvatorelli. *Per tutte le destinazioni.*"

Inside, the front part of the building was walled off from the operating area by moveable, six-foot-high partitions. Here there was a tiny reception area staffed by a short-skirted, bouncy woman of perhaps twenty-five; a conference room with massive flow charts and schedules pinned to the walls; and a small private office. Everything was modern and well-maintained, but utilitarian in the extreme. No pictures on the walls, no flowers on the desks. The only object there for its cosmetic value was a lonely, failing rubber plant in a corner near the copier. And possibly the receptionist. From beyond the far partition came the thumping, creaking, and cursing to be expected in a busy shipping firm. I was cheered.

The conference room was occupied by three shirtsleeved men engaged in heated conversation, all more or less at the same time. The portly gentleman in the tie, the receptionist informed me, was signor Salvatorelli, who was expecting me. However, a scheduling crisis had unexpectedly arisen. Something about the way she said it told me that they were not unusual at Trasporti Salvatorelli. The signore would be only a few minutes, she was sure, but if I wished, she would interrupt him. No, I told her, I would be happy to wait. I accepted a cup of tea and took a seat in one of the two visitors' chairs, where I could watch Bruno Salvatorelli in action.

He was a complete surprise, totally unlike what I'd expected. I know—I shouldn't have been so astonished only a few days after having had a similar experience with Colonel Antuono, but as a matter of fact this happens to me all the time. The thing is, not only do I have this gift for coming up with stereotypes at a moment's notice, but I always seem to do it along embarrassingly hackneyed lines. So what I'd conjured up for Bruno Salvatorelli was a swarthy, furtive, shifty-eyed shyster with glossy black hair; someone who went around shooting his cuffs, or shrugging his skinny shoulders while saying "Eh!"

To my relief I couldn't have been further off the mark. Not that Bruno Salvatorelli was a reassuring sight. Fat, rumpled, excited, he looked like a man well on the way to an ulcer if not already there. Bald except for an ear-level fringe, he had meticulously teased a few long, shellacked strands of graying hair from one side to the other over the top of his scalp and somehow plastered them in place. At least half a dozen pens were stuffed into a shirt pocket already stained beyond hope of restoration. Stubby, similarly stained fingers held yet another pen, a thick green one, which he jabbed intermittently at one of the flow charts.

His two foremen held clipboards packed with papers, and while Salvatorelli ranted and poked at the chart, they ranted back and slapped their clipboards. "*Impossibile!*" one or the other of them would say every few seconds and turn away in exasperation, but Salvatorelli held firm and eventually prevailed. He was obviously the boss; I had to say that for him.

When his employees had marched grimly out, dominated if not won over heart and soul, Salvatorelli came to shake hands with me. With his other hand he dabbed at his head with a grubby handkerchief, taking care to avoid displacing a single, lovingly arranged strand.

"This is a terrible business to be in," was his greeting to me in Italian. "Don't ever take up the shipping business. It's one problem after another."

I promised him I wouldn't and followed him into his office, where he waved me into a chair and, with a great sigh, plumped heavily down behind his desk. For a few seconds he sat there, grimacing and digging his middle finger into a spot at the base of his sternum. If not ulcers, he certainly suffered from heartburn. "I have to stop drinking wine," he told me. "My liver, it can't handle it anymore. It's all right if we speak Italian?"

In my best accent I told him I was reasonably fluent.

My best accent isn't all that good. "I'll talk slowly," he said.

The receptionist came in with two thick folders of papers. Salvatorelli looked at them the way a treed coon looks at the frothing hounds. He practically cowered.

"What is that?" he asked her, his voice rising.

Here, I saw, was a harried man, a man who felt himself beset on every side, who wondered *when*, not *if*, the next disaster would strike. Every now and then my life gets like

107

that, too, but with Salvatorelli I had the impression it was business as usual.

"It's only the papers to do with signor Norgren," she told him soothingly. "You told me to bring them."

"Yes, of course. Good." He winced slightly. "There's nothing wrong with them?"

"No, everything is in order."

"Fine, fine, put them down."

Oddly enough, his nervousness wasn't worrying me; if anything, I was encouraged. It wasn't a suspicious sort of agitation, if that makes any sense; not the skulking fear of a thief, or the terror of a crook in trouble with the Mafia. It just seemed like the sincere concern of a respectable, if frenetic, businessman who took his business to heart.

This was borne out by the fastidious way he went through the arrangements with me, making sure that I was aware of and approved everything that had been agreed upon between him and Ofelia Nervi, and that I understood the purpose of every form in the files. It took an hour and a half, and although I can't say it was fun, it was comforting. Bruno Salvatorelli knew his stuff.

Which made the mix-up with Clara Gozzi's Rubens all the more puzzling. How could it possibly have been sent accidentally to Blusher as part of a shipment of otherwise unadulterated junk? What was it doing at Trasporti Salvatorelli in the first place, without Salvatorelli's being aware of it? Or *was* it a scam of some kind, as I'd surmised with Clara? But that seemed improbable. Bruno Salvatorelli just didn't come across as a crook. Not that my judgment in these matters was perfect.

"I understand there is also a gentleman in Sicily who is contributing paintings," he said. "Did you wish us to handle them? I have an agent in Palermo."

"No, I think Ugo's arranging that himself, but I'll be flying down to see him Saturday, before I head back home, and I'll ask him. Signor Salvatorelli, may I ask you a question?"

"Ask, ask." He was expansive now, replete with the satisfaction of minutiae properly executed. The last document had been signed, we had shaken hands once more, and the receptionist had come in to take away the papers and bring us pungent cups of *caffè alla Borgia*. (Salvatorelli's liver was apparently selective: wine, no; apricot brandy, yes.)

"As you may know," I said, "I'm the one who identified the painting in signor Blusher's warehouse as—"

He stiffened. The anxiety-antennae popped back out on his forehead and quivered. "This is intolerable!" he said. "Intolerable!"

I backpedaled. "It's only that I couldn't help wondering, signore, how such an accident could happen in so—so well-run a company, so—"

He wasn't fooled by this mealy-mouthing. The cup was banged into its saucer. Brandy-laced espresso sloshed onto the desk blotter. "I have spoken freely to the police!" he shouted. "I have spoken freely to the insurance company! I have welcomed their investigations! I have *embraced* their investigations! They ascribe no blame to me! I know *nothing* of stolen paintings! I will not permit—will not permit—"

A commotion at the entrance to the building had thrown him off the track. He half rose to peer over my shoulder. "What, what, what . . . ?"

I turned too, looking out through the space between the partitions. The receptionist was unsuccessfully trying to hold off five uniformed men, two in the military-style khaki outfits of the carabinieri, three in the natty uniforms of the municipal police: dark blue berets and jackets, gray pants with thin red stripes, and white Sam Browne belts with handcuffs and holstered pistols. One of the carabinieri carried a semiautomatic machine gun propped barrel-up against his shoulder.

With an effort Salvatorelli finally managed to get something out. "What do you want?"

"Signor Salvatorelli?" said one of the policemen, sweeping the complaining receptionist casually aside.

"Of course I'm signor Salvatorelli. Who else would I be?"

"I am Captain Barbaccia." He held up a sheet of paper. "I have authorization from the special prosecutor's office to make a search of this property."

Salvatorelli's cheeks puffed out. Red spots appeared on the sides of his neck. He raised a fat, clenched, quivering hand. "*Puh* . . ." he said, ". . . *puh* . . ."

Captain Barbaccia took advantage of this interlude in the conversation to step into the office. He looked down at me thoughtfully, a craggy handsome man with an air of quiet authority, and a uniform that must have been tailored for him. Now *here* was someone who would have made a respectable Eagle of Lombardy.

"And who are you, please, signore?" he asked me pleasantly. I told him.

"And your business here?"

But by this time Salvatorelli had found speech. "This is too much!" he cried. "I am being persecuted, hounded to death, as was my sainted brother! What do you want here? What do you hope to find? How can I run a business if—"

"We believe there may be several missing works of art on your property, signore," Barbaccia said calmly.

Salvatorelli's mouth fell open. His face went from dull red to sick gray. He sagged back into his chair. "You . . . you accuse me . . ."

"No one accuses you, signor Salvatorelli. We have no reason to suspect you of anything." After a moment he added, "I tell you the truth."

Some of the color came back into Salvatorelli's cheeks. He took a breath. "What paintings?" he asked.

"Perhaps you would show us the way to your Lot 70?" Barbaccia suggested.

"What paintings?" Salvatorelli demanded. He might be excitable, but he wasn't a pushover. "I insist that you tell me."

The captain paused, then complied with a small bow of his head. "A landscape by Carrà and a small still life by Morandi; stolen from the municipal gallery in Cosenza five years ago."

Carrà and Morandi, along with the better known De Chirico, were painters of the quasi-surrealist *Pittura Metafisica* movement of the 1920s; distinctly minor figures in a short-lived school. Hardly worth stealing, you might think, but given today's bizarre market, I had no idea what they might be worth—or rather what they might sell for. Two or three hundred thousand dollars each, I supposed.

"*Cosenza?*" Salvatorelli echoed, sounding genuinely amazed. "What have I to do with Cosenza? I demand, I insist—"

But Barbaccia's patience had worn through. "Please get up, signore. We wish to see the lot in question." He stepped briskly out of the office and waited, stiff and commanding, for Salvatorelli to follow.

The businessman jumped up and scurried out. "I go," he muttered, "but under protest, under protest."

Without looking at me, Barbaccia leveled a finger in my direction. "This one remains. The others, too," he said to the policeman with the machine gun, who nodded and took up a position in the hallway, presumably to guard me, the receptionist, and a couple of big-eyed workers who had drifted in to see what the commotion was about. Barbaccia and the others followed a grumbling Salvatorelli into the back of the building.

In accord with what appears to be prevailing Mediterranean police custom, the vicious-looking, black semiautomatic had been entrusted into the hands of the youngest, most jittery-looking carabiniere, a downy-faced, nervous kid who seemed to be all of seventeen. As always, this had a markedly quieting effect on those in his charge. No one talked to anyone else. No one made anything remotely like a sudden move.

But after a while, when he'd relaxed a little, I smiled at the youngster. "How's it going?" I said, dropping my classical Italian for a cozier, slangier version. "What's up, anyway? Do you think—"

Either he recognized my accent, or he had heard me tell Barbaccia that I was an American. Whichever, he seized the opportunity to practice his English.

"Shuddup, you," he said, with a concise but expressive jerk of the black machine gun.

I decided my questions could wait after all.

In twenty minutes they were back, with a noisily expostulating Salvatorelli leading the way. It was a mark of just how unsettled he was that he had allowed one of the hair strands to work loose and slip down, so that it now clung curving to one temple, like a Caesarean laurel wreath. Italian was flying thick and fast, with not much attention to syntax, so I couldn't understand all of it, but I got the gist: He, Salvatorelli, had no way of knowing that the two paintings were there. How could he? Lot 70 had been deposited the previous month for eventual shipment to Naples, by a man who said his name was signor Pellico. No, Salvatorelli had never seen him; the business had been conducted entirely by mail. A three-month storage fee had been paid, and the crate had remained on the premises until such time as signor Pellico directed that it be shipped. How could Salvatorelli know what was inside? What did the captain expect of him? That he would search through the effects of his clients?

The captain assured him that he didn't expect it at all, that no suspicion attached to signor Salvatorelli or his firm, that the carabinieri were in fact grateful for his excellent cooperation in the recovery of these valuable works of art. It was clear to anyone with eyes that Trasporti Salvatorelli had been the innocent pawn of a slippery criminal who would, with luck, soon be brought to justice.

Slowly, Salvatorelli became more composed. The handkerchief was applied to his forehead and neck. The nonconforming hair was detected and smoothed back into place. He was, he said, happy to have had the opportunity to be of service. The captain could count on his continuing cooperation in this matter.

The captain was pleased. Perhaps the signore would be kind enough to show him the correspondence with signor Pellico?

At this point Salvatorelli noticed with apparent surprise that I was still there.

"Ah, signor Norgren," he said, "I hope you will forgive this intrusion. But our business is concluded, no? You will understand if . . . ?" His gesture took in Barbaccia and the others. He became solemn. "It is my civic duty. . . ."

"Of course," I said. But before standing up, I looked at Barbaccia to make sure it was all right to leave. I still wasn't about to make any unexpected moves around the adolescent with the weapon.

Barbaccia gave me a cordial nod of dismissal. "Perhaps we'll meet again," he said pleasantly.

CHAPTER 11

Outside in the parking area there were three cars that hadn't been there when I'd arrived. Two were white and blue, with POLIZIA MUNICIPALE on the sides; the other, large and black but unornamented, had its rear door open. One of the two carabinieri—the grown-up, the one without the machine gun— was leaning into it, evidently reporting to someone in the back seat on what had happened. The carabiniere's clipped speech and rigid posture made it obvious that he was reporting to a superior officer.

As I passed by, hoping to find a taxi stand on Viale Lenin, I could just see the crossed legs of the listener, clad in khaki trousers and softly gleaming boots. "*Capisco*," he was saying. "*Sì, capisco. . . . Benissimo. . . .*"

Something about those hollow, dessicated *capiscos* made me cock my head. As I did the voice floated forth again.

"Do my eyes deceive me," it wondered dustily in English, "or can this be Dr. Norgren?"

The Eagle of Lombardy, on the spot. So he did come out of his warren sometimes.

I stopped and came back to the car. "*Buongiorno, Colonnello.*"

"*Buongiorno, dottore.*" He subjected me to an unamiable examination. "You're feeling better?" he asked indifferently.

"I'm feeling fine, thanks." These cool, empty conventions were just that. We seemed to be starting off on the same foot on which we'd concluded our previous meeting.

"Good." The dispassionate scrutiny continued. "I must say, I'm surprised to find you here. Would you be kind enough to tell me what brings you?"

"Salvatorelli is shipping the paintings in our show," I said. "I had to go over the arrangements with him."

"Ah. Wholly understandable. Thank you. My mind is now at ease."

Why wasn't his mind at ease before? What the hell was he implying? "Colonel, is something bothering you? Why shouldn't I be here?"

"No, no, I was thinking only that you have a wonderful talent to be present at critical moments. When your friend was attacked—you were there. Now, at the very moment two paintings are seized at an out-of-the way shipping company— you are here. I was merely contemplating these facts."

"Sheer coincidence," I said.

"No doubt, yet such coincidences unnerve me. Understand me, signore, I suspect you of no complicity—"

Hey, thanks a lot, I thought but didn't say.

"—but I don't like coincidences. They can upset finely laid plans, as can the meddling of the most well-intentioned of people. I hope they will not continue."

"Well, I'll certainly avoid all coincidences in the future." Not much of a retort, but I never seemed to be at my best with Antuono, who continued to demonstrate his remarkable knack for nettling me. My chief consolation was that it seemed to work both ways.

"I'm relieved to hear it. You're returning to the city center?"

I nodded. "To my hotel. I have a meeting later this afternoon with Amedeo Di Vecchio at the Pinacoteca." I thought I'd better let him know ahead of time, in case another "critical moment" occurred.

"Would you like a ride?" he asked unexpectedly, and, without waiting for my reply, slid aside to make room.

I almost turned him down, but I had no idea where the nearest taxi stand was, and I wasn't quite up to walking the couple of miles into town yet. Besides, I was naturally curious to see where further conversation with him might lead. Resolving not to let him irritate me, I got in. The interior smelled faintly of cloves, as had Antuono himself the other day, now that I thought about it.

Although he might smell the same, however, he didn't look the same, or even seem like the same person. It was amazing what a well-tailored uniform could do. Now his 135 pounds or so looked spare, not scrawny. His arid, whispery voice no longer seemed beaten-down and querulous, but self-assured and reserved, even commanding.

"Alberto?" he murmured to the carabiniere who had been standing at attention and now managed to stiffen even more alertly in preparation for the colonel's next words.

There were no words. Antuono merely nodded his head faintly toward the open door. The carabiniere closed it. Antuono tipped his head minutely toward the driver's seat. The carabiniere quickly trotted around the back of the car, got behind the wheel, and started the engine.

This was fascinating. Obviously, Antuono had considerable cachet, at least with the rank and file. During the recovery of the two pictures, he had remained outside, like a soldier-king, while his minions carried out the operation. And just now the carabiniere had waited, practically quivering, for his command, then jerked like a mechanical soldier at his delicate gestures. What was more, Antuono was very clearly used to this treatment. Yet the higher-ups had assigned him to a disgraceful mole-burrow of an office—an old storage area, as he himself had said—and left him to spend his time riffling through the papers in his precious cardboard boxes like Silas Marner with his hoard. And Antuono seemed quite used to *that*, too. Content with it, in fact. Suited to it.

So who was he, really? How much weight did he carry? Or was I making too much of what were simply the concomitants of rank? When colonels spoke, corporals jumped. And when generals decided, colonels concurred. The carabinieri was, after all, not a civilian police force but a military body. Most of the corps still lived in barracks.

Antuono had wedged himself up against the far side of the car and sat holding on to the strap above the door, his doleful, droop-nosed profile backlit by the window, his tunic buttoned across his narrow chest. He looked out the window and sighed, his mind somewhere else. For someone who had just executed the recovery of two stolen, reasonably valuable paintings, his spirits hadn't been perceptibly raised.

"Congratulations, Colonel," I said as the car slipped out into the traffic. I was determined to get us on a better footing.

"On?" he said absently, still looking out the window.

"Retrieving the Carrà and the Morandi."

He gave a deprecatory shrug. "*Pittura Metafisica.*"

I understood his feelings. It was hardly the same thing as finding, say, a couple of missing Raphaels. Another bit of data about Antuono registered. He knew something about art, which isn't necessarily true of art cops: enough to know the term *Pittura Metafisica* in the first place, and enough to have an opinion on its merit. I also realized he hadn't even bothered going into the building to see the pictures they'd retrieved. That seemed odd, *Pittura Metafisica* or not.

"In any case," he said, "locating them was little more than luck."

"But your men walked in knowing what they were looking for. How did they know where to find them?"

"In the usual way," he said, covering a yawn as he watched the traffic. "An informant. A dealer from Ferrara, new in the area."

"Filippo Croce?"

He kept looking out the window, but I saw his eyelids whirr briefly. "You know Filippo Croce?"

"I just met him yesterday. At Clara Gozzi's house."

"I see. Yesterday."

One more mark in Antuono's mental black book. Christopher Norgren, perpetrator of unlikely coincidences. Still, I had to admit to myself that I did seem to be in the thick of things. If I were Antuono, maybe I'd have been wondering about me, too.

"And just why did you assume it was to this gentleman I referred?" he asked.

"Well, he's a dealer from Ferrara, and he mentioned being new, so I just, uh, took a stab."

"Sheer coincidence."

"That and the fact that I didn't trust the guy."

He turned to regard me keenly. "And why not?"

"For one thing, he was pushing Clara to buy some paintings against her better judgment."

"And trustworthy dealers do not do this?"

"No, they don't. And for another—" But how could I tell the Eagle of Lombardy that my suspicions had been aroused by his pointy-toed shoes and polka-dot bow tie? "It's hard to say, Colonel. There was just something that didn't seem right about him."

"You think not? And yet his information was reliable, as you saw for yourself."

"How did *he* know about the paintings?"

"On that, he provided great detail. He was seated near two men talking in a bar on the Piazza Garibaldi in Parma. He heard them mention the name of Morandi. As an art dealer who had heard about the theft from Cosenza, he was naturally curious and listened more closely. They began whispering. He tipped his head closer still. And eventually he heard them say 'Trasporti Salvatorelli' and 'Lot 70.' Thinking it might be important, he wrote it down. He also tried to see the speakers, but they were seated behind him and he was unable to do this. Afterward, he came immediately to us with the information. Do you see anything untrustworthy in that?"

I was flabbergasted. I hadn't expected any substantive

answer at all to my question, let alone this torrent of particulars. Why all the information? Was he testing me to see how much I knew about this kind of thing? As it happened, this was a quiz I thought I could pass; I knew, or thought I knew, most of the usual ways art thieves conducted their business.

"He'll get a reward, won't he?" I asked.

"Certainly. Twenty million lire has been offered, and signor Croce has expressed interest."

Twenty million lire. Roughly thirteen thousand dollars. Not quite in the same league as the reward for missing Rubenses. That was a relief anyway, an indication that some things were still right in the world.

"And you find something improper in this?" he prompted.

"Colonel, I'm sure it's occurred to you that his story is a little pat. I mean, he just happens to be in a bar where he just happens to overhear the name of an artist that not one person in ten thousand would recognize, coupled with a few words that pinpoint an exact location. . . . Doesn't it strike you as too much of a—"

"Coincidence?" Antuono said with the most meager of smiles. Not playful, exactly. Not even chaffing. But all the same a smile.

What do you know, I thought. Does a sense of humor lurk in there somewhere?

"And your conclusion?" he asked, turning again to the window. We were now on the trafficky Via Mazzina, swinging around one of the half-a-dozen grandiose gates on the perimeter of the Old City; all that was left of the thirteenth-century city walls.

"My conclusion is that there never were any talkative, careless thieves—they were careful enough to be unseen, you notice—in any bar, and that Croce either stole the paintings himself or he's in league with the people who did. He comes to you with this story, which was probably part of the plan from the beginning, and he and his friends collect the reward. Croce gets commended as a public-spirited citizen, winds up a lot richer, and nobody at all gets arrested or even accused. My conclusion is it's a scam, a hoax."

This succinct description of a hoary and often-used scheme was received in moody silence, with Antuono hanging on to the strap and staring out the window, nodding rhythmically as I spoke. When we stopped at a traffic light, he swung around to look at me again with an expression that told me I'd passed the test; I wasn't quite the naive academician he'd supposed me to be on first acquaintance. I got the impression it didn't make him like me any more.

"Of course it's a hoax," he said abruptly. "It's more of a hoax than you realize. Would you like to know what I think our friend signor Croce is up to?"

I said I would.

"I think these two paintings, the Carrà and the Morandi, are not in themselves significant; I think they function as an advertisement."

Antuono's accent, although slight, clouded his pronunciation enough to make me think I'd misheard him. "Did you say an advertisement?"

He nodded. "I think in this way he sends a message to the underworld here."

"I'm afraid I don't get it. What message?"

"The same message that you seemed to find in his actions."

"That he's a crook?"

"Exactly. It's a subtle way of telling those who know about such things that he is approachable in matters of this kind; that he can deal skillfully with the authorities without implicating others; that for a reasonable consideration he might help in disposing of other missing artworks; that he is—"

"Bent."

"*Eccoti*, bent," Antuono agreed with another pale smile— two inside of five minutes! "My belief is that he hopes that those behind the robberies of two years ago will approach him to make contact with us or perhaps with the insurance company regarding the return—the profitable return, to be sure— of the paintings. I tell you frankly, *dottore*," he said resolutely, "I hope in my heart it works. I would like to have those paintings back."

"But how could he do that? If he comes to you *again*, you'll *know* he's a crook."

"Of course we'll know. We already know." He snorted. "Two men in a bar! So? Next time he'll come up with another story. He'll tell us someone called him anonymously on the telephone, or someone—also anonymous—tried to sell him one of the paintings and the selfless, virtuous signor Croce wormed the location out of him and ran straight to us with it. He will not be too selfless to accept the reward, however."

He hunched his bony shoulders. "So what? How could we prove anything? But we would have the paintings; that's the important thing. The paintings would be preserved."

And to hell with finding the thieves, with prosecuting Croce himself, with worrying about the millions that the insurance company would shell out. Forget about catching the thugs who broke Max's legs, or punishing the murderers of Paolo Salvatorelli and old Giampietro the watchman. The paintings were the only thing that mattered, that was Antuono's philosophy.

Tony Whitehead has told me many times that I'm a rotten negotiator (it's true) because I'm no good at hiding my feelings. My face gives me away. As it apparently did now.

"You don't agree?" Antuono asked with a tinge of acid. "You think I look at this in the wrong way?"

"No, it's just that . . . Well, sure, the paintings are important, but does that mean we just write off the human costs? That we hand these creeps their ransoms, collect the paintings, and call it square? Until next time, when we play the same game all over again?"

It was more than I'd meant to say. Antuono had defended his position cogently enough in his office the other day, and who was I to quarrel with him? Especially when I had no alternative to offer.

He waited sourly for me to finish. "Do you happen to know what the recovery rate is for stolen art in America?" he asked.

"About ten percent."

"That's correct. Interpol's rate, too, is ten percent. France does better: almost thirty percent. Do you know what our rate is?"

"More than thirty percent or you wouldn't be asking me."

"Almost *fifty* percent. Since 1970 our unit has recovered

120,000 works of art—120,000! Italy recovers more stolen art than any other country in the world."

"Maybe that's because it has more stolen art to recover," I said. "What other country even *has* 120,000 stolen works of art?"

Why was I being contentious? Possibly because I was still smarting from his cavalier treatment of me in his office on Wednesday. Or maybe I'd never forgiven him for not being the imposing Eagle of Lombardy I'd expected (although he was doing a lot better today). Or—most likely—because I kept seeing Max, lying mustacheless and wax-fleshed with pain in the clutch of that monster-contraption, and I wanted somebody to pay for putting him there. As far as that goes, I wouldn't have minded seeing someone called to account for my own lumps and bruises. Antuono responded with surprising moderation. "You're right," he said with a sigh. "It's a hopeless task. You know what we say here? We say: 'Come and see the wonderful art treasures of Italy—only don't wait; they might not be here next month.' " He sighed again, sagged against the seat, and went back to gazing out the window.

And suddenly, uniform or no uniform, Antuono was Antuono again. Tired, crabby, defeated. Scrawny, not spare. The Turkey Buzzard of Lombardy. I was sorry for what I'd said.

"Colonel, I apologize. I don't know what I'm quarreling with you about. Your record speaks for itself."

He glanced quickly at me to see if I'd intended a double meaning, which I hadn't. "You know, Dr. Norgren," he said slowly, "it's not that I wouldn't like very much to put my hands on those responsible. It's only that we have learned— learned in the hardest possible way—to go about it in our own manner."

"Who do you think *is* responsible?" I asked. "Could Croce himself be behind it?" Antuono had been surprisingly forthcoming so far. Maybe he'd keep it up.

He laughed; a single, scornful note. "Not Croce. We know all about Croce. A minor figure. No, he simply offers his services, and he accepts a commission. He has no idea where the paintings are. He has no idea who took them. He advertises, and he waits."

121

"What about Bruno Salvatorelli?"

"You know him better than I. What do you think?"

"I hardly know him at all. But if you ask me, he was genuinely surprised when the Carrà and the Morandi turned up. Either that or he's a hell of an actor."

"In Italy everybody is a hell of an actor."

As if to illustrate the point, our driver suddenly stamped on the brakes and shouted a few staccato syllables at a car that had cut in front of us. We were in the Old City now, at the foot of Via Maggiore, where seven narrow, crowded streets converged, without benefit of traffic lights, at the base of the two strange, leaning 800-year-old towers that were even now the tallest structures in Bologna. The driver of the other car responded in kind, and a series of furious, rapid-fire gestures were exchanged: Chins were flicked; temples were dug at with spiraling index fingers; forearms were jerked. The cars moved apart, and our driver returned whistling to his work.

"You see, to perform is part of our national character," Antuono said. "I understand it's part of our charm. But I believe you're right about signor Salvatorelli. I have no reason to think he knew anything of this robbery or of any other. I can also tell you that the paintings are not in his warehouse. That we know."

"What about his brother?"

"His brother?"

"Paolo, his dead brother. Look, there's obviously something funny going on with Trasporti Salvatorelli, and if Bruno isn't behind it, then the chances are it must have been Paolo."

"No, no. You're unfamiliar with these things. There are other more reasonable explanations. That Morandi, that Carrà—they could easily have been—"

"I'm not talking about those, I'm talking about Clara Gozzi's Rubens. How did that get there? Do you have a reasonable explanation for that?"

"No," Antuono said mildly, "do you?"

"No, I don't have an explanation for that," I said with more irritation than I intended, then lowered my voice. "But it stands to reason Paolo had something to do with those robberies, doesn't it? The Rubens wound up in their warehouse, didn't it? And Paolo was attacked—murdered—because he was about to pass some kind of information about it on to you, wasn't he? He *must* have been involved."

The car had pulled up on Via Montegrappa, in front of my hotel. Antuono let go of the strap he'd been clutching for the entire ride, turned to face me, and folded thin arms over his chest.

"First," he said, "your conclusion as to the reason Paolo Salvatorelli was killed is surmise."

"Maybe, but it's a pretty reasonable surmise."

"Second, if we do assume it to be correct, then does not the same logic force us to conclude that your friend signor Cabot was also involved?"

"Look, Colonel—" I said hotly, but it was from force of habit. He was right; being targeted by the bad guys hardly proved you were one yourself. "Yes, you're right," I admitted. "Well, thanks for the lift." I climbed out and stood at the open door, smiling. "Something tells me maybe I just ought to leave it to you."

"*Tante grazie, dottore,*" Antuono said dryly. "*Grazie infinite!*"

With my fingers on the door handle, I paused. "Colonel, I'd like to propose something. You told me once before that you think the Mafia is behind the thefts."

"The Sicilian Mafia, yes," he said warily.

"Well, I'll be going to Sicily this weekend—"

"And why would that be, please?"

"I have to see Ugo Scoccimarro. He's lending some pictures to our show."

"All right. And your proposal?"

"I was just thinking that if it would be any help, I'd be glad to dig around a little, to see if I could pick up any rumors in the art world down there."

He stared at me as if I were crazy. "You'd be glad ... !" The rest was choked down with a visible effort. "*Dottore*, if you happen to learn of something pertinent, of course I will be happy to hear from you. But I beg of you, don't extend yourself. We have agents in Sicily, skilled undercover agents, who have been gathering information for months."

"But I could ask questions, get into places that your agents never could. I could—"

"*Dottore*, we are speaking of an operation of great delicacy, great complexity. There is physical danger, as you well know. The smallest error of judgment could—"

He reached across the width of the automobile to grasp my forearm. Entreaty hadn't been his strong suit so far, but it shone in his eyes now.

"I beg you," he said. "Don't meddle. Attend to your business and let us attend to ours."

CHAPTER 12

Sure, just leave it to Antuono—who kept telling me that he didn't expect, didn't even intend, to bring anyone to justice. The people behind the thefts—the Mafia, if he was right—would just wind up a few billion lire richer, the insurance company a few billion lire poorer, and that would be the end of it; an inconsequential redistribution of wealth that Assicurazioni Generali was apparently happy to go along with, given the alternative.

Too bad about Max, and about a couple of murders along the way—but you couldn't make an omelet without breaking a few eggs, could you?—and all's well that ends well. *We would have the paintings; that's the important thing. The paintings would be preserved.*

Except of course, that they *wouldn't* be preserved. Oh, we'd have them, all right—maybe—but you can't hack a stiff, fragile, five-hundred-year-old Giorgione out of its frame, roll it up, and stow it away God know where, and expect to have quite the same painting when you unroll it two years later. Even that would be hoping for the best. Art thieves have been known to fold canvases (not salutary for aged pigment) or cut them into pieces, or even worse. And what about the future? If people committed theft and murder and got paid for it, weren't you just asking for it again? Was it really 120,000 works of art the carabinieri had recovered, or 1,000—each one stolen 120 times or so?

And these reflections, discouraging as they were, assumed that the paintings would actually be located, that Antuono had matters in hand, as he'd been at such pains to imply. But did he? Then why, with his months of information-gathering, with his "operation of great delicacy, great complexity," was he reduced to hoping that Benedetto Croce's crude "advertisement"—if that was really what it was—worked?

Such were my thoughts as I brooded over a bowl of seafood stew and a plate of stuck-to-each-other-any-which-way Italian rolls. I did have a stake in this, after all, over and above my normal curator's concern for the paintings. My friend had been crippled, and I myself hadn't been handled any too gently. It was only natural that I'd care how things turned out.

And, well, yes, all right, I was a little ticked off—or maybe not such a little—by Antuono's treating me as if I were some bungling do-gooder that kept getting underfoot. Twice now he'd referred to me as a meddler. Why couldn't the guy see I had something to offer? Did he really think his agents with their fake mustaches and sham spectacles could gain the kind of entree into the art world that I could? Or was he just too much of a prima donna to accept help from anyone?

I muttered something along these lines at the last of my *zuppa di pesce*, ordered an espresso, and tried to get Antuono out of my mind. As he'd said, he had his affairs to worry about; I had mine. Fine, the hell with him. I finished the bitter, bracing coffee in two swallows and headed for my appointment with the dour, orange-haired director of the Pinacoteca.

The Pinacoteca—the word is Greek for *picture gallery*—was located a few blocks from the Piazza Maggiore, in a well-maintained old building, now painted a mustard yellow, that had once been a Jesuit convent. At the end of Via Zamboni, it was just down the block from the crumbling palazzo that had been the seat of the University of Bologna since 1710, and the small square at the foot of the street was crowded with long-haired, studious-looking youngsters, book bags over their shoulders, engaged in what appeared to be weighty conversations with their peers. There was a fair amount of litter on the pavement, and, except for the Pinacoteca itself, the buildings in the area were showing their age. Peeling plaster, decomposing stucco, and general grunginess were all around, and the walls and columns were covered with tattered posters, most of them notices for concerts or lurid calls to arms. "*Rivoluzione!*," "*Indipendenza!*," and "*Giustizia!*" appeared frequently, as did warlike photographs of Fidel and Che.

It was, in other words, a lot like Telegraph Avenue in Berkeley, and by the time I stepped onto the Pinacoteca's portico, I was feeling right at home, even a little nostalgic for my graduate years at Cal.

Inside, it was sharply different; no noise, no garbage, no picturesque seediness. All very serene and modern. The cellblock interior of the old convent had been gutted and replaced by spacious, off-white rooms in which the art treasures were expertly shown off against uncluttered settings. I was fifteen minutes early for my meeting with Di Vecchio, so of course I took the time to wander through. I'd been there before, but never with the theft on my mind, and this time I found myself heading for the two rooms from which the paintings had been stolen.

As Di Vecchio had said, there was no "junk" in the 6,000-piece collection, but most of what the museum did have was work by regional artists who, however good, had never achieved worldwide recognition. These the thieves had left alone; understandably, in my opinion. Would *you* risk pursuit and prison to steal a Bugardini, a Garofalo ("the Raphael of Ferrara"), a Marco Zoppo?

This is not to say that the Pinacoteca was a second-rate

museum. Most of the world's great art museums are equally provincial: the Uffizi, the Prado, the Rijksmuseum—all are primarily showcases for their native sons. It takes a museum without much of a cultural pedigree of its own (the Metropolitan in New York), or with a long history of big spending (London's National Gallery), or with one of the world's preeminent looters in its past (the Louvre), to be truly eclectic. And even the Louvre is a little overrepresented in its Rigauds and Prud'hons, if you ask me.

The thieves had also bypassed the famous paintings in the gallery given to the work of Guido Reni, Bologna's foremost artist. All of these had been created to hang in churches and be seen from a distance, so they were huge, averaging twelve feet by twenty-five. Even when cut from their frames and rolled up, they lacked portability—imagine hurriedly stuffing one in the trunk of a car. The same for a large Raphael in another room.

What had they taken, then? Those paintings small enough to tuck under an arm when cut free and rolled up, that were by artists famous enough to bring real money in Riyadh or Tokyo or Cleveland. The Pinacoteca had lost works by Corregio, Tintoretto, Botticelli, Giorgione, Titian, the Carracci, Veronese—eighteen great masterpieces in all.

Well, seventeen. The Botticelli, a Pietà, had been painted in the clumsy, semihysterical style of his sadly degraded sixties, thirty years after the glorious days of the *Primavera*. Definitely Mickey Mouse stuff, to use the appropriate art-historical terminology. Not that I'd tell that to Di Vecchio, of course. Anyway, a Botticelli was a Botticelli. One didn't take its theft lightly.

Most of the pictures had been taken from the second-floor room in which I was now standing, and the one next to it. These rooms were different from most of the others in that they had no windows, only skylights. Assuming the thieves had used a rope ladder, the skylights would have made it easy to enter and leave the gallery without being observed, and the absence of windows would have given them privacy while they worked. The question was, how had they gotten in, and gotten the pictures off the walls, without tripping the alarms? Surely their security system hadn't just happened to be off, like Clara's. And where had the night guards been? It was something I'd never asked Di Vecchio about before; but then I'd never been put into the hospital in connection with it, either.

From the corner of my eye I saw a guard watching me steadily. I thought it best to stop studying the skylight and instead focused on the wall in front of me, on which hung a large wooden altarpiece, a *Christ Enthroned* by the thirteenth-century Florentine master Cimabue. Cimabue is one of those artists I know I *should* like, I really should. Very important historically. A splendid craftsman, the teacher of Giotto (maybe), the man who bridged the gap between the art of antiquity and the new humanistic world view, etc., etc. But I just don't like him; he gives me the creeps.

Tony Whitehead has pointed out that this is hardly an apt sentiment from a curator of a major art museum, and that the least I could do would be to come up with a more felicitous way to put it. So I suppose I ought to rattle on about the frozen Byzantine angularity of Cimabue, or the grim, Gothic starkness. But the long and short of it is that Cimabue gives me the creeps. Sue me.

Not that I didn't stay there studying the altarpiece under the eye of the guard. I seem to spend a lot of time studying paintings I don't like under the eyes of museum guards. The problem is, I always feel rotten just striding through a gallery, however wretched, in which some poor guard spends most of his working life. As a result, I usually feel compelled to demonstrate some appreciation, even if it's pretense. Just one more sign of insecurity resulting from my infantile anaclitic redefinition of love objects, I suppose.

When I'd stood there long enough to make him feel better (all right, Louis, to make *me* feel better), I walked back to the elevator landing and went through the frosted-glass double doors that led to the administrative wing. Di Vecchio was in his office, severe and upright behind his steel desk in the armless, no-nonsense secretary's chair he favored. He glanced up from a letter he was reading and waved me into a rigid, molded-plastic chair, also armless. Three years ago, when the amiable, elderly Dr. Sorge Begontina had still been director, this office had been a homely, clubby place reeking of cigar smoke and stocked with ratty, comfortable furniture: a battered wooden desk with a row of cubbyholes at the back, threadbare Persian carpet, even a couple of sagging, horsehair-stuffed armchairs that were probably older than Begontina.

But with the coming of Amedeo Di Vecchio, the horsehair had gone, as had the cigar smoke and the friendly clutter of Etruscan pottery shards and odd bits of Roman sculpture—a marble forefinger, half a sandaled foot, a fold of toga—that had weighted down open books or piles of paper, or simply sat there. Now the lines were clean and the furniture steel and plastic in simple primary colors. No more arms on the chairs. The only art on the walls was a set of engravings of the Greek ruins at Paestum. Beyond those frosted glass doors Di Vecchio might live in a Renaissance world of vibrant, subtle colors and bursting forms, but when it came to decorating his personal workspace, his own austere socialist's taste came to the fore.

I settled myself into the hard chair as comfortably as I could while he signed the letter and placed it on a tray. He adjusted his gold-rimmed glasses on the bump at the top of his nose and sat more erectly in his own comfortless chair. With his fringe of a beard, his gaunt limbs, and his glittery eyes he looked like something from a Byzantine mosaic himself.

"Good afternoon, Christopher."

"Amedeo, do you happen to like Cimabue?"

He blinked. "Of course. I find him deeply moving. Cimabue is superb, without peer; the greatest of all the Duecento masters. Why do you smile?"

"Was I smiling?"

"You *are* smiling." But he didn't pursue it. Di Vecchio, I knew, considered me insufficiently serious-minded; not as bad as Max, but not adequately professional, either. He raised a finger to touch his cheek in the same spot where my most visible bruise was. "You're all right now?"

"I'm fine. I can't say the same for Max."

"I know," he said grimly. "I went to see him yesterday. Why wouldn't he listen to me? Why wouldn't he listen to Dr. Luca?"

"He's listening now. He won't talk to Antuono."

130

He glanced sharply at me. "I didn't tell him not to talk to Antuono. I told him not to shout to everyone in Bologna that he was going to do it. I *want* him to talk to Antuono if he knows something. You think I don't want those pictures back?"

I said something soothing. Di Vecchio scratched irritably at the grizzled edge of his red beard and grumbled.

"Well," I said, "let's get down to business."

My business with Di Vecchio was the same as it had been with Clara Gozzi: going over the particulars arising from the loan of paintings to Northerners in Italy. This took a lot longer to get through with Di Vecchio than it had with Clara. Partly this was because the Pinacoteca was lending us twenty-four pictures, compared to Clara's four, but mostly it was because Clara was an easygoing sort who was happy to trust the details to others, while Di Vecchio was a fussy stickler who—well, Di Vecchio was Di Vecchio. It took us two hours, most of which was spent trying to answer his finicky questions on insurance; specifically, on the federal special indemnification grant we'd gotten over and above the usual National Endowment of the Arts funding. Like Clara, I'm not too detail-oriented, and it was rough going.

"Very good," Di Vecchio said, terminating the exacting discussion at last. Folders and binders were shoved into a desk drawer, and he leaned back—that is to say, he sat up straighter—in his unyielding chair. "I understand you were at Salvatorelli this morning when the Eagle of Lombardy swooped down on his prey. Is it true you rode back to Bologna with the great man?"

I wasn't surprised to learn he already knew about it. The art world grapevine is amazing, practically instantaneous. "It's true," I said. "We had a chat."

"And is he getting anywhere, our Eagle?"

"Well, as I understand it, the Morandi and the Carrà—"

He jerked impatiently. "I'm not talking about the Morandi and the Carrà. He hasn't been sent to Bologna to recover Morandis and Carràs."

"He thinks there may be a connection, though, or at least that one could develop. He thinks Filippo Croce set this up as a sort of advertisement to the people who have the paintings."

"It could be. What is he doing about this?"

"I don't know. I suppose he's keeping an eye on Croce to see what develops."

He made a hissing sound. "To see what develops," he repeated disdainfully. "Forgive me, but I don't feel cheered. Christopher, they've already had those paintings for almost two years. Who knows what's happened to them by now? For all we know, by now they've been—"

Don't say it, I thought.

"—carved up and recombined. Would we even *know* them?"

Carved up and recombined. Words to strike dismay into the heart of the most steel-nerved of curators. Di Vecchio was referring to the barbaric, increasingly common practice of mutilating art to make it more saleable and less recognizable at the same time. A skillful and corrupt restorer, for example, might take a five-by-seven-foot late-Renaissance mythological painting, too big for today's rooms, and chop it into fragments, creating three or four smaller pictures, and usually throwing away—throwing away!—twenty to forty percent of the original canvas as unusable.

Or a beautiful old French cabinet might have the *maindron*—the proud stamp of its maker—removed, and the rich old finish stripped and redone. Or the signature of a famous sixteenth-century painter might be changed to that of a lesser-known one. Or the painting itself might be altered in any of a thousand ways.

At first glance, these alterations don't seem to make much sense. Don't they drastically reduce the value of the art pieces? Yes, but art thieves—or rather the receivers or dealers who hire them, which is usually the way it's done nowadays—can cheerfully absorb the losses. The economics are simple: Say you hire a gang to steal five paintings worth $800,000, for which they're paid $10,000. You then pay your crooked restorer $5,000 apiece to change them, or $25,000 in all. Now they are much less traceable, but of course they're only worth, say, $300,000,

So what? When they are sold you will have invested $35,000 and gotten a return of $300,000. Even an unenlightened business mind like mine knows a good deal when it sees one like that.

"You don't really think that's what happened to them?" I asked, looking for reassurance. The idea that someone might have butchered those Tintorettos, the Giorgione, the Veronese . . . my God, it didn't bear thinking about.

"We must face the possibility," Di Vecchio replied.

"But the Rubens," I said, forced to reassure myself. "Clara's Rubens. It turned up whole."

"True, but of all them it's the picture least able to be altered. How can you cut up into several paintings a portrait of a single subject? And the subject, Hélène Fourment, is well-known, and associated with Rubens and only Rubens. She would be very difficult to disguise."

I resigned myself to the fact that I wasn't going to get any reassurance.

"Perhaps that's why it was returned," he continued. "It was the only way to collect any money."

"But nobody collected any money. Blusher donated it to the museum."

"Oh? Well, that's very puzzling."

"Amedeo, how did they ever get in here? Weren't the alarms working?"

He bristled. "Of course they were working. We have four separate systems on individual circuits."

"Then how did they manage it?"

He glowered angrily at me for a moment, then sighed, took off his glasses, and wearily rubbed the lumpy bridge of his nose between thumb and forefinger. "They used a ladder to enter through the window of a bathroom here on the upper floor."

"Not through a skylight?"

"A bathroom. Sometime earlier, from inside, they had used tape to deactivate the alarm-latch of this window."

"From *inside*? But if they'd already gotten in, why didn't they just take the paintings then and there? Why risk coming back and fooling around with ladders?"

"I must assume that the window was modified during the day, while the museum was open and people were about. The theft itself took place between twelve-thirty and one-thirty at night."

"I don't get it, Amedeo. Even if they took care of the window alarm, what about the inside systems? I mean, you must have sensors that pick up people walking around. Infrared beams . . ."

"Photo-electric barriers, movement sensors, pressure alarms, everything you could wish. But," he said, looking pained, "every night at twelve-thirty come the people who clean, or so they did at the time. We could not have them setting off bells at every step, so when they would arrive, security became somewhat . . . well . . ."

Sloppy, I said to myself.

"Flexible," Di Vecchio said.

I leaned forward. "Amedeo, if they knew about that, then there must have been some inside involvement, someone on the museum staff."

"That is extremely unlikely," he said stiffly.

I didn't think so. The art world had a long, unhappy history of betrayal by its own.

"But didn't the police question them?" I asked.

"Of course. Aren't the workers always the first to be hounded? The police, the carabinieri, the prosecutor, every conceivable arm of the politico-commercial apparatus. Naturally, nothing of value was learned."

When Di Vecchio started going on about workers and the politico-commercial apparatus, there wasn't much to be gained from continuing the discussion, and I stood up, thanked him, and began to say good-bye.

"Can you stay a moment?" he asked. "Dr. Luca asked to see you. I think he would simply like to hear that everything is going well. You know where his office is?"

"Somewhere in this building. I forget just where."

"It's downstairs. You have to go around the temporary exhibit area . . . Come, it's simpler to take you."

Benedetto Luca's office was behind a door the frosted glass segment of which was almost completely taken up with his title: "*Soprintendente per i beni artistici historici per la provincia di Bologna-Ferrara-Forlì-Ravenna, Repubblica Italiana.*"

Inside, the decor befitted this august appellation: green-shaded brass lamps, roomy chairs of deeply polished wood and copper-studded burgundy leather, a massive nineteenth-century desk. Luca got up from behind the desk to murmur a mellow, dignified welcome, and lead us to an informal grouping of soft chairs—with arms, I was glad to see—against one of the handsome paneled walls, under a softly backlit Etruscan funerary head mounted in a shadow box.

"Well, Christopher," he said, "you're all right? Your injuries aren't serious?"

"No, sir, I'm fine."

"Good. Poor Massimiliano. Terrible thing, terrible. And the arrangements for the exhibition?"

"No problems there. I saw signora Gozzi about her loan yesterday, and Amedeo and I just finished discussing the state collection. And your deputy, signora Nervi, took care of all the details with the shipper."

"Fine, fine," Luca said, his deep, marvelous voice resonant and, as always, a little vacant. "And the four paintings to be borrowed from Ugo Scoccimarro? What of them? You need to take special care there. Signor Scoccimarro is . . . well, shall we say, not experienced in these matters."

"I'll be seeing him tomorrow. I'm catching a noon flight to Sicily."

"Ah, good. I see there's no reason for me to be concerned. You have everything under control." He stood up and shook hands with me. "Perhaps we can have lunch when you return? Monday?"

"I'm sorry, I can't. I'm coming back to Bologna just to pick up my things late Sunday night. Then I fly back to Seattle early Monday. But I'll take you up when I come back."

"Fine." His creased, aristocratic features arranged themselves into an expression of concerned gravity. "Tell me, Christopher: You saw our friend Colonel Antuono in action today. Were you impressed? Do you have hopes he'll recover our paintings?"

It took me a second to answer. "I have hopes, yes."

A derisive bark of laughter came from Di Vecchio. "Hopes," he said.

CHAPTER 13

From the Pinacoteca I took a taxi to the Ospedale Maggiore to visit Max and work another installment of my cheer-up magic on him. I had meant to see him the day before, but somehow with the trip to Ferrara to talk with Clara, and with Calvin's arrival, I'd never gotten around to it. To be honest, I'd shrunk from it. I just hadn't wanted to face looking at him in that hospital gown, with that pale, bare upper lip, and his swollen tongue poking at the hole where his front teeth had been, and his naked legs skewered on that ferocious machine.

But by now, deservedly, I was feeling guilty. Tomorrow I was leaving Bologna for Sicily, then I was going home, and it would be months before I'd be able to see him again. I'd be going merrily about my business in Seattle and Max would

slowly, grimly, be learning to "adjust." I was worried about
how well he'd succeed at it. He was energetic, impatient. I
didn't think he'd bear up well under a physical handicap. And
being crippled over here wasn't the same thing as it was in
the States. You don't see many people using aluminum walkers
in the streets of Europe's old cities, or blind people, or
extremely elderly people. It's just too hard to get around. Traffic is too fast and too frightening, and there are all kinds of
obstacles on the sidewalks: old stone posts from the days of
horses and coaches, bicycle racks in oddball places, wildly
uneven paving, unexpected stone steps to connect modern and
ancient street levels.

Assuming he stayed in Italy, it was going to be tough on
Max. Not so easy if he came back to America, either.

They say that when patients start complaining it means
they're getting better. If so, Max was well along. He started
the minute I walked in. Not about the pain, or the difficulties
to come, but about the little things hospital inmates like to
gripe about: the rotten food, the forcible awakenings at 10:00
P.M. to proffer sleeping pills, the nurses who twittered instead
of speaking, the many offenses against one's modesty.

"You ought to see the production when I need to take a
crap," he said. "First, two guys have to come in with— You
probably don't want to hear this, do you?"

"Not really," I said. Then, nobly: "But I'll listen if you want
to talk about it."

Max laughed. "Not really."

He lay back against his cranked-up bed with a sigh. He
really did seem better. His face was no longer corpse-gray,
and the bruised flesh of his legs wasn't quite so lurid; a dull
yellowish-brown now, instead of raw purples and reds. Black
scabs had begun to form along the edges of the punctures and
incisions. And I had the impression the grumpiness was pro
forma; a way of showing me he was on the mend.

"Are you still on pain pills?" I asked.

"Yeah, but they've cut way down. It really isn't that bad,
Chris." He glanced down at his bear-trapped legs. "Dis-
gusting, yes; agonizing, no. Now they're telling me I'll be up
and out of this by the end of this month."

"That's terrific, Max." It sounded a lot more realistic than the end of the week. "Hey, did you hear that Blusher's donating his reward to the Seattle Art Museum?"

You don't often see somebody's jaw literally drop, but Max's did. "*Blusher* is? How much?"

"A hundred and fifty thousand."

"A hundred . . ." He tipped back his head and laughed. "Well, what's his angle?"

"What makes you think he's got an angle?" I said, as if I hadn't been wondering the same thing since the minute I'd walked into Blusher's office.

"Come on, I've met the guy. So have you."

I smiled. "He claims the publicity he's getting from it is worth it."

"Worth a hundred and fifty thousand bucks? Wouldn't you love to handle his PR account?" He shrugged. "What do I know. Maybe it is worth it to him. I'm glad it worked out for the museum." Suddenly he was tired, subdued. The muscles around his mouth had flattened. The pain was back, I thought.

I searched for something to make conversation about. "There was some excitement on the art-theft front today," I told him, feeling like the aged Cyrano reciting the news to Roxanne. "I got to see Colonel Antuono in action."

"Is that right?" he asked dully.

"Max, do you want a nurse? Do you need some pills or something?"

He shook his head. "I'm not due until seven o'clock, and I'm not about to let them make a junkie out of me. So go ahead. What did Antuono do?"

"He recovered a couple of stolen pictures from Cosenza. *Pittura Metafisica*, nothing big, but he thinks it might turn out to be related to the Bologna thefts. He told me—"

"Chris—" He started to sit up, grimaced, and sank back. "Look, I don't want to know anything about this."

"Well, he didn't mean there was a direct connection. But he thinks the dealer that tipped him off, Filippo Croce—"

"Chris, please!" He seemed really agitated. "Don't tell me any names. The less I know, the better, that's all. The less *you* know, the better. Why the hell don't you go home? What are you doing talking to Antuono? You don't know anything. Why take a chance on making them think you do? Jesus, you want to wind up like me?"

I tried to settle him down. "It's okay, Max, don't worry. All I was going to tell you—"

"Never mind, don't *tell* me." His eyes fluttered and closed. "Oh, God."

I leaned closer to the bed, put my hand on his wrist. "Max, listen. I understand why you don't want anything to do with this anymore. I'd feel the same way if I were you. Look, those five names you were going to pass along to Antuono—or anything else for that matter—*I* could tell him for you. Your name wouldn't have to come up. How can you just let them get away with it? What about Ruggero Giampietro? Just let them get away with murdering him when he got in their way? Max, I wouldn't tell Antuono where I got the information if you didn't want me to."

His eyes had remained pressed closed. He was breathing through his mouth.

"Max?"

"You know," he said softly without opening his eyes, "maybe I could use a nurse after all."

I had dinner again with Calvin. Then we walked back to my hotel for coffee and dessert in the bar. As we passed the front desk the clerk waved me down.

"A message for you, signor Norgen."

He pulled a form from a slot behind him and handed it to me. Tony Whitehead had telephoned. From Tokyo. I was to call him back at the Imperial Hotel. That seemed odd. He had telephoned just last night from Seattle, full of concern about my condition. It had gotten me out of bed, and we had talked for over half an hour.

I asked the clerk to have cappucinos sent to my room and took the elevator up with Calvin.

"What's he doing in Tokyo?" I asked.

"Thinking about putting in a bid on that late Tokugawa screen, I guess."

"Good-bye, hundred and fifty thousand," I said.

Calvin peeked at the note. "The Imperial Hotel," he read admiringly. "The guy really knows how to travel. No dumps for Tony."

The glance at the hallway with which he accompanied this was patently disparaging. The Europa wasn't Calvin's kind of hotel. Nor mine. It was a commercial hotel, a big barn of a place, clean enough but shabby when you looked too closely at anything. I had made a reservation at a pleasant hotel called the Roma, where I always stay, but there had been a mixup and no room was waiting for me. With a big trade fair going on—Bologna has a lot of them—I'd been lucky to get this place. Of course, Calvin wouldn't have approved of the cozy, unpretentious Roma, either. He was staying at the four-star Internazionale a few blocks away.

I opened the door to my room, motioned him into one of the two worn armchairs, and picked up the telephone.

"Wait a minute," I said. "It's ten-thirty. Tony could have called hours ago. What time is it in Tokyo?"

The question delighted him, giving him as it did an opportunity to employ his high-tech wristwatch. He did something to his ratcheted safety bezel, pressed a micro-button on the minikeyboard, and consulted one of the dual LCD displays.

"Well, um, it's two-thirty in Karachi," he said slowly. "A.M."

"Hey, that's good to know, Calvin. I guess we better not call anybody in Karachi."

"Wait a minute, wait a minute." He fussed some more with the watch. "Tokyo! Ha! It's eight-thirty in the morning. Tomorrow, according to this." He hesitated. "Or is it yesterday? Which way does the international date line go?"

"I don't know, but we better get it straight. I don't see much point in calling him yesterday."

Calvin grumbled something and I punched in the thirteen digits it took to reach room 1804 at the Imperial Hotel.

"Tony? It's Chris."

"Everything okay there?" he asked. "You didn't get run over again or anything?"

"No. Oh, I've had a few interesting adventures with the Eagle of Lombardy, but that can wait till I get back."

"Who the hell is the Eagle of Lombardy?"

"*Colonnello* Cesare Antuono—the man who was so anxious to hear any shreds of information I might be willing to pass along?"

"Oh, Antuono, sure. Are you going to tell me what that tone of voice is supposed to mean?"

"Come on, Tony, the guy didn't have any use for me. The further I stay away from him the happier he is. That business about meeting with him to report 'pertinent' information—*you* set that up."

"Me? What for?"

"To get the museum some good press, I suppose. You contacted the FBI to offer my services, and the FBI contacted him, so he went along with it. But he didn't want to."

"Chris—"

"Tony, he told me."

"I don't give a damn what he told you. *I'm* telling you this FBI guy called me—I can't think of his name—Mr. . . . I can't remember. Out of the blue. Watfield, it was. Then he came over to my office. No, Sheffield. He told me he'd just gotten a call from New York, I mean from D.C., that this Colonel Antuono in Rome was looking for all the help he could get— that is, he was going to be assigned to a case in Bologna, and seeing as how we were involved in the art scene there—in Bologna, I mean . . ."

Now Tony, as I mentioned earlier, has been known to deviate from the unadorned facts in the interest of the greater good, but I thought I knew him well enough to sense from his voice when I was being led astray, even over the telephone. When Tony lied, he was straightforward and fluent; it was when he was telling the truth that he tended to trip over his tongue and sound shifty. Which meant, unless he was being even more devious than I gave him credit for, that this was probably the truth. Which meant that Antuono had lied about it; he had asked the FBI for my help, then told me that he hadn't.

Which made no sense at all, whichever way I came at it.

". . . is all I know about it," Tony finished up defensively.

"I guess it was just a misunderstanding," I said.

"Of course. We're dealing with two different languages here. You didn't think," he said, sounding hurt, "that I'd purposely mislead you, do you?"

That was another question, best left alone. "Tony, what am I calling you about?"

"Well, I've had some news from Seattle I thought you might be interested in. You know that painting of Mike Blusher's—"

"Calvin told me. Blusher donated the reward to the museum."

"Not that one, the other one. The van Eyck. It—"

"The fake van Eyck," I said.

"Well, the thing is, it isn't a fake, not exactly. It—"

"What? Of course it's a fake! The techniques are eighteenth-century at the earliest, to say nothing of the *craquelure*, which is—"

"Will you let me say something, for Christ's sake? The van Eyck painting is a fake, yes. But Blusher took your advice and took it into the university to have it examined, and the panel that it's painted over turns out *not* to be a fake. Eleanor Freeman—"

"Of *course* the panel's not a fake! It's early seventeenth-century, manufactured for the Guild of St. Luke in Utrecht. I told Blusher it was real. I told *you* it was real—"

"You told me it was real," supplied Calvin, who was listening to my side of the conversation from his chair.

"I told *Calvin* it was real. Everybody agrees it's real. The *International Herald Tribune* says it's real—"

"*Time* says it's real," Calvin supplied.

"*Time* says it's real—" I said, then stopped. I hadn't heard anything from Tony for a while. Now there was a long, full sigh, deeply indrawn, slowly let out. An expensive one, considering that it was delivered from Tokyo to Bologna.

"Are you actually going to let me say something now?" he asked. "Like maybe two complete sentences?"

"I'm sorry, Tony, go ahead."

"In a row?"

I laughed. "What did Eleanor come up with?"

"Chris, the X rays show a painting under the van Eyck."

And not just any painting, either. Eleanor Freeman, the uni-

versity radiographer–art historian whose specialty was Old
Master fluoroscopic analysis, had concluded that the painting
beneath the forged van Eyck "appeared in all probability"
to be Hendrik Terbrugghen, an important seventeenth-century
Dutch painter and a member of the Utrecht Guild from 1616
until he died in 1629.

"I don't believe it," I said flatly.

"Why not?"

"Because it's all too weird, that's why. Every time I turn
around there's another update on the story that's more bizarre
than the one before. I don't know what kind of scam Blusher
is pulling, but there's something."

"Chris, he just pledged the museum $150,000," Tony said
reproachfully.

"Well, I'd spend it pretty fast if I were you."

"I'm working on it. Look, it's weird, all right, but it's true
all the same. Neuhaus and Boden agree with her."

I relented slightly. "What's it look like?"

"Half-length portrait of a young man playing a lute, seen
three-quarters from behind; very Caravaggist. You know the
type; Terbrugghen's done a bunch of them. This one's mono-
grammed and dated 1621. I haven't seen the X rays yet myself,
but Eleanor tells me even the brush strokes and the construc-
tion are right. She says if it's not by Terbrugghen it's by the
world's greatest Terbrugghen scholar."

No, I thought stubbornly, not necessarily the greatest, just
a Terbrugghen scholar. Eleanor knew the Old Masters' meth-
ods; so did a lot of other people, including forgers. You can
check books on the subject out of the library.

"Any *craquelure?*"

"Yeah, and this time it runs the right way. And of course,
as you pointed out, the thing is done on a Utrecht guild panel,
complete with logo, from the first third of the seventeenth
century—which isn't exactly easy to lay your hands on. So if
what you're thinking is that it's a forgery, I don't see it."

I relented some more. "It sounds authentic," I allowed, "but
I still—"

"Chris, listen. Would someone paint a first-class forgery,

143

then cover it up with another one so nobody could see it? That's crazy. Look, tell me, just what is it you think the guy's pulling?"

"I don't know. How much reward money's involved?"

"None, as far as anybody knows. There aren't any missing Terbrugghens in the Interpol list or the carabinieri bulletin. It may never have been stolen. For all anybody knows, somebody painted over it a hundred years ago because he didn't know it was worth anything."

I still wasn't satisfied. "Tony, have they done any physical tests for age, any pigment analysis, any—"

"No, apparently Blusher jumped three feet off the ground when he heard the X-ray results, and he didn't want anyone fooling with it anymore. He had a truck there for it inside of an hour. I hear it's in a bank vault now."

"So what's going to happen to it?"

"Who knows? It's up to him."

"You mean he gets to keep it?"

"I don't see why not. Who else has a claim? The shippers say they don't know how it got into the shipment or where it came from, and nobody knows who owned it."

"What about the Italian government? There's a law about taking art out of Italy."

"Wrong, there's a law about taking *genuine* art out of Italy. You can take out all the fakes you want to. Blusher's saying that when it left Italy it was a forged van Eyck, not a genuine Terbrugghen, so Italy has no claim. Personally, I think he's right, and from what I hear so far, they're not going to contest it."

"There you are, Tony," I said excitedly, "that's the scam! It's genuine, all right, and he had it painted over to get it out of Italy. Then, once it's here he sets up this elaborate routine that winds up with the supposedly amazing discovery that there's a valuable work of art underneath—and he gets to keep it."

"Oh, sure, nice and simple. All it leaves is one or two inconsequential little questions."

"Like what?"

"Like where did it come from in the first place? Nobody's reported it missing."

"Maybe it wasn't stolen. Maybe he bought it from somebody but couldn't get it legally out. Maybe—"

"And what was that business with the Rubens all about? How did he get hold of that? And if this is all a scam, how do you explain his giving us the $150,000? I wish we'd get taken in by a scam like that every week."

"Okay," I said wearily, "you're right. I don't know what the answers are. I can't figure out what's going on."

"Nothing's going on, at least not the way you mean. When will you be back in Seattle?"

"Monday. I'm all wrapped up here, but I'm catching a noon plane to Sicily tomorrow to pin things down with Ugo Scoccimarro."

"Fine, good. See you then."

"Don't spend that whole hundred and fifty thousand in Japan, Tony. Remember, we're buying that Boursse from Ugo. Sixty thousand."

"Absolutely. A deal's a deal. And Chris—I can still hear those gears spinning in your head. Forget about scams, will you, and just concentrate on business. All right?"

"Right," I said. "See you next week."

The coffee had already been delivered and begun to cool by the time I hung up. I drank mine and ate a couple of the orange-flavored *biscotti* that had come with it, while I filled Calvin in on the parts of the conversation he'd missed.

"I thought you said," he told me, "that there couldn't be any big-time artist's work underneath."

"Well, Terbrugghen's only recently gotten to be a big name. Until lately he hardly got any attention. You don't find him in the standard art history texts until the sixties or even the seventies. Whoever forged the van Eyck could easily have painted over it back then, just wanting the panel itself, and an authentic old ground to work on. The Terbrugghen itself would have been next to worthless."

"Is that what you think happened?"

"I don't know. I've been instructed twice today, by two

authority figures on two continents, to mind my own business. I think maybe that's what I'd better do."

Calvin leaned back and stretched. "Fascinating. Well, I guess I'll call it a night."

"Early for you, isn't it?"

"Yeah, but I have to get up early. This girl I met at the museum is driving me up to the Riviera for the weekend. Her folks have a beach house in Portofino. Hey, have fun in Sicily, and I'll see you back in Seattle."

CHAPTER 14

This girl I met at the museum is driving me up to the Riviera for the weekend.

How, I wondered glumly, did the guy do it? I'd been at the museum most of the afternoon myself and nobody'd invited me on any weekend jaunts. I hadn't even spoken to a woman. I didn't remember even *seeing* a woman. But Calvin had seen, spoken, and conquered (had he used his nifty little pocket translator?), and tomorrow he was off to the Riviera with her.

Life was like that for him back home, too. In Seattle I'd attributed it to his Porsche, but he didn't have his Porsche here, so it wasn't that. I don't mean to say there's anything wrong with Calvin; looks and brains aren't everything and he's a nice enough guy in his own way, but I just couldn't understand why he seemed to turn up at every show reception with a new woman, while I came alone. And left alone.

Since Anne and I had broken up I'd been in a funk as far as females were concerned. Oh, there'd been a few, but I just didn't seem to have the energy anymore, or maybe it was the patience, for the get-acquainted routine: the games, the goofy questions, the tedious self-histories ("So—now tell me about *you*"). I suppose if I'd stuck with it I might have met somebody, but the chances were so slim—the number of normal-looking, superficially rational screwballs wandering around had astonished me—that it just didn't seem worth the effort.

With Anne it had been different: no games, no goofy conversations. I still had no idea what her sign was. There had just been a sweet, growing appreciation and attachment, a sense when I was with her that the world was a pretty fine place after all. Until that miserable episode in San Francisco had turned everything sour.

But now, back in Europe where we'd met and things had gone so well for us, San Francisco no longer seemed to overshadow everything. There had been extenuating circumstances. Making an end to a ten-year marriage, no matter how rotten, was unlikely to bring out the best in anybody. So there'd been a few bad days. Anne had never thrown them up to me; I was the one who'd made all the fuss at the time, and I was the one who was still making a fuss about them. She'd even called me, and here I was, still dithering.

Now look, Norgren, I said, you know you're going to call her back, so instead of cerebralizing for the next hour, why not save yourself the time and the angst and just do it? The hell with what Louis might think about it.

And so I did. I got out my address book and dialed her number at the U.S. Army installation at Berchtesgaden. Finally.

"Hello?"

She had answered promptly on the first ring, startling me into a tongue-tied panic. I almost hung up. It occurred to me I could have done with a few more minutes of cerebralizing. Stricken mute, I stood there with the telephone at my ear.

After a moment she spoke again, softly. "Chris?"

That tentative, quiet syllable flowed over me like warm, perfumed water. The tension drained out of my neck. My shoulders unhunched. I sat down heavily on the bed. "God, it's good to hear your voice."

The next twenty minutes were a blur of laughter and explanations, of cut-off sentences as we both tried to talk at once, of catching up with each other and trying to find our old familiar groove again. Then, gradually, the momentum slowed. We caught our breath.

"I've wanted to call a hundred times," I said.

"I know. Me too."

"It's just . . . well, I felt so bad about the way things went."

"We picked a rotten time to get together, that's all. It was my lousy idea, if you remember."

"It wasn't a lousy idea, it was a good idea. I was lousy company."

"You were *awful* company. Where are you calling from, Chris? Are you still in Europe?"

"I've been here all week." Briefly I told her about the show I was working on, omitting several of the more colorful experiences of the last few days. "I only got your message last night."

"When do you go back?"

"Monday—"

"Monday!"

That little cry of dismay did me a lot of good. Until then, I hadn't been sure if she wanted to see me again, or if that initial call to say hello had been a civilized way of saying good-bye.

"I'm in Bologna right now," I told her, "but I'm going down to Sicily for the weekend. Is there any chance you could come, too? You'd like Ugo, and he'd love to have you. And I don't have that much to do; we'd have some time to ourselves. Maybe drive around and see some of the island." I held my breath.

"Ah, Chris, I'd love to, but I can't. I'm tied up all weekend with a NATO subcommittee meeting in Rotterdam, at the Naval Institute. Things are like a zoo right now. Damn."

"Look," I said, "I'm supposed to leave for home Monday morning, but I can shift it to Monday night. Will you still be in Rotterdam then?"

"I can be."

"All right, save Monday for me, will you? Maybe I can fly out through Amsterdam and stay for most of the day. It's just a quick train ride to Rotterdam."

"Don't bother about that. I'll meet you in Amsterdam. Oh, Chris, could you really do that? It'd be wonderful!"

"Don't worry," I said, my spirits higher than they'd been in months, "I'll work it out. Give me a number where I can reach you tomorrow. That'll give me a chance to figure out the logistics, okay?"

The telephone rang the next morning at about eight, just as I finished shaving. I toweled off the shaving cream and picked up the receiver. "*Pronto.*"

"Dr. Norgren," the prissy voice said in English, "I am sorry to disturb you. I am Mr. Marchetti, the assistant manager. You are leaving your room today, this is correct?"

"'Yes, that's right." With the towel I dabbed at some cream behind my ear.

"We are having a small problem at the desk. Through a misunderstanding, a shortage of rooms has developed. May I ask if you will be staying until check-out time?"

"I can check out early if that would help."

I heard a relieved sigh. "Thank you so much."

"What time did you have in mind?"

"Would ten o'clock be too early? We don't want to inconvenience you."

"No, in fact I can be out of my room in half an hour if you like."

"Ah, that would be wonderful. You're sure it's no trouble? If you wish, you can leave your luggage with the bell captain until you need it. I will send up a boy."

"That's all right, I'll take it down myself."

"As you wish. You will be going to the airport? You would like a taxi?"

"Yes, it takes about half an hour, doesn't it?

"On Saturday morning, about twenty minutes."

"All right, could you have one here at eleven-thirty, please? Or better make that eleven-twenty to be on the safe side."

"With pleasure. *Molte grazie, signore.*"

"*Non c'è di che.*"

By eight-thirty I had settled my bill, made arrangements for a room when I got back on Sunday night before flying on to Amsterdam the following morning, and left my bags with the bell captain, who wrote out a receipt and placed them with the rest of the luggage that lined one wall of the reception lobby. Then I went into the dining area and had breakfast, a good one: juice, a bucket-sized cup of strong *caffè latte*, and a basket of crusty, warm rolls, toast, jam, and cheese.

All the same I didn't linger over it. This was, in fact, the first meal I'd had there. The Hotel Europa, as Calvin had implied, was not big on ambience. The building was an early nineteenth-century palazzo that had been reasonably well maintained, with large public rooms, head-high paneling, and decent nineteenth-century fakes of good eighteenth-century paintings hung high on the walls. But there was a depressing, anonymous feel to the place, perhaps from the 1950s imitation-leather sofas, or from the total absence of amenities like flowers, or vases, or rugs, or ornaments on the tables. If you've ever stayed in a Moscow hotel, you know the feeling. Everyone else in the place seemed to be a businessman in for the trade fair, which apparently had to do with mattress and cushion manufacture, or so it seemed from the snatches of conversation I heard around me.

I finished the last of the coffee and walked to the Municipal Archaeological Museum a couple of blocks away on Via Archiginnasio. It was the only museum in Bologna I'd never been to, and I was anxious to see the well-known head of the Pharaoh Amenhotep IV it had on display. Well, moderately anxious. And once I'd seen it my interest in the remaining Egyptian exhibits quickly waned. There is, you have to admit, a certain numbing sameness about pharaonic heads. After you've looked at them for a few minutes, you're no longer sure if you're looking at Thutmose II or Thutmose III, or maybe even Amenhotep I. You don't much care, either.

There I am, being provincial again. I apologize. Pharaonic heads can be terrific, but I guess I just wasn't in a museum mood for once. After a few more minutes, with over two hours to kill, I walked several hundred feet farther down Via Archiginnasio, sat down at an outdoor table at the crowded Caffè Zanarini, ordered an espresso that I didn't really want, and thought about how to pass the time.

The café looked out over the Piazza Galvani, already buzzing with streams of well-dressed people, mostly women, mostly elegant, who had the steely look of serious Saturday shoppers in their eyes. At the center was a modest statue of the locally born Galvani, and beyond that, at the corner of Via Farina was an ancient but ordinary-looking apartment building with a marble plaque that was too small to read from where I sat. I knew what it said, however: Guido Reni had died there on August 18, 1642. At the other end of the piazza loomed the facadeless back of the basilica with its crazy jumble of 600 years' worth of changed plans, there for all the world to see in the stops and starts and metamorphoses of its naked brickwork.

It was the kind of scene that ordinarily would have occupied me for a reflective hour, but this morning I was restless, impatient to get on to Sicily. I jumped up after a few minutes, went to a telephone, and called the airport. Yes, I was told, there was an earlier Aer Mediterranea flight to Catania, departing at 10:15 A.M., and yes, they would be happy to reassign me to it.

That left an hour. I walked quickly back to the hotel, picked up my bags, and got the desk clerk to get me a taxi. I was at the Borgo Panigale Airport at 9:45, which left barely enough time, because security precautions in Europe, and in Italy in particular, are painstaking. If I'd been on an international flight, or had had anything but carry-on luggage, I wouldn't have had a chance to make it. As it was, I had to stand in a men-only line (the women had their own) to enter a booth where I was patted down and gone over with a metal-sensitive wand. Then I was directed to another line, this one heterosexual, first to have my bags go through the X-ray scanner, and then to put them on a counter where they would be opened like everyone else's and meticulously gone through.

Almost. I got as far as the X-ray machine. My suit bag had just come through the scanner without incident, and I was waiting for my old red duffel bag, when the conveyor belt stopped moving. A few seconds passed.

"C'è una problema?" I asked the woman behind the machine.

She stopped her whispered conference with a guard. *"No, davvero,"* I was told with a cheerful smile. *"Va bene."*

All the same, the conveyor wasn't moving. I checked my watch, wondering if I'd make the flight after all. Well, no real problem if I didn't. I'd just catch the one I'd originally planned to take. I realized I'd forgotten to call Ugo about the change, so it might not make a difference anyway. Still, I would have preferred to be up and away rather than waiting around the airport.

My thoughts were going along in this lazy manner when the area erupted into noise and activity.

"Everybody out!" one of the nearby guards shouted suddenly in Italian. "Hurry, back to the lobby!"

Travelers in this part of the world do not need to be told such things twice. The orderly line flew apart as people scrambled helter-skelter for the main terminal. The woman behind the X-ray scanner turned and fled with the rest of them. I started to do the same thing but found myself tangled up with my neighbors, as did many others. There was quite a bit of yelling going on now as people tried desperately to unsnarl their arms and legs from other people's luggage straps.

"Scusi," I shouted above the noise, and tugged hard to free my arm. It didn't budge. The grip on it tightened. So did the grasp on my other arm. Startled, I glanced around and found a uniformed guard, a big one, on either side of me, holding tight.

"Che c'è?" I stammered. *What's the matter?*

For answer I was pulled roughly out of the line and pushed down the passageway in the opposite direction from everyone else.

153

"Faccia presto!" I was told. *Hurry up.*

It wasn't as if I had any choice. They had never let go of my elbows, and now they hustled me down the aisle between them. I can't say my heels were actually dragging on the floor, but if I'd tried to hold my ground they certainly would have been. These were big men, and they meant business. I could see two other uniformed guards trotting close behind us with semiautomatic weapons unslung and at the ready. Not teenagers this time, but grown men, square-jawed and intense. Their eyes roved nervously, looking for—what? Fellow terrorists trying to rescue me?

Another guard, a senior officer from the look of him, also moved grimly along with us. Five armed men, for God's sake, and all of them convincingly out of sorts. A bomb, I thought dazedly. Somebody's planted a bomb in my duffel bag.

"Che c'è?" I pleaded again. *"Sono americano!"*

This had all the effect it deserved, which was none, except possibly to increase the tempo of the quick-marching. At such times one's life flashes before one's eyes. In my case it was the previous two hours, starting with the request from Mr. Marchetti that I leave early. Even at the time, it had struck me as unusual, and now all I could think about was how my bags had lain in the packed lobby for almost an hour, nominally under the supervision of the bell captain, but in reality available to anyone who chose to tinker with them. The duffel bag would have been especially easy prey. I'd lost the key to the tiny padlock years ago, and had never bothered to get another. I used the bag for underwear, socks, and shoes; nothing valuable.

I was brought to a jolting stop in front of a gray metal door that said PRIVATO on it, then made to wait while one of the guards unlocked it, and then shoved roughly inside. The older officer and the guards with the semiautomatics crowded into the bare little room with me. There was only a metal table in the center with a couple of battered chairs around it. These were not put into immediate use. Instead, I was jammed up against a wall and patted down again, this time more harshly.

"Il passaporto," the officer said and stuck out his hand.

I handed it to him. He barely glanced at it before putting

it in his pocket. He was a bulky man of about fifty, tense and breathing hard.

"*Parla italiano?*" he asked. His lips barely moved when he spoke. He was keeping a tight rein on his anger. With each breath his nostrils flared.

I nodded. I was feeling less flustered, more pointedly frightened. The room was very small and private, the guns very big, the men hard-bitten and tough-looking. I knew that one of the reasons the police forces of Italy had put together their admirable record against terrorists was that they did not always observe the same niceties of behavior toward accused or suspect persons as did, say, the police in America.

If you had asked me how I felt about that a few minutes earlier, when I was just another passenger at an airport in a city that had suffered more than its share of terrorist horrors, I would have told you I felt just fine about it; no problem. But now that I appeared to be a suspected terrorist myself, I seemed to have developed a finical concern for the civil rights of detainees, or prisoners, or whatever I was.

"I don't know what you found in that bag," I began in Italian, "but—"

Sit down, I was told.

I sat. One of the guards moved behind my chair, out of my sight. The other continued to watch me coldly from across the table. I could smell the oil from the guns.

"This morning," I said, "my bags were left in the lobby—"

Abruptly the senior officer took off his cap and slammed it on the table. I jumped.

"I want to know what activates that bomb," he said tightly. "I want to know how to dismantle it."

So there actually was a bomb. In my old red duffel bag, traveling companion since my college days. I'd understood that, of course, yet I hadn't really believed it. I still didn't really believe it. A single, cold drop of sweat rolled down my side.

"I don't know anything about a bomb," I said numbly. "All I know—"

He leaned forward suddenly and twisted the collar of my jacket in his hand. "You bastard, I've got two good men on that thing, you understand?" He was a squarish man with close-cropped gray hair that grew low on his forehead, and thick, curled ears. When he spoke, knobs of gristle shifted and crackled in his cheeks like lumps of tobacco. He gathered more material into his fist and twisted, hurting my neck, forcing my face closer to his. "Do you know what's going to happen to you if they get hurt?"

You will understand when I tell you that I felt very much alone at that moment, and scared, too. Big, angry, powerful men and brutal weapons seemed to fill the anonymous little room. I felt like a character in a Kafka story, intimidated and confused and acutely aware that the situation was not under my control. But I was offended, too, and that stiffened my spine. I stared steadily back at him, waiting for him to let go of my jacket.

When he did, I spoke. "I don't know anything about a bomb," I said as coolly as I could. "My bag was left in the lobby of the Hotel Europa for an hour this morning. This was at the instruction of a Mr. Marchetti—or somebody who called himself Mr. Marchetti—the assistant manager."

"You left it *open?*" Even the skepticism was an improvement. At least he was listening.

"Unlocked. There wasn't anything valuable in it. Look, I'm an art curator. I'm here working with the Pinacoteca and the Ministry of Fine Arts. The carabinieri will vouch for me. You can talk to Colonel Antuono."

His heavy gray eyebrows unclenched themselves for the first time. "You're working with Colonel Antuono?"

"Uh . . . well, yes, you could say that."

It was delivered with less than perfect assurance. The heavy eyebrows drew ominously together again.

Antuono had given me his card, on which he'd penciled his Bologna telephone number. I took it out of my wallet and handed it to the officer. "Go ahead and call him."

There was a telephone on the wall. He went to it at once, but turned and leveled the card at me before picking up the receiver. "If you're wasting our time, if one of my men is harmed . . ."

"Look, if I knew there was a bomb in that bag, do you

think I'd calmly walk up, put it on the X-ray counter, and just hang around waiting to see what happened?"

He considered this for a moment, then picked up the telephone and spoke without dialing. "Cristin, get me a Colonel Cesare Antuono, two-three-nine-two-eight-five. I'll take it in the west office."

The receiver was slammed back into its holder. "You wait here," he told me, and headed for the door.

"I have a ten-fifteen plane," I said, not very hopefully.

"Not today." He turned to the guards. "Stefano, you stay here. Be careful. Don't speak to him. Call me each ten minutes until I return. Maurizio, I want you outside. Both of you, be alert; we don't yet know what's happening."

Stefano followed his instructions to the letter. He pushed one of the chairs against the far wall, about ten feet from me, and sat down to watch me relentlessly, holding the semiautomatic in his lap, one hand on the barrel, the other at the finger guard; a posture that did not encourage conversation. His eye never left me, even during the telephonic check-ins. There were four calls in all; forty slow, silent minutes, lots of time to think.

With more than enough to think about. Somebody wanted me dead. Enough to blow up a few hundred innocent people who happened to be on the same airplane. There were other possibilities, of course: that someone else on the plane was the target, or that this was a terrorist action not aimed at any individual, and that—in either case—the selection of my bag for the bomb was random, or if not quite random, then merely a matter of convenience and accessibility.

The second telephone call hadn't been made yet before I rejected this as not credible. If I were just a tourist, or on some other business, then maybe it might have happened that way. But I'd been asking a lot of questions about the thefts, I'd been seen with Antuono, and I'd already been involved in a murderous street assault—during which, as Max had pointed out, I'd seen the faces of our attackers. I'd even tried to identify them at the police station. With all of that going on, it was asking too much to treat the finding of a bomb in my bag as no more than an unhappy coincidence. There was no question in my mind that I was the target, and that it was related to the thefts.

Yet the idea of killing so many people just to get to me was so monstrous I couldn't make myself believe that either. What could I know that anyone found so dangerous? Max's idea that I could identify the two thugs didn't hold water; I'd already failed to do it once. Did someone think he'd told me the names of the five people who knew his security arrangements? Well, he hadn't, not that I hadn't asked, and even if he had, how was anyone to know I hadn't already been to Antuono with it? So what did I know? What did someone *think* I knew? Or was someone afraid of what I might find out? Well, like what, for instance? And if it wasn't something I knew or might find out, then what was it?

This got me nowhere. I took a different tack. Who knew that I was flying to Sicily this morning? That question gave me more answers than I knew what to do with. When I thought back over my conversations of the last few days I realized I'd blabbed to everyone about it. I'd told Salvatorelli, I'd told Luca and Di Vecchio, I'd told Clara, I hadn't missed anyone. I'd told Max, I'd told Calvin, I'd told Tony. Not that I entertained any suspicions about the last three, but who knew whom else they'd mentioned it to?

Of them all, in fact, there was no one, even Salvatorelli, whom I could seriously cast as a murderer in my mind. Certainly not as a mass murderer. Yet one of them must have . . .

Croce. Filippo Croce, the sleazy art dealer from Ferrara, the man with the pointy-toed shoes who'd come to Antuono with his story about the *Pittura Metafisica* paintings in the Salvatorelli warehouse. Had he still been in the room when I'd told Clara I'd be visiting Ugo, or had he already left? No, he'd been there. It had been right at the beginning; he hadn't yet delivered his harangue on revolutionary perspectival structure. Filippo Croce . . .

When the door finally opened, it wasn't the senior officer who came in, but Colonel Antuono, in his natty uniform, but looking cross and tired in spite of it. "You can go," he muttered to Stefano, who rose meekly and left. I heaved a sigh, grateful to see the last of the semiautomatic.

"You understand I have no jurisdiction here, in this matter of the bomb," he said. "My official concern is with the pictures."

"I understand." Whatever the reason he was there, I was glad to see him. Under these circumstances he qualified as an old friend.

He pulled the vacated chair up to the table and wearily sat down. The tunic strained across his stooped shoulders. He undid a button. He tapped slowly on the table, regarding me with something close to resignation.

"Why do you do these things?" he said at last, very quietly.

"Do what? What did I do?" I said, not that he seemed to expect an answer. "All I know is, at eight o'clock this morning I got a call from a man who said he was Mr. Marchetti, the assistant—"

"There is no Mr. Marchetti. The name of the assistant manager is Pugliese."

"Well, sure, it was just a ploy. I've already figured that out. It was just a way for someone to put a bomb in my bag." When I heard my own words, I came perilously close to letting out a nervous giggle. What was I doing in a situation like this?

Antuono wondered the same thing. "And why," he asked with testy patience, "would someone wish to do such a thing?"

"I have no idea why, but I think I might know who." I told him what I'd been thinking about when he came in.

"Again you persist with Croce," he said when I'd finished. "Why would Filippo Croce want to do you harm?"

"I don't know, goddammit! Didn't I just say that?" I was getting a little testy myself. It hadn't been my idea of a wonderful morning, and the idea that someone had tried to end my life—and was likely to try again—was still filtering through the unreality of the last hour. "But he was right there when I told Clara I'd be on that plane."

"And no one else knew? Only Croce and signora Gozzi?"

"Well, no, I also told Salvatorelli—"

"Ah? Is that so?" He took out a little notebook and scribbled in it.

"—and Benedetto Luca and Amedeo Di Vecchio."

"Luca . . . Di Vecchio." He nodded without looking up and kept on writing.

"And Ugo Scoccimarro, of course. And I think I mentioned it to Tony Whitehead . . ."

The pen stopped. He glanced up at me under lifted eyebrows.

" . . . and Calvin Boyer—he works with me in Seattle. He's here in connection with the show."

"I see." The notebook was snapped closed and put away. "Perhaps we go about this the wrong way. Is there anyone in Bologna you forgot to tell? It would make not so long a list."

I wasn't in the mood for Antuono's arid wit. "Well, why the hell would I keep it a secret?" I said. "Why should I think anyone would try to kill me, let alone blow up an entire planeload of people, just to get to me?"

"No, no, they are not such monsters as that. You were carrying a time bomb, *dottore*. It has been disarmed. The detonation was set for eleven thirty-five."

"At which time the plane would have been over the middle of the Tyrrhenian Sea."

"Yes, but that would have been your fault, not theirs."

"My— I don't understand."

"Your reservation was on Alisarda flight number 217, no? You were to leave at noon."

I shook my head. "No, I changed that to a ten-fifteen flight."

"Yes, but when did you change it?"

I realized what he was driving at. I had called the airport at 9:15, after my bags had been in the lobby for almost an hour. Then I'd gone quickly back to the hotel—no more than a three-minute walk—to get them. If someone had put a bomb in the duffel bag, which someone had, it had been done between 8:30 and 9:15, at which time "Mr. Marchetti" had believed that I was booked on the noon flight—half an hour *after* detonation.

"The taxi," I murmured. "He ordered a taxi for me. At eleven-twenty. The bomb would have gone off while I was on my way to the airport."

"Yes, that's what it was designed for. It's not a subtle device; it had no chance at all of getting through airport security—a point in your favor with Captain Lepido, by the way. Also, it was not large. It was what is called an antipersonnel bomb, capable of demolishing the inside of a taxi, yes; of bringing down an airplane, highly unlikely. So you see, we are not dealing with a monster after all. It was you alone he was after."

"He was willing to sacrifice the cabdriver."

"One person, not hundreds."

"Well, that's very comforting, Colonel. I can't tell you how much better I feel knowing that."

He allowed himself a wry smile. "Signor Norgren, I have a favor to ask you. I think it might be helpful if the person who tried to kill you were to believe he succeeded. It would be safer for you if he thought you were, ah, out of the way, and it would perhaps be useful to the police in apprehending him."

"All right. What's the favor?"

"As I said. To pretend you are killed, at least insofar as Bologna is concerned. For a few days only. Go to Sicily and do your business, but no telephone calls back to Bologna, no contact of any kind."

"I don't get it. You said the Sicilian Mafia is involved. If I go to Sicily and do my business, they're likely to find out I'm alive, aren't they?"

"Not the people that matter. They're here in Bologna."

"But you told—"

"I told you the Sicilian Mafia is behind the thefts. They are. But those concerned are now here." Even in that tiny, secure room, with no one else around, he leaned forward and lowered his voice. "Things come to a head; we will very soon have those paintings back. The arrangements have already been made." He held up a finger. "I speak in confidence."

Arrangements had been made, and word of my survival might somehow spoil them, so would I kindly shut up, stop poking around, and play dead; that was what he was telling me. Still, I dearly wanted to see those paintings back, too. So if it would help, I would go along with it even if I didn't like it.

"All right," I said tentatively, "but I'd like to let my friends know I'm all right. I wouldn't want them to hear I'd been killed."

He waved his hands. "No, no, no, don't worry, they won't think so. I will see to it that the newspapers and the television report only that a taxi was blown up on its way to the airport, resulting in the death of the passenger, but that his name is being withheld until his family is notified. I will say that terrorists are believed responsible. To your friends, it will mean nothing. To the people who planned it, it will mean everything."

I nodded. "Okay."

"There is one more thing. I hope I am correct in thinking that you will go directly home from Sicily, that you are not returning to Bologna?"

The back of my neck prickled. Since coming there, I had been beaten up by thugs and run down by a car; I had very nearly been blown up; I had been told that things would be better if I were dead, or failing that, if I could at least have the good grace to act as if I were. Now I was being given the carabinieri version of a get-out-of-town-by-sunset-and-don't-come-back speech.

"Are you telling me not to come back here?" I said hotly.

"I merely ask the question. You will admit my work has not been made simpler by your presence."

It was hard to argue with that. "There aren't any direct flights from Sicily to Seattle," I told him. "I'm coming back Sunday night at ten o'clock and I'm getting the first plane Monday morning—six-thirty, I think. I've already booked a room for Sunday night at the Europa. They're holding the rest of my luggage." I didn't feel I had to tell him about Anne and Amsterdam.

"You arrive at ten at night and you leave at six-thirty the next morning?"

"Yes," I said. "You have to admit, even *I* couldn't screw things up too much in that amount of time." You wouldn't guess it, but I was feeling pretty surly.

He nodded and rose. "That will be acceptable. If you make your statement to Captain Lepido now, you can still be on the noon plane."

"Fine." God forbid that my continued existence in Bologna should complicate his life any more than necessary.

As we were going out the door he put a hand on my arm. "A word of advice?"

I paused.

"When you get your luggage from the Europa . . . ?"

"Yes?"

"Look inside."

CHAPTER 15

Ugo Scoccimarro's frank, happy face was enough to expunge most of the morbid thoughts with which I'd been occupying myself on the flight from Bologna, and any gloomy remnants were blotted out by his exuberant Mediterranean bear hug of a greeting. This was not Clara Gozzi's discreet northern version, but the full Sicilian treatment: bone-cracking embrace, thunderous back-pummeling, noisy kiss on each cheek. And no slack mouthing at the empty air for Ugo, either. When he kissed you, he kissed you. The sensation was something like getting your cheek caught in a vacuum cleaner.

I hugged him in return. Seeing Ugo always made me feel that the world wasn't such a complicated place after all, that there was still room for simple pleasures, simple motives—

maybe even simple explanations to complicated-seeming things, although I was starting to doubt it.

With a cupped hand he gently patted the side of my face where some bruising was still visible. "You're all right now?" he asked in his broad Italian. "It doesn't hurt?"

"Not at all." I'd called a few days ago to fill him in on what had happened.

"And Max? He's better?"

"A little. It'll take time, though."

"Ah, Cristoforo, if only I didn't ask the two of you to come get a drink with me, to walk with me to the station. If only—"

"Forget it, Ugo; it's not your fault. They were after Max. If they didn't get him then, they would've gotten him some other time."

On the other hand, some other time I might not have been with him to absorb a great deal of gratuitous punishment. But this I dismissed as an unworthy thought. I clapped Ugo on the back. "I'm glad to see you," I said honestly.

"And I you. Look, here's Maria."

"Chris, hello!" Ugo's wife called in English, and I received an embrace as openhearted if not quite as suffocating as Ugo's. "You poor man!"

An animated, wiry woman a year or two older than Ugo, Mary Massey had been an accountant employed by the Americans at the Sigonella Air Force base when she'd met him at a St. Agatha's Day party in Catania. A few months later they were married, Mary for the first time, the widowed Ugo for the second.

It was a relationship of opposites: Mary's father was an American master sergeant from Pennsylvania, her mother an Italian bookkeeper from Messina, up the coast from Catania. Mary had spent eleven years in Philadelphia. Well read, well traveled, she had two college degrees (one American, one Italian), an inquisitive, intelligent mind, and a sometimes biting sense of humor. Ugo, as blunt as a watermelon, had left school in the fourth grade; had never been north of Naples or had the least desire to do so until Mary began dragging him off on yearly vacations; and still possessed, as far as I could tell, a world view better suited to the simple olive-grower he once was than to the business titan and international art collector he'd become.

The marriage shouldn't have lasted a year, but somehow they had clicked. Ugo, with plenty of native intelligence and his own rough charm, tolerated and actually seemed to enjoy Mary's barbed wit, and Mary was equally broad-minded about Ugo's Neanderthal opinions. When they didn't agree, which was all the time, they laughed and went on to the next subject. It had worked for them for six years, and from the look of them as we walked to the parking area—Ugo's hefty arm tenderly encircling Mary's fragile shoulders, Mary leaning into him—they were still going strong.

The airport was on the Plain of Catania, some distance south of the city. For the first few miles Ugo drove through a string of small villages and decaying stone farmhouses over-looking rocky land that would have seemed untillable if not for the evidence of scraggly rows of grapevines or stunted olive trees. The dark, small people with their creased faces; the hard land; the unadorned, whitewashed buildings made it seem like another world from Bologna. If not for the occasional *caffè* and *tabaccheria* signs in the villages, I would have thought we were in the Greek islands.

It was a sunny day, the first after two days of rain, and there were knots of women sitting outside to gossip and enjoy the warmth. Fashions hadn't changed much down here. Most of them wore the same black dresses and black shawls that I'd seen in photographs from their grandmothers' generation. And all but a few of them had their chairs turned away from the street so that they faced the blank white walls of the build-ings a few feet behind them. It seemed odd to me, and I com-mented on it.

Ugo laughed. "You don't find that in Catania or Palermo. These villages—they're centuries behind. The women keep their eyes away from the streets, the cars, so that they don't catch the eye of a man even accidentally. Quaint, don't you think?"

"Oppressive, don't you think?" Mary said in English, then translated for Ugo's benefit.

He shrugged. "The old ways. There's a lot to be said for them. At least the women didn't talk back." With another rumbling laugh he reached across and squeezed Mary's knee.

The open country gradually gave way to the sprawling southern reaches of Catania. Ugo went screeching through the twisting, narrow streets at the death-defying speed with which everyone down here seemed to drive, even in the city. It seemed a dreary place, with long rows of dark, low tenements and a lot of garbage in the streets. Many of the buildings were made of a repellent muddy-purple stone. These, I knew from my *Michelin*, were built from the lava with which Mt. Etna sporadically engulfed the city. Several times on the drive I had seen the conical volcano looming to the north, an elongated pancake of steam trailing from its peak.

Twice I watched in surprise as small, three-wheeled automobiles were pushed over the sidewalk and through what appeared to be the double front doors of ground-floor apartments. Another time I saw one of the cars through a window, standing in the middle of what was unmistakably the kitchen. A few feet away an aproned woman was chopping vegetables at the sink.

When I remarked on this, Ugo shrugged again, but didn't smile this time. "Eh, it's an old city. The apartment buildings don't have garages."

"Why not leave the cars out on the street?"

Ugo grumbled something unintelligible, and pressed the accelerator even farther down. My question hadn't pleased him.

"You can't leave a car out all night in Catania," Mary said. "At least not around here. It's not such a great idea in our neighborhood, either. The car might still be there in the morning, but forget about hubcaps and mirrors. Ugo, do you remember what happened to Silvia?" She turned to look at me over her shoulder. "I have a cousin who parked one of those little cars in front of a restaurant and went in to eat. Five big men came along, picked it up, and simply ran off with it. She actually saw them do it, but she couldn't catch them."

Ugo pouted. "Any big city has a little crime. New York is worse." Down went his foot on the accelerator.

I resolved to ask no more questions about curious native customs.

There is no quick way through or around Catania. One must wind through the heart of the city to get to the other side. This we did, and after a while the dismal streets broadened into clean, pleasant avenues, and the neighborhoods took on an affluent sheen. We stopped for a few minutes near the Via Etnea, a posh commercial street that might have been in Rome or Paris, so I could buy some socks and underwear. The ones I'd started out with were being held in Bologna along with my duffel bag as material evidence. These purchases naturally required some explanation. Ugo and Mary were shocked, of course, and insisted on going over the same ground I'd covered with Antuono a few hours before. To equally little avail.

A few miles north of the city we finally pulled into a seaside neighborhood of handsome villas and small apartment buildings, and parked in an unpaved alley bordered on both sides by eight-foot stucco walls topped with broken glass.

"We'll leave the car here," Ugo said. "We're going out for dinner later."

Half a dozen boys of nine or ten trotted up. Cigarettes dangled from several of the small mouths. Ugo gave one of the smokers, a hot-eyed kid wearing a torn Hard Rock Cafe T-shirt, a 1,000-lire note.

"Protection money," Mary told me. "They watch the car. The Mafiosi begin early here."

Ugo scowled at her. "Very funny," he muttered. "See, I'm laughing. I'm going inside to get the pictures ready for Cristoforo."

He unlocked a tall, spiked gate in one of the walls and stalked down a path through a sparsely planted rock garden toward the house, a modern, boxlike three-story structure painted pale blue.

"Oh-oh, now I've made him mad," Mary said with no sign of repentance. "I'll have to be good for the rest of the day." As usual, when Ugo wasn't there, she spoke English to me.

She closed the gate behind us and shook it to make sure it

was locked. As we followed a few yards behind Ugo a star-
tlingly large bulldog gallumphed out from behind a corner of
the house and made fearsomely for her, spittle drooling from
its dewlaps and lovelight shining in its eyes.

"Hello, Adamo, how are you, dog?" she said, tugging hard
on both its ears and accepting with apparent enjoyment a
slobbering show of affection. "Say hello to Christopher."

I gingerly patted the monstrous head and tried without success to avoid the frantic wet-mop of a tongue. "More protection?" I asked.

Ugo, who had paused a few feet ahead of us, made the
connection to "protezione" and answered in Italian. "Yes," he
allowed, "there's some theft around here."

"*Some* theft?" Mary echoed. "You have to nail everything
down if you want to keep it." To me she said: "We've been
lucky, but twice last year they robbed the neighbors across the
way."

Ugo, never one to stay in a snit for very long, burst out
laughing. "After the first one," he told me, "they got a watch-
dog, a big expensive Doberman. They thought that would
take care of the problem. So what happened? Well, the next
time the crooks came, along with everything else they stole
the dog."

Adamo, who had calmed down enough to notice Ugo, wad-
dled amiably over to him. Ugo knelt, grasped its flaccid chops,
and fondly rocked the big head from side to side. "But nobody
would steal you, would they? You're too ugly to steal, aren't
you?" The dog grinned and wagged its stump of a tail.

Mary put one hand in the crook of Ugo's elbow and one
in mine. "Come on, let's go in. Chris has had quite a day. I'm
sure he'd like to relax and have a drink."

True enough, but I didn't get much time to relax. Their
housekeeper had barely set down three glasses of a sweet,
musky marsala, and Mary had just begun to ask polite questions about the show, when Ugo started fidgeting. He crossed
his right leg over his left. He reversed them. He uncrossed
them and tapped his toes restlessly against the tiled floor. He
pulled up his shirt cuff to look with ostentatious anxiety at
his watch. He sighed.

"Is something bothering you, love?" Mary asked. "You have an itch in an indiscreet place, perhaps? Would you like to be excused?"

"No, no. It's just the time. It's after four o'clock, and the light won't be good much longer. I want Cristoforo to see the paintings before it goes."

"Of course. I'd like that." Not that I thought for a minute that it had anything to do with the light. Ugo was like a big kid; he just couldn't wait any longer to show off his picture gallery. And I was happy to oblige; I'd rather look at old paintings than drink wine anyway. Especially when I know the wine will still be there when I come back. I put my glass down on a marble-topped sidetable. I'd been flattered to see that Ugo felt comfortable enough with me to serve the marsala in big, square tumblers instead of the stemmed wineglasses he found too dainty for his yeoman's hands.

Mary stood up. "I'll leave the two of you to it, then. Don't forget about the time up there. We have early dinner reservations: eight o'clock."

Ugo sprang out of his chair, grabbed the bottle by the neck, and tucked it under an arm. "Bring your glass," he told me. "We'll have a toast."

I complied. Looking at old paintings *while* drinking wine was even better.

I assumed we were going to spend a leisurely hour or two in his top-floor gallery, but instead he led me on a double-time tramp through it, allowing only hurried pauses in front of the four paintings he was lending us for the exhibit, and another stop before the Boursse he would be selling to the museum.

The little Boursse was as exquisite as I remembered it, a meticulously executed interior scene along the lines of his *Woman Cooking* in London's Wallace Collection. But this one was even more intimately domestic: *A Mother Ridding Her Child's Hair of Lice*—not a hugely appealing subject to today's art lover, but in seventeenth-century Holland a frequently used image of maternal love and a homely metaphor for good government. Sipping the fragrant wine, I looked at it lovingly (no longer covetously), but I could hear Ugo behind me, shifting impatiently from foot to foot, could feel him psychologically yanking at me.

I turned away from the picture. "Ugo, are we in some kind of hurry?"

"No, no. Well, yes. Don't you want to see my surprise?"

"Surprise?"

His face fell. "You don't remember?"

I did, dimly. "In Bologna, at that bar. You said something about a surprise. . . ."

"Yes, come!" Now he was physically yanking me. "You can look at your Boursse some more later." We bypassed the elevator (too slow?) and started down the steps. "Do you remember," he said with a nervous laugh, "you once told me there was somebody missing from your show?"

"Uytewael," I replied.

More properly Wtewael, Joachim, made fractionally more accessible to the nonspeaker of Dutch by its alternate spelling. Uytewael was another painter of the Utrecht School, one of its leaders in his day, but little-known now. He was a legitimate part of Northerners in Italy, having spent two formative years in Padua when he was in his twenties. Originally, a single rare Uytewael had been included in the loan we were getting from the Pinacoteca, but the picture had proved too fragile to travel, so the show was without one. Or had been until now.

I stopped him on the stairs and stared at him. "You haven't gone out and bought an Uytewael, have you?"

He grinned again and tugged at me to move along.

I held him back. "You're going to lend it to the show? That's great, Ugo! But where—"

He put a fist on each hip. "Hey, Cristoforo, you want to talk about it, or you want to see it?"

CHAPTER 16

I wanted to see it. We took the lower flight of stairs in what seemed like two strides, and Ugo pulled me into a big ground-floor room that served as a workshop and storage area. There, in the center, clamped to an easel by wooden vises, it was: a small, unframed mythological scene, *Venus in the Forge of Vulcan*, a favorite subject in those days.

I began to move closer, but Ugo grabbed me by the arm again. "Wait. Look at her eyes." He led me, not to the easel, but from left to right in front of it. "You see?" he whispered reverently. "Wherever you move, the eyes follow you."

"Ah," I said, "so they do."

So they did. So do the eyes of the Mona Lisa (as any self-respecting Louvre guard will tell you if you let him), of the

Rembrandt self-portraits, of Hals's *Jolly Toper*—and of ten thousand other pictures in the galleries of the world—including several others in Ugo's collection. So, for that matter, do the eye-dots on a six-year-old's Happy Face drawing. The fact is, any two-dimensional rendering of a three-dimensonal face looking directly out of a picture will appear to be looking at you wherever you stand, if you take the trouble to notice. It is an artifact of human perception.

But of course I wasn't about to tell Ugo and spoil his pleasure in it. I was filled with gratitude. Ugo's generous gesture was going to eliminate a significant gap in the show. I moved slowly closer, looking at the picture of the near-nude figures: two bearded men, Venus, Cupid. It was painted on a panel, like Blusher's van Eyck-*cum*-Terbrugghen, only on this one the crackling ran the way it was supposed to. With time, an irregular groove had appeared down the center, marking the separation between the two planks beneath, and some of the glue used in joining them had leached to the surface, staining the figure at the anvil.

I walked around it to look at the back. The panel was from the Utrecht St. Luke's Guild, I thought, which was as it should have been. Besides the guild logo there were a couple of brands on it; one I recognized as an old quality-control mark, the other I thought was the stamp of the panel maker. A few strips of linen, brown and cracked with age, had been glued into the joint for support. I shifted to examine it from the sides.

And I began to feel a faint, intuitive stirring of doubt. Was there something not quite right here? Or was I getting paranoid? Was I going to be seeing forgeries every time I turned around now?

Ugo was busy pouring wine at a worktable. He came to my side with the two tumblers. "You're surprised, yes?" he burbled. "You like it? It's not such a terrible painting, is it?"

"Mm," I said. Abstractedly I took the glass he offered. What was holding my attention was not the painted surface, or even the back, but the very edges of the panel. You don't often get to see panel edges. They're usually glued solidly into sturdy frames, not just for appearance but for bracing. But this one was unframed, and the edges were coated with what looked like a compound of tangled yarn embedded in tar. This in itself was not extraordinary. In those days masses of plant fibers were sometimes glued to the hidden joints of a panel for additional stability. However, I couldn't recall seeing them cover the entire perimeter the way they did in this case.

My silence was getting to Ugo. "Cristoforo, what's the matter? You don't like it?"

"I don't like this," I said, fingering the edging.

"I'll have it taken off," he said anxiously. "Right away, don't worry."

"No, I mean I don't like the way it feels." I pressed a finger gently into it.

Ugo did the same. "How should it feel?"

"After four hundred years? Brittle, dry. It shouldn't still give this way. When did you say you got this?"

"In January, why? What's wrong?"

"January," I repeated. "Four months ago. Ugo, I could be wrong, but I don't think this stuff can be any older than that. Maybe newer."

His lips jerked. He didn't quite see where I was heading, but he didn't care for the general direction. "What do I care about this . . . this substance? What does it matter?"

I explained. What I was worried about was a waggish little caper that went back at least three hundred years. Toward the end of the seventeenth century the city council of Nuremberg had given permission to a painter to take down and copy Dürer's great self-portrait, which hung in the town hall. To make sure he didn't do something dastardly, such as swiping the original and substituting his own copy for it, they marked the back of the panel with various seals and hard-to-copy brands. Whereupon this resourceful crook carefully sawed off the front panel with Dürer's painting on it. He then used the thinned boards as the base for his copy, which was dutifully returned to the council complete with certified seals and markings still on the back, and made off with the famous original. (Not to worry; as often happens, it eventually found its way back into public hands and is now the showpiece of Munich's Pinakothek.)

174

Ugo took my undrunk wine back. He put both tumblers on the worktable with the bottle, returned, and looked soberly at the little painting.

"You think someone sawed off the front of my picture," he said slowly, "and painted a copy of it on another piece of wood, and then glued the copy on the panel? And then they stole the real picture and covered up what they did by putting on this black stuff?"

That was what I was thinking, all right. It wasn't only the freshness of the black adhesive, it was the painting itself that was worrying me. It wasn't an obvious forgery, like Blusher's fake van Eyck, but there were things about it that made me wonder: the washed-out colors, the flatness of the forms, a lack of the elaborate detailing that usually characterized Uytewael. True, I hadn't seen much of his work, and what I'd seen had varied in quality from picture to picture, so maybe I was imagining things. Besides I was by no means expert in this obscure Dutch Mannerist's work. But taken all together, I was uneasy, and I was truthful about it with Ugo.

"But, Cristoforo, look how *old* it is," he said. "See the cracks, see how it's stained, see the patches? Look how it was fixed up—here, and here, and here—a long time ago."

"Yes, I see." The trouble was, I told him, those were just the sort of "imperfections" a knowledgeable forger would supply. "Where did you get this, Ugo?"

"From Christie's, in London. Clara was there for an auction, and she called me to say it would be offered. She knew," he added proudly, "that I am a collector of the Utrecht School."

"Clara?" I said. Clara Gozzi?"

"Sure, Clara Gozzi. She said it was going to go for a low price, a bargain. She wanted to know, did I want her to act as my agent."

"And you told her to?"

"I said yes, all right, up to £100,000."

"And what did you wind up paying?"

"I got it for £93,000."

About $150,000. A bargain, all right—if it was really an Uytewael.

"Where did it come from? What's its provenance?"

"What the hell do I care where it came from?" He grabbed me roughly by the shoulder and swung me around to face him. "What are you saying, they stuck me with a fake? That's impossible!"

Max once told me that he'd seen Ugo genuinely worked up only once, and that had been over a ridiculously trivial matter, when someone had tried to overcharge him a few hundred lire for theater tickets. The overriding imperative of Ugo's life, Max had said, was *non farsi far fesso*—not to be made a fool of. It was a result, Max had airily supposed, of social insecurity stemming from a peasant background.

Whatever the root cause, Ugo was thoroughly worked up again. His face was splotched with red; in his temple throbbed an artery I hadn't seen before. I felt guilty for upsetting him, sorry that I'd been so blunt. I should have eased into this, kept my suspicions to myself until I had something more to go on.

"I don't think there's any reason to worry, Ugo," I said with more confidence than I felt. "I'm just naturally suspicious. If something does turn out to be funny about this, Christie's will take it back."

"What are you talking about?" he shouted. "How could anything be funny? The people at the museum, they checked it over."

"What museum?"

He snorted and waved his arms at the walls. "What museum, what museum—the Pinacoteca, what else? Di Vecchio examined it himself."

He quieted down enough to explain that the purchase had been conditional on Ugo's having the painting examined by experts of his own choosing. He had left it with the Pinacoteca for a few days, and Di Vecchio and his staff had concluded that there was no basis on which to dispute the painting's authenticity. There was a high probability that it was a genuine Uytewael, but if so it was an inferior one; perhaps unfinished, maybe a study, probably just an unsuccessful effort that had been discarded but not destroyed.

Di Vecchio had told him to forget his plans of offering it to Northerners in Italy; it was simply not exhibition-quality.

"So I did," Ugo said. "But then, when you said you would come here to Sicily anyway, I figured, Amedeo doesn't know everything; why shouldn't I let you decide for yourself?"

"No reason at all. But didn't he say anything about this black stuff?"

"Nothing."

I hunched my shoulders. "Well, forget what I've been telling you. All I can say is, it would never have gotten by Amedeo. He'd have noticed it, and looked into it, and he must have been satisfied with the answers he got. Maybe it was restored just before it was auctioned, maybe—"

"Notice? How could he notice? With the frame on it you couldn't see the edges."

"It had a frame when it was auctioned?"

"Sure. Over there." He pointed to the disassembled parts of a simple old frame on a worktable a few feet away.

"Why did you take it off?"

"Me, I didn't take it off. Vittore took it off."

Vittore Pinto, Ugo explained, was his Catanian restorer, and it had come off because one of the panel's long-ago owners had apparently seen fit to preserve the deteriorating wood of the frame by bathing it in olive oil. It had worked fine for the frame, but over the years a greasy film had spread onto the margins of the painting.

Ugo halted. "Wait, doesn't that prove it's old? Vittore said it would take years and years for such a film to form. Doesn't that prove it's real?"

Unfortunately, I told him, it proved nothing. It was just another touch a clever forger would throw in.

"You're just like these damn psychiatrists!" he exploded. "Everything proves what *you* say. You hate your mother too much? Sure, that proves you wanted to have sex with her when you were a little kid. You love your mother too much? Sure, that proves you wanted to have sex with her when you were a little kid."

I laughed, glad to have him making jokes again, and leaned over to look at the picture. "I don't see any film now."

Pinto had removed it, according to Ugo, and had touched up the rest of the painted surface as well. The frame had undergone an oil-evaporation process, had been coated with sealant, and was now drying. On Monday the restorer would come back and refit it to the panel.

"Ugo, maybe I've been making us crazy over nothing," I said hopefully. "Could Pinto have touched up this black edging, too?"

"No, I don't think so. Vittore's good at his job, but he makes sure to charge plenty. There's nothing on his statement about this, so take my word for it, he didn't do it."

Unless he did it *without* telling Ugo. The copyist that forged the Dürer hadn't charged the council for alterations, either. But this seemed too unlikely to pursue. If Pinto had sliced off the face of the original Uytewael and made off with it, he would hardly have left the evidence of his tinkering sitting around Ugo's workshop for a week.

Besides, who in his right mind would go to all that risk and trouble to make off with a Joachim Uytewael, for God's sake? What kind of market was there for Uytewaels? Even in Ugo's relatively modest collection there were paintings worth nine or ten times as much. Was I inventing all this?

Tentatively, I fingered the tarry black border again. No, I wasn't inventing anything. Something wasn't right here. Maybe there was a simple and legitimate explanation, but something wasn't right.

"Ugo, tell me: Does it look exactly the same as when you first saw it? I mean exactly."

He studied it, lips pursed. "Yes. A little nicer since Vittore cleaned it."

"You're absolutely sure it's the same painting Clara brought back from London?"

"Ten minutes ago I was sure," he grumbled. "Now, with all these questions, who knows?" He chewed on a plump underlip. "You're starting to worry me, damn it. The fact is, Cristoforo, I didn't see it when she brought it back. I was in the middle of moving back here from Milan. I had no time for it. Clara took it straight to the museum. The first time I saw it was when it got here a week, two weeks, later." He grabbed up his tumbler and gulped down the rest of his wine. "But so what? What are you saying?"

"I don't know. How did it get here from the museum?"

"It came with the rest of my paintings. Max arranged with the shipping company there, I forget their name—"

I looked at him. "Salvatorelli?"

"No, not them. From Milan. Albertazzi."

Another theory bit the dust. Albertazzi & Figlio were also well-known transporters of fine art. But unlike the Salvatorellis, they were incontestably upright; not a shred of rumor about underworld connections attached to them.

"The Pinacoteca's in Bologna, Albertazzi's in Milan," I said. "How did it get from Bologna to Milan? Or did the movers just pick it up at the museum on their way south?"

"How do I know? Can I take care of every detail? Can't I trust the Pinacoteca?"

He banged down his glass, threw up his hands and stumped angrily around the little room, lapsing into a muttered dialect I couldn't understand.

Two circuits calmed him. He stopped, facing me. "Cristoforo," he said quietly, "let me get this straight. You're worried that if we could see under that black stuff, we'd see two pieces of wood, two layers of wood."

"Right."

"But if you're wrong, there'd be one solid piece, the way there's supposed to be."

"True."

He smacked his hands together. "Fine! So then let's see. What are we standing here talking for?"

He went quickly to the workbench, rummaged for a moment, and came back, freshly energized, with a wood chisel in his hand. Ugo was first and foremost a man of action.

"*Wait!*" I jumped between him and the picture. Chisels being addressed to seventeenth-century paintings tended to turn curators into men of action, too. "What are you going to do?"

He blinked at me. "I'm going to scrape it off and see what's underneath. Why not?"

"For one thing, you just paid millions of lire for this. Hundreds of millions."

"So? It's mine, isn't it? Don't worry, I'm not going to hurt the picture. Just this crap on the edges."

We were dancing absurdly around, Ugo trying to bull his way past me, me holding him off.

"Ugo, I just *think* the painting might be a forgery. You can't just chip away at it when you feel like it. Besides, it isn't yours."

He stopped shoving and peered skeptically up at me. "Who says, not mine?"

"Not yours to do anything you want with. It's yours as an article of public trust. You're its custodian, its guardian, not its owner. You're the one who's responsible for preserving it for posterity—not scraping away at it with a chisel to see what's underneath."

Okay, it was a little windy, but this kind of thing has a better ring to it in Italian. And being exactly what I really believe, it was delivered with sincerity. In any case, the appeal to Ugo's better instincts did the trick.

"Cristoforo, you're right," he said, lifting his jowls a little, as befitted a guardian of the public trust. He put down the chisel. "So what do we do?"

I'd been giving this some thought. "The top person I know on early sixteenth-century Flemish painting is Willem van de Graaf at the Mauritshuis."

"At the what?"

"It's a museum in The Hague. I'd like him to see this."

"Sure, tell him to come down."

"No, I mean I'd like to take it there. That's where his laboratory is. I could fly up there with it on Monday morning. If it's genuine, I'll take it gladly, and I can have the Mauritshuis ship it on to Seattle for the show. If it isn't—well, I'll call you, and we can figure out what to do from there."

"But what about the frame? I wouldn't like to see it in the show without a frame."

"I'll take it along with me. One of their conservators will be glad to mount it."

He hesitated only briefly. "All right, sure."

"Good—hold it, what am I thinking of? This won't work. You'd have to get a rider on your insurance."

"Don't worry. I'll take care of it tomorrow."

"In one day? On a Sunday?"

"Sure, why not?"

I shook my head. "Well, maybe you can, but you're not going to take care of getting customs approval in one day. No, we'd better—"

"I'll take care of it," he said.

I smiled. "Obviously, you've never had to deal with the Italian government on—"

"I told you, don't worry. I'll take care of it, you'll see." He puffed out his plump chest. "Me, I'm on very good terms with the officials here. They'll do anything for me."

CHAPTER 17

La Vecchia Cucina was a homey, rustic place—floors and beamed ceiling of dark wood, walls of rough, whitewashed stucco, a stone fireplace—given a touch of elegance by black-tied waiters and thick white linen. Ugo, ever sensitive to social nuances, basked in being fawningly received as a man of importance, and grandly introduced me to Fabrizio, the proprietor, as a great art scholar from America.

We were shown to a prominent table by Fabrizio himself, who pulled out Mary's chair for her and raised a scandalized fuss when he discovered a faded wine stain at the edge of the snowy tablecloth. The maître d' was summoned and castigated. Two waiters rushed up. One whisked the offending cloth away; the other slung a new one onto the table with the deft, snapping flick of the wrists that is practically an art form among Italian waiters. Places were rapidly reset while Fabrizio murmured apologies for the inconvenience.

Ugo lapped it all up, dismissed Fabrizio with a forgiving, seigneurial wave of the hand. Glasses of the infamous Jazz! were brought to us. Ugo toasted my health, downed the aperitif with every sign of genuine pleasure, smacked his lips and said "Ah!"

I steeled myself, tossed the stuff back, smacked my lips, and said "Ah!" too.

It was as bad as I remembered. I noticed that Mary took only a small sip and set her glass off to the side.

Ugo rubbed his hands together. "I thought you would enjoy an authentic Sicilian restaurant," he told me, "not a fancy place. You feel adventurous? You want to try some of our traditional foods?"

I was hungry, not adventurous. The last meal I'd had was a Continental breakfast at the Europa twelve hours before. What I wanted was the biggest plate of lasagna the kitchen could make, but not at the cost of disappointing my host. "Absolutely," I said. "I've been looking forward to it."

Others were helping themselves from a self-service antipasto table, but Ugo, who may have felt such behavior in my presence would have been déclassé, had a waiter deliver a platterful to us. Almost everything on it was from the nearby sea: a marinated salad of shrimp and octopus; mussels baked with olive oil and bread crumbs; thin, fried cakes made of tiny, transparent fish complete with heads and tails; fresh tuna, fresh sardines; sea urchins in the shell—all at room temperature and all delicious, except for the sea urchin, which I regarded doubtfully, not quite sure how to approach it.

"One eats only the eggs, this orange stuff," Ugo explained, turning over a shell on his own plate. "It's like caviar. One scoops it up with a piece of bread, so."

I tried one and found it like a mouthful of unflavored gelatin, nothing remotely like caviar. The bread was good, though. "Interesting," I said.

"Now," Ugo said brightly, "a test for freshness. If we turn it over"—he did so with the tip of a knife—"we should find

183

that the spines still move. And so they do." He leaned toward me, over the purple, feebly waving spines, happy and maybe just a little malicious. "You ate it while it was alive! What do you think of that?"

Not a lot, really. What we were looking at was reflex activity in the rudimentary nerve fibers under the exoskeleton, unconnected to any central nervous system. (You're right, this is not the sort of thing I'd ordinarily know, but I'd once done a project on the Echinodermata for a high school biology contest; I'd gotten an honorable mention for it.) Once again, though, why disappoint Ugo? Who could blame him for a little jovial malice after the way I'd ruined his day over the Uytewael?

I looked down and grimaced. "My God, it's still wriggling!"

For some people it would have been overkill, but Ugo beamed and showily tossed the insides of another urchin into his mouth.

"And look at these little fish!" I went on, shuddering. "You can see their *eyes!*"

Ugo delightedly shoveled in a dozen of them, eyes and all. Mary watched my performance without comment, but with one eyebrow infinitesimally raised.

His good humor restored, Ugo ordered the other courses for us, and the rest of the meal went well: spaghetti with fresh sardines, and grilled mullet with fennel, accompanied by two bottles of Corvo Bianco that went quickly to my head. Then coffee with a gigantic *cassata Siciliana*—a heavy, iced cake made with ricotta cheese and jellied fruit. We all ate and drank heartily and laughed a great deal.

Ugo and I were in the middle of telling Mary about the Uytewael (by this time it seemed quite funny) when the restaurant went tense and quiet. Ugo stopped in mid-guffaw. I turned to follow his gaze and the gaze of everyone else I could see.

Two men in dark, conservative suits had entered and sat down at a table near the fire. They were conversing with Fabrizio in low voices.

"What is it?" I asked. "Who are they?"

"Sh!" Ugo said severely. "They are politicians."

"Politicians?"

He looked at me. "You don't understand what 'politician' means here?"

"The Mafia?"

It was Mary who answered. "The grown-up variety this time," she said in a low voice. She had switched to English. "Not just your plain old everyday Mafia, either. You're looking at the big wheels themselves, the *padroni*."

The Sicilian Mafia. Right there in the room with me. The people who had tried to blow me up that morning. Well, not precisely. Antuono had said that the ones who were directly involved were now in Bologna. Still, if these men were the *padroni* here, then it could hardly have happened without their knowledge, probably not without their authorization. These were the shadowy figures who pulled the strings, or at least the figures for whom the strings were pulled.

I shifted my chair to have a better look. They couldn't have been less intimidating. One was in his fifties, pudgy and bald, with thick glasses and a black fringe of baby-fine hair. The other, white-haired and fragile-looking, was about seventy, with elegant, long-fingered hands that he waved as he spoke, like a man leading a Haydn quartet. They had ordered a bottle of wine and were sipping from small glasses while people from other tables—almost in procession—came to them, bobbed, said a few words, and departed. Most left small offerings from their own tables: fruit, or pastry, or more wine.

A third man, in a flashier, double-breasted suit, stood a step behind them, his back against the fireplace wall. This one was younger, more fit, olive-skinned. Now and then he would lean over to whisper a few words to one of the Mafiosi, but mostly he let his expressionless eyes wander over the room. Periodically, he would nod peremptorily at someone; the person would eagerly hop up to come pay his respects at the table.

"Who's that other guy?" I asked.

"Secretary," Ugo said.

"What does that mean, bodyguard?"

"It means secretary," Ugo said crossly. "They don't need bodyguards."

He wasn't really paying attention to me; he was watching

185

the newcomers intently. When his own signal to approach came, it was not from the "secretary," but from the white-haired man, who nodded to him with a smile, as a courteous monarch might motion a subject to approach. It was Ugo's turn to pay homage. He licked his lips, straightened his tie, and stood up.

"You think they would enjoy to try the *cassata?*" he asked Mary.

"Sure," she said, "it's pretty good."

We watched Ugo, all smiles and deference, take the cake to them and put it on a table already loaded with tribute.

"They'll never be able to eat all that stuff," I said.

"Don't worry about it," Mary said. "Fabrizio gives doggie bags."

"Mary, what did Ugo mean, they don't need bodyguards?"

"They don't need them, that's all. Nobody would dare hurt them."

"I see."

"No, you don't see. Nobody would dare to, but nobody would want to, either, or hardly anybody. Sure, these creeps have turned every third Italian kid into a dope addict, but they also make it possible for everything to work around here. Without the Mafia everybody would be after his own graft, there'd be gang wars all over the place, there'd be a thousand little Mafias. They'd eat us up alive."

"So one big Mafia is better than a thousand little ones, is that the idea?" I usually thought of Mary as an American married to an Italian. Sometimes I forgot she was half-Sicilian herself.

"You better believe it."

"Well, I see your point, but—"

"Look, there was a back road we took today, coming in from the airport. A few years ago there used to be this gang, like pirates. They worked the road late at night. They used two cars with walkie-talkies, one at either end, and when they got a lone car, they'd head it off and block it from in front and behind at this narrow bridge, to rob it. Sometimes they killed the passengers. It went on for months; nobody could do anything."

"What about the police?"

"Come on, the Catanian *polizia* are something else. The only thing that made any difference was when a few people got together and went to the Mafia, to those guys sitting right there. There was no protection fee involved, you understand, no subscription, no Mafia interest. But the gang was giving the area a bad name, and people just expected the Mafia to do something about it."

"And?"

"And a few mornings later they found the cars the gang was using, burned to crisps near the bridge. Three bodies inside, likewise fried. And that was the end of that. I'm telling you, when these guys go after you, you can forget it."

"Oh, wonderful. Did I tell you Colonel Antuono thinks it's the Mafia that's trying to kill me?"

She blinked at me. "The . . . oh, piffle, why would—"

At that moment Ugo returned, flushed and pleased with himself. "I told them all about you," he said proudly. "They were tremendously interested."

"I'll bet," I muttered. "They probably loved finding out I was still in one piece."

He looked at me peculiarly. "What?"

"I'll explain later, Ugo."

"They invite you to their table," he said. "They would like to meet you." He put a hand on my forearm. "It's an honor, Cristoforo."

"Well, I'd like to meet them, too," I said, pushing my chair out from the table.

The dark secretary was standing right behind me, smooth and snaky. "I am Basilio," he said in English. "When they sit down, you sit, too. When they stand up, you go. You are to ask them nothing, only answer. This is understood?"

Basilio, it seemed, was not only secretary but protocol chief, too. He waited, blocking my way until I nodded, then turned and led me to their table.

The two men rose. There were smiles and handshakes and friendly noises. If they were annoyed to find me still breathing, they didn't show it.

The older man with the graceful fingers was mild and

courtly. *"Benvenuto a Catania, dottore,"* he said. He smelled of soap and cologne.

It occurred to me that I might fare better if they thought I didn't understand Italian. *"Molte grazie,"* I said haltingly. *"Mi dispiace, io non parlo bene l'italiano."* I tried to make it sound as if I'd memorized it out of Berlitz.

Both men laughed pleasantly. The white-haired one waved me politely to a chair and we all sat. I accepted a small glass of dark, sweet wine. The pudgy one spoke quietly over his shoulder to Basilio, who stood at his side.

"They say," Basilio translated, "how long do you stay in Catania?"

"Only four days, unfortunately." It was actually only two days, but I'd learned my lesson: I wasn't going to start advertising my departure time again.

The information was conveyed by Basilio, who was given a second message, this time from the white-haired man. "They ask, what is your special competence, your expertise?"

"The Renaissance and Baroque periods."

This seemed to interest them, especially the older man.

"They say," Basilio said, "have you familiarity with Sicilian artists of the time?"

"Of course. Montorsoli, Pietro Novelli—they're known throughout the world." Not household names, perhaps, but why quibble? And oddly enough, I found myself wanting to please the older man.

He was pleased. He chuckled and nodded at me. "Known throughout the world," I heard him repeat in Italian.

For a while the three of us sipped and smiled at each other. I was conscious of envious stares from other tables. People were coveting my time with them, fretting that their own turns might be bypassed. Not that mine was doing me much good. For all the information that my clever no-spikka-da-Italian ploy had produced, I might have dispensed with it. There had been no muttered byplay in Italian about bombs or loot or anything else.

I decided to take hold of matters. "I had an interesting flight here today," I said.

Basilio translated.

"Ah?" said the pudgy one politely. Either his attention was beginning to wander or he was craftier than I thought. No doubt the latter.

"Yes," I said, "I was almost killed by a bomb."

With a quick stab of his cold eyes Basilio advised me against the propriety of this. I repeated it.

Basilio shrugged. "He says," he told them in Italian, "that he encountered many difficulties and delays on his flight."

There were murmurs of sympathy, bland and perfunctory; nothing more. Something was peculiar here. Even with no more than Basilio's bowdlerized version to go on, their ears should have pricked at mention of the flight, but there had been nothing. Was Antuono wrong? Despite his "skilled undercover agents" and their months of information-gathering, had he come to the wrong conclusion about who was at the bottom of it all? Or—a fresh, unsettling possibility—had he been purposely misleading me? But why?

The bald one said something to Basilio.

"They say, where you are from in America?"

"I was born in California."

This produced the first real show of interest in a while. "They say, you know of Sylvester Stallone the actor?"

"What? Yes."

"*Cugino!*" the bald man exclaimed.

"Cousin," Basilio translated dutifully. "A distant cousin. His people come from nearby."

The bald man nodded vigorously, "*Sí!*" he said. "*Sí!*"

"Ah," I said. The conversation had edged over into the surreal. "Very interesting. *Molto interessante.*"

More smiles, and the white-haired man stood up and held out his hand. Basilio looked meaningfully at me. I got up, too. There were bows and handshakes all around.

"Good-bye," said the white-haired man in labored, almost impenetrable English, "and good luck."

Half an hour later, as Ugo, Mary, and I were leaving, Ugo was summoned briefly back to their table. He joined us outside, all smiles.

"They liked you," he told me blissfully. "The insurance is arranged, the customs are taken care of."

I stared at him. "You mean *those* are the officials you were talking about? It's the Mafia that's helping me get that picture to The Hague?"

"Sure," he said. "Who else?"

Possibly it's occurred to you to wonder why I was so willing to personally convey a suspect painting to The Hague (even, as it now appeared, under the dubious sponsorship of the Mafia). Why not simply have it shipped there for van de Graaf's inspection? There was plenty of time, after all; Northerners in Italy was still months from opening. Why complicate my life?

If, however, you know your European geography, then all is clear. The Hague is even closer to Amsterdam than Rotterdam is; a mere nine miles, with fast, frequent trains between the two. This isn't to say that I manufactured an excuse to go there. Everything I'd told Ugo about the painting and about van de Graaf was true. All the same, my scrupulous if malleable conscience was not displeased at having a justifiable, work-related reason for a diversion to the west coast of Holland. I would fly there directly from Sicily.

From Ugo's I checked with Alitalia to make sure there was an early Monday morning flight with seats available. There was. I thanked the clerk without making a reservation; this time I would do my booking just before I boarded. Then I called van de Graaf to set up a 10:30 meeting at the Mauritshuis. And finally, saving the best for last, I called Anne to ask her to meet me at The Hague museum at noon.

"Can you be there?" I asked.

"With bells on," she said.

CHAPTER 18

"Hm," said the eminent Dr. Willem van de Graaf.

The remark was wholly in character. A stringy, puckered old man, dry as ashes, his taciturnity had been a joke among my fellow students at Berkeley. Not his expertise, however. He had taken part in a colloquium on the Early Netherlandish School, and whenever a few sequential sentences could be wrenched out of him, he had bowled us over with the depth and specificity of his knowledge. Since then he and I had been friends of a sort, and I had turned to him more than once for help.

We were leaning over a table in the basement of the Royal Picture Gallery Mauritshuis, having just gotten Ugo's Uytewael out of its carton and unwrapped it.

"What do you think?" I asked when he straightened up after a few minutes.

He repeated his earlier opinion: "Hm."

I asked what he thought about the black material encrusting the edges.

It was called *cañamograss*, I was tersely informed. It was typical of Catalan panels, less so of those from the north. The fibrous material in it was usually hemp. It was unusual for it to be so lavishly applied. As to whether it was too soft to be four hundred years old, he preferred to reserve judgment until some tests could be applied.

I pressed him. What about the picture itself?

What did I think was wrong with it? he wanted to know.

"I'm not sure if anything is. I don't know Uytewael that well, but the colors seem flat to me. The whole thing seems . . . well, insipid, pedestrian. Not up to his standards."

"Not up to his standards. Did you ever hear what the painter Max Liebermann had to say about us poor art historians?"

I shook my head. Laconic he might be, but all the same van de Graaf had a sizable store of obscure but pithy quotations.

" 'Let us honor the art historians,' " he quoted. " 'It is they who will later purify our *oeuvre* by rejecting less successful works as "certainly not by the artist's own hand." ' "

He cackled and I laughed along with him. "All the same, I'm just not comfortable with it, Willem."

He leaned over it again. His nose wrinkled. "Don't I smell copaiba balsam? Has someone been working on it?"

"It was just cleaned. 'Touched up,' according to Ugo. I'm not sure just what that means, but I don't think that's what hurt the colors. According to Ugo, the guy is an expert."

"Ah, but you know what Max Doerner said about experts."

I didn't, of course.

" 'There *are* no experts in the field of picture restoration.' " van de Graaf said. " 'There are only students.' " He tucked in his chin, folded his arms, laid a forefinger vertically along his upper lip, and continued to peer at the painting with lidded eyes. "Hm," he said.

We were back where we started. "What now?" I asked.

"Now? As soon as you give me some peace, I'll take this in back and see what I see."

"Will you be able to tell me anything today? At least whether or not there are two panels glued together under all the gunk?"

He hunched his shoulders. "Today, tomorrow, next week. It can't be hurried."

He meant *he* couldn't be hurried, but I'd known that when I'd come. Still, there wasn't any particular rush, no reason the painting couldn't be left with him and shipped later.

"I'll call you, then," I said.

He was already heading for the double swinging doors to the work area, holding the picture in front of him, studying it intently.

"Hm," he replied.

I went upstairs to the museum's public galleries. Anne would be there by now.

If anyone ever asks me, not that anyone is likely to, what the finest small art museum in Europe is, I will unhesitatingly name the Mauritshuis. There isn't a second-rate piece of work in the place. Not one. Every painting, every object, is a jewel. It's like the Wallace Collection in London or the Frick in New York: a limited but superb collection in an elegant old town house. Walking through the building would be a pleasure even without the pictures. And with them, one can see them all— really see them—and be done in under two hours, still fresh and appreciative. Try that in the Louvre.

I had arranged with Anne to meet in one of the second-floor galleries, but at the foot of the staircase I hesitated, suddenly apprehensive. Our recent telephone conversations had been exuberant and happy, filled with laughter. But now, in retrospect—and faced with actually meeting her—I'd begun to wonder if there hadn't been something counterfeit about them; an edgy, forced glitter stemming more from the awkwardness of not having talked for so long than from anything else.

What were we going to say to each other now? When you came down to it, what had we actually said on the telephone? That we were looking forward to seeing each other. That was

193

what second cousins said, or business acquaintances who meet at a convention once a year. Were we—was I—trying to drag out past its alloted time something that wasn't there anymore? How did I know that Anne *didn't* intend this as a civilized farewell, the final tying up of a few troublesome strings before she went on with her life?

I turned away from the staircase, chewing my lip. This was no way to approach things. I needed to calm myself down, compose my thoughts. Fortunately, I had a tranquilizer at hand. No, I don't carry around a handy vial of Valium. But I was standing in a gallery full of eighteenth-century Dutch paintings, and if browsing for a while in that lovely, peaceful, orderly world didn't unruffle me, nothing would. I took a slow breath and began to wander through the small ground-floor rooms.

And within a minute or two, I thought I could feel it working. With a few monumental exceptions, Dutch artists painted little to raise the blood pressure or inflame the spirits. Nobody ever got overexcited looking at *Still Life with Turkey Pie* or *Cheese Seller's Stall at Dordrecht.* Josef Capek described Dutch art as the work of seated artists for sedentary burghers. Just the thing for the fevered mind. Knee-deep in metaphor, of course, but only the scholars worried about that nowadays.

I went slowly, stopping only twice, once to pay homage to Vermeer's *View of Delft,* the wonderful townscape that revolutionized the painted depiction of light. And then again, before his simpler *Girl with a Blue Turban,* which has no particular claim to fame other than its being so achingly beautiful. If that didn't soothe me, I decided, I wasn't going to get soothed. So at last I made for the stairs, looking back over my shoulder at the *Girl.*

Her limpid brown eyes, you will be interested to learn, followed me every inch of the way.

Anne had her back to me when I saw her. She was standing in front of a picture of a cow, her face turned up to look at it. Her honey-colored hair was darker than I remembered it, and a little shorter; her shoulders more delicate. She was in civilian clothes—a belted jumpsuit, fashionably baggy at the hips and tight at the ankles, with a jacket over her arm. She looked absolutely terrific. My confidence level, such as it was, ratcheted down another notch.

I came up behind her, my heart in my mouth. "Hi there, Captain."

She turned. "Dr. Norgren, I presume."

"Sorry I'm late."

"Oh, that's all right. You look wonderful."

"So do you—just great."

From that fatuous beginning things got worse. We walked through the museum, hardly seeing it, both of us timid, skating clumsily around each other, searching for something riskless to talk about. How was my flight? What had her meeting been about? How had I liked Sicily? Had she had any interesting assignments lately? Had her brother-in-law recovered from his kidney-stone operation? Had she—

Finally, she put a finger to my lips to get me to shut up. "Let's sit down a minute."

Docilely, I sat next to her on an out-of-the-way bench. Around us were peaceable little scenes by de Hooch and de Heem and Terborch—ordinarily the names alone would have been enough to lull me—but they weren't doing me any good now. I was filled with misgiving, terrified at what she might be going to say to me.

"Chris," she said soberly. "I've been giving things a lot of thought." Her eyes, usually as near to violet as eyes come, had deepened to a glowing blue-black. She looked down at her hands, clasped on her lap.

"And?" I said, or squeaked.

"I've been miserable since San Francisco," she said, talking rapidly. "I miss you awfully. I want us to give it another try— that is, if you want to."

"Me too!" I blurted, practically dissolving into jelly with relief. We leaned our foreheads together and laughed, a little jerkily from the release of tension. I realized that she'd been as worried as I had. A few museum visitors glanced at us with understandable irritation.

"Whew," I said, and grabbed her hand. "Come on, let's get some air."

We left the museum, walking around the corner and then along the edge of the Hofvijver, the square, fountained "lake" that sets off the dignified old Parliament buildings.

"So," I said, "what do we do?"

She smiled and squeezed my hand. "Seems to me we're already doing it."

"I mean after today. How do we handle it? You have to stay in the Air Force—"

"I *want* to stay in the Air Force. For one more year, anyway."

"And I have to and want to stay at the Seattle Art Museum, six thousand miles away."

"True. What would you suggest?"

"We could get married," I said, startling both of us.

"Married?"

I shrugged. "In for a dime, in for a dollar."

She burst out laughing. "You just got divorced. You've been single all of five months."

"Right, I gave it a fair try. Between you and me, it's not what it's cracked up to be."

She stopped and studied me. "Are you serious?"

"Of course. Well, I think so. I just thought of it."

"But how would getting married change anything? I'd still be in the Air Force, you'd still be in Seattle."

"So what are we supposed to do?" I asked again. "Just see each other from time to time, whenever I get over to Europe or you get to the States?"

"Why not? Why do we have to *do* anything? Why can't we just take it as it comes, see how it turns out? When my tour of duty's up, we can see how we feel."

"Well, sure, I suppose we could," I said doubtfully, "but—"

"Chris, did anybody ever tell you you have this need to tie everything up into nice, neat, black-and-white packages?"

"Yes," I said.

Only Tony called it "trying to deoptionalize nonprogrammable contingencies." Louis saw it as "a counterproductive aversion to ambiguity due to faulty self-esteem." I forget what Bev called it, but she had a name for it, too. I was starting to think maybe they had a point. Either that or everybody liked ganging up on me. And even Louis had never accused me of having paranoid inclinations.

"Isn't it enough to just be together again?" she asked. "To be friends again?"

She had moved closer to me, putting her hands against the lapels of my jacket and looking directly up into my face. There was a barely noticeable little twitch in the soft skin below her eyes, something that showed up when she was anxious or insecure. Anne wasn't even aware when it was there, but for me it always had a compelling, waifish poignancy. I embraced her; for the first time in five months I wrapped my arms around her and pulled her close. Unexpectedly trembling, I bent my face down to her hair and inhaled the fragrance. I could feel her shaking, too.

It was more than enough.

The paintings had put us in the mood for some plain, hearty Dutch cooking; the sort of thing that would have looked right on one of those scarred old tables in a scene by Jan Steen or Adriaen Brouwer. In most Dutch cities it would have been easy to find an appropriate restaurant. Dutch cooking may not often figure in discussions of the world's great cuisines, but of plain and hearty there isn't any shortage. The Hague, however, is the least Dutch city in Holland, as the Dutch themselves like to say. Full of foreigners on expense accounts, it's easier to find a plate of *escargots à la bourgignonne* than a bowl of humble, nourishing *erwtensoep*.

All the same, with half an hour's diligent perusing of the sedate, embassy-lined streets, we managed to locate a signboard with a red, white, and blue soup tureen on it. In Holland this signifies a small restaurant promising just what we were looking for: traditional food and old-fashioned cooking.

The promise was delivered on. We ordered smoked herring and *hutspot*, a beef-and-vegetable stew that gave robust new meaning to "plain and hearty." And while we ate, I told her the long, tangled story of my last few weeks, from Blusher's Rubens through Ugo's dubious Uytewael. As you can imagine, this took a while. By the time I finished, we were done with our stew and had moved on to a nearby *pannekoekhuis* for crepes and coffee at a sidewalk table under the plane trees.

"Somebody's tried to kill you *twice?*" she said, stirring sugar into her coffee. "My God."

"Only once. They weren't trying to kill me on Via dell'Independenza."

"They ran you down with a car but they weren't trying to kill you?"

"I mean it was Max they were after. I was just incidental. If I hadn't run back to help, nothing would have happened to me."

"All right, once, if it makes you feel better—"

"It does."

"—but why even once?"

I shook my head. "It's got to have something to do with the thefts. That's all I can think of."

"But what? Were they trying to keep you from finding out something?"

"I don't think so. Once I left for Sicily I wasn't planning on coming back to Bologna, except to catch a plane to the States, and everybody knew it. So there wasn't any risk that I'd uncover anything new."

"What then?"

"All I can guess is that it's something I already know. Or that they think I know."

"Like what?"

"Maybe they're afraid Max told me the names of the people on his list; the people who knew his security systems."

She shook her head. "No, if that was it, why would they wait until you were leaving? If you were going to tell the police at all, you'd already have told Antuono."

"Yes, you're right."

"Chris, could it have something to do with the Uytewael? Could someone have been trying to keep you from finding out it's a fake?"

"Who? Ugo's the only one who's likely to suffer over it."

"Well, Ugo then. I know he's your friend and you like him—"

I laughed. "You and the police; you both keep trying to pin it on Ugo. Look, if he didn't want me to find out the picture was a fake, he didn't have to blow me up. All he had to do was not show it to me. I didn't even know it existed."

She took a halfhearted stab at her jelly-filled crepe. "Colonel Antuono must have a theory about all this. What does he think?"

"I'm not sure he does have a theory—about why someone would want to kill me, I mean. What he's interested in is the paintings, period. Any corpses that happen to get produced along the way are incidental nuisances."

"All right, what's his theory about the paintings? Who has them?"

"According to him, the whole thing was organized by the evil masterminds of the Sicilian Mafia."

"But you don't think so."

"No. When I was in Sicily I had a conversation—more like an audience—with the Mafia *padroni* and unless I got led down the garden path, they don't know anything about it."

She sat back and eyed me quizzically. "An audience with the Mafia *padroni*." She sighed. "Tell me, Chris, is this what life is like for other art curators, too, or is it just you?"

"It's just me. Anyway, the only time these guys showed any interest was when they thought I might know Sylvester Stallone."

"Maybe you were talking to the wrong *padroni*."

"Maybe. Antuono claims the ones involved are in Bologna now. Apparently, he's close to some kind of deal with them to get the pictures back."

"Chris . . . should you really be going back to Bologna, even for a night? Somebody tried to kill you there."

"No problem. They think I'm dead."

"They—?"

"Oh, did I forget that part? Yes, Antuono 'disappeared' me. He put out a story to the press that I'd been successfully blown up. So I'll be safe. In any case, I have to go back. I wound up coming straight here from Sicily; most of my things are still in Bologna."

"Oh." A perceptible hollowness had come into our conversation. Anne was looking down at her empty cup, turning it slowly on its saucer. "What time do you have to go?"

"I'd better head over to the train station at four," I said. "It takes about an hour to get to the airport."

She looked at her watch. "Fifty minutes," she murmured.

I cleared my throat. "What about you? When do you leave?"

"I've got a military flight at a little after eight." She suddenly looked up at me. That delicate, oddly affecting tic below her eyes was back. "Chris, couldn't you—"

"Anne, couldn't we—" I said at the same time, and we both laughed.

We could and we did. Anne had some time off due her, and there wasn't any pressing reason I couldn't take a few days' vacation, too. The post office across the street had a rank of international telephone booths from one of which Anne convinced the United States Air Force that they could get by without her until the following Monday. I wasn't able to get through to Seattle, but I'd try again later. We came out of the post office hand in hand, delighted with ourselves, but as yet undecided as to where we would spend the time.

"We could stay here," Anne suggested. "Maybe in one of the beach hotels."

"Except that my things are still in Bologna."

"What about going back there, then? All that good eating."

I made a face. "Maybe we can do that another time. For the moment, Bologna seems to have lost its charm for me."

Besides, although I saw little danger in returning for a single night, I wasn't keen on being seen around the city by anyone who was under the happy impression he'd killed me. Especially not with Anne at my side.

"Well, how about going back long enough to get your things?" she asked. "I can try and get a seat on your flight. Then tomorrow we can go someplace else. Have you ever been to Lake Maggiore?"

I shook my head.

"It's wonderful. I know a hotel in Stresa that's straight out of the eighteenth century. You'd love it—stuffy and old-fashioned—"

"Thanks a lot."

"—and romantic as they come."

"That's better. Uh, you've been there?"

"Yes; by bus, as part of an R and R group tour, not that it's any of your business. It can't be much more than three hours from Bologna by train. The water is this incredible turquoise green, and there are lemon trees and pomegranates and coconut palms, and the Borromean Islands are like a set from Sigmund Romberg. We could just laze around and take it all in. What do you say?"

What would anybody say? We went directly to the KLM terminal in the central railroad station to get her a seat on the plane. Then we picked up the bags we'd both left in the luggage room and boarded the train for the airport. I couldn't seem to stop grinning.

And no longer, even in my heart of hearts, did I carry a shred of resentment toward Calvin for his long weekend on the Riviera. Poor Calvin, with his dreary, eternal flitting from woman to woman. My heart went out to him.

CHAPTER 19

When we arrived at the hotel in Bologna, there was a note in my box: Willem van de Graaf had called. I was to telephone him at home if I got in before eleven. And, I was informed at the desk, another gentleman had telephoned that morning. Although he had become somewhat agitated at missing me, he had left no message except to say that it was quite important and he would call again.

"An Italian gentleman or an American gentleman?" I asked.

"Italian," I was told.

"Maybe it was Colonel Antuono," Anne suggested a few minutes later in our room.

"Not likely. The Eagle of Lombardy doesn't get agitated."

She stretched and covered a yawn with the back of her hand. "I'm beat. I think I'll take a hot shower."

I smiled happily at her. How quickly we had relaxed into the old rhythms, the old, easy intimacy. On the flight from Amsterdam I'd begun to get a little anxious about how comfortable we'd be with each other once we were alone. I'd even considered raising the possibility of separate rooms, at least for the first night, until we got used to one another again. Fortunately, good sense had prevailed.

"Go ahead," I said. "I'll give Willem a call and see what he's come up with."

The receiver was picked up on the third ring. "Willem, this is Chris Norgren. Is it a fake?"

"A fake?" Surprisingly, he laughed. "Yes, I suppose you could call it that. Amusing, in a way."

I wasn't sure I liked the sound of that. *Amusing* wasn't a word I associated with van de Graaf. Willem didn't have a sense of humor so much as a sense of irony.

"The *cañamograss* around the edges is no more than a few months old," he told me, "and not real *cañamograss* at that."

That was what I'd thought from the beginning. What was so amusing about it? "And?" I asked warily.

"And the panel is actually two separate layers laminated together, the process being disguised by the *cañamograss*."

Also as I'd thought. "Willem," I said, "why do I feel as if I'm waiting for another shoe to drop?"

"Shoe?"

"Willem, is the Uytewael a fake or isn't it?"

"No," he said, "the Uytewael is not a fake."

I sat down on the edge of the bed. "What?"

"It's not Uytewael at his best, but it's Uytewael, without question."

Just what Di Vecchio and his people had concluded. "But you said—"

"The Uytewael is authentic. The back to which it's glued is not. It's an imitation, a very good one, of a seventeenth-century Dutch panel. But it's quite recent."

This took a few seconds to sink in. "You're telling me

someone took a genuine Uytewael, sawed off the front of it—"

"Evidently."

"And then glued it onto a *fake* panel-back?"

"Precisely."

"Why? What could possibly be the point?"

"I was hoping," van de Graaf said, "that you could tell me."

"The question is, what did they do with . . ."

Whatever I was going to say trailed away. I stood frozen and mute, the receiver pressed against my ear. I was at long last having a moment of real insight, obvious and startling at the same time—what the psychologists call an aha experience. There *was* a link between at least some of the disparate happenings of the last few weeks; specifically, a link between Sicily and Seattle, between Ugo Scoccimarro and Mike Blusher. How could I have failed to see it, or even to guess at it, before?

"Have to go, Willem," I mumbled. "Hold on to that painting. I'll be back in touch soon."

More thoughts crowded their way in; more links, more possibilities. Hypotheses sprang from hypotheses, like a crossword puzzle being filled out every which way at once.

The telephone rang the instant I put it down.

"Chris, is that you? It's Lloyd."

"Lloyd?" I was still tracing out the crossword puzzle.

"As in 'Lloyd from the Seattle Art Museum'?" Your place of employment? Lloyd, the director's faithful administrative assistant—the director who, I might add, has been seriously concerned about you since you failed to arrive on your scheduled flight, and has had me searching hither and—"

"Oh, God, I forgot to call, didn't I? Look, I'm back in Bologna—"

"No, really? Do you mean Bologna, *Italy*?"

I sighed. This was Lloyd's typical mode of conversation, and I was generally up to it. But not now. "Lloyd, I'm sorry. Something important came up. Is Tony in? I have to talk to him."

"I'm not sure. Just a minute." There was a pause for muffled conversation. "Chris? I'm afraid our leader is out, but Calvin

Boyer is just pulsing to speak with you. Hold on, he's going to his desk."

A few seconds later Calvin came on to the line, pulsing. "Chris—hey, did you hear about Mike Blusher?"

It took me a moment to respond. The talk with van de Graaf was still rumbling around my mind. "No, what now?"

"They arrested him, can you believe it?"

That cleared my head. "You bet I can," I said with enthusiasm. "For what, fraud?"

"You got it. The FBI was in here talking to us about it this morning. They got him in a sting. He's selling the Terbrugghen all over the place. There are four of them, at least. They nailed him with a fake Uruguayan. This guy from Oman—"

"Wait a minute, will you, Calvin? Slow down. What's a fake Uruguayan?"

"Well, a real Uruguayan. You know, an Uruguayan-American. He was supposed to be a millionaire from Montevideo or someplace, but he's really an FBI agent. *Capisce?*"

"No," I said irritably. "Slow down, will you?"

"All right, pay attention, don't interrupt." There was a pause and a slurp; his afternoon Coke, straight from the can. Then, more slowly, if not that much more coherently, he explained. In the end, after many questions and explications, a more or less intelligible story emerged.

A week earlier, an Omani hotel magnate and novice art collector, Mr. al-Ghazali, who was in New York for several days of auctions at Sotheby's, had gone to the New York Police Department to express certain reservations about a purchase he had tentatively agreed to make—not from Sotheby's, but from a Mr. Michael Blusher, who was also there for the auctions.

According to Mr. al-Ghazali, he had recognized Blusher at a cocktail party at the Central Park South apartment of a Manhattan art dealer and had approached him on the terrace to congratulate him on the spectacular discovery of the Terbrugghen. Blusher had asked him if he collected Old Masters, and al-Ghazali had replied laughingly that he was thinking about it inasmuch as the Impressionists and the Moderns seemed to be priced beyond reach. They had then each gone on to talk with other people, but as the party was winding down, Blusher had suggested they have dinner together.

Afterward, over *truite fraîche grillée* at Lutèce, Blusher had revealed that he was interested in quietly selling the painting to a discreet buyer. He had come on strong—"like a yacht salesman," al-Ghazali disapprovingly said later—but the Omani's interest had been aroused all the same and they had talked price. Blusher had asked $850,000, al-Ghazali had offered $300,000, and they had settled on $425,000, contingent on al-Ghazali's later examination of the painting in Seattle.

Blusher, too, had a condition: that the sale not receive any publicity, at least for the time being. The only reason he was letting the painting go, he had explained, was that he was in a financial hole, and if word of it got out, others would guess the reason, something that would do his business no good. Al-Ghazali had accepted the condition, and they had shaken hands on it over the *soufflé au Grand Marnier*.

But later the Omani began to have second thoughts. He was new to collecting and unsure of himself, and the hard sell hadn't sat well with him. Nor had the secrecy, the emphasis on discretion. The following evening, at another party, he had chatted with a South Korean newspaper publisher who, like al-Ghazali, was in New York for his first major auction. The Korean had astonished him by saying that Blusher had offered *him* the Terbrugghen over lunch. The Korean, in fact, was under the impression that his own conditional offer of $330,000 had been accepted.

Stung by this evidence of bad faith (and very likely by the lower price the Korean had gotten), al-Ghazali went to the police. He was referred to an art-squad detective who in turn contacted the FBI's white-collar crime squad, which had already been following Blusher's much-publicized art adventures with skepticism if not outright suspicion.

"Ha," I said on hearing this.

"What?"

"I said ha. They weren't the only ones. Didn't I say all along he was pulling something?"

"Did you?" Calvin said. "I don't remember that."

"Go ahead, Calvin."

The FBI had quickly gone into action. A few days after Blusher returned to Seattle, he was approached by a Portland art dealer claiming to be an intermediary for a rich Uruguayan interested in making some, ah, discreet art purchase, preferably without the usual bothersome and time-consuming forms and declarations

Blusher had leaped slavering for the bait. The mysterious Uruguayan had been shown the Terbrugghen, with the over-painted "van Eyck" now removed, and a price of $400,000 had been agreed upon. The Uruguayan, who preferred to deal in cash (Blusher had cheerfully agreed to this), would return with the money the next day.

Instead, a team of FBI agents and Seattle Police Department detectives had arrived at Venezia with both a search warrant and an arrest warrant. In a closet next to Blusher's office they had found the Terbrugghen. Within an hour they'd uncovered three identical copies. "Exact duplicates, front and back," was the way they put it in their report.

At first, Blusher had claimed that they were all part of his legitimate authentic-simulated-masterpiece business. Then he had changed his mind and gone to a modified version of his mistaken-shipment-from-Italy story. Then he had decided that he wanted to talk to a lawyer, after all, and had said no more.

I sighed with satisfaction. It was just as I'd thought. The panel on which Blusher's Terbrugghen was painted had, of course, come from Ugo's picture, the back of which had been sawed off and replaced with an imitation. The Terbrugghen had then been forged directly on the genuine panel, which would have been a little thinner than before, but so what? Old panels were hardly uniform in thickness. Then, to spice up the eventual "discovery," the Terbrugghen had been painted over with the van Eyck.

Blusher, after gulling me into suggesting that he have it X-rayed, had taken it to the university. There, Eleanor Freeman had been startled to see (in a shadowy radiographic exposure) what looked very much like a Hendrik Terbrugghen painting underneath the fake van Eyck. Who could blame her for leaping to the conclusion that she'd found a lost masterpiece? As

Tony had said: "Why the hell would anyone paint a first-class forgery, then cover it up with another one so nobody could see it? That's crazy."

Not so crazy, it seemed.

"So he had three copies of the original made," I said slowly, "maybe even more, and he was selling them off as the original at three or four hundred thousand dollars apiece. He makes over a million dollars, and the joke is that even the original was a fake to begin with."

"Some joke," Calvin said.

After he hung up I kicked off my shoes, lay back on the bed with my hands clasped behind my neck, and closed my eyes. I was beat, too, but my mind was buzzing.

"Sounded interesting," Anne called from the bathroom. I could hear her brushing her hair.

"The Terbrugghen's a fake," I said dreamily.

"I heard."

"A fake seventeenth-century Dutch painting on a real panel."

"Uh-huh. Chris, you can talk normal-speed. I think I'm capable of following this."

"And the Uytewael is a real seventeenth-century Dutch painting on a fake panel."

I heard her come out of the bathroom, still brushing. "So I gathered. Quite a plot."

"Damn, I should have figured it out long ago. I knew Ugo's picture'd been tampered with the minute I looked at it, but I got going in the wrong direction and I couldn't get turned around. I couldn't get off the idea of a forged painting. I hardly looked at the back. It never occurred to me the *panel* was forged."

"Well, of course not," she said supportively. "It wouldn't occur to anyone." She brushed without speaking for a few seconds. "Chris, do you think that's why they tried to kill you? To keep you from finding out?"

"I guess so. I just wasn't as smart as they gave me credit for."

More brushing, slow and silky. What a lovely sound, I thought.

"Anne, I'm starting to think I might know who 'they' are. But I still haven't put all the pieces together. I need a little more information. And I think I can get that tomorrow."

The brushing stopped. "Chris . . . shouldn't you just tell Antuono and let him handle it?"

"Not quite yet, I think. Don't worry, I'm not going to do anything dangerous. I just need to stop by the hospital first thing in the morning and get one more piece from Max. Then I'll go straight to Antuono, I promise. And then we'll be off to Lake Maggiore. Noon at the latest."

"Well . . . all right," she said doubtfully. The sound of hair being brushed resumed. I opened my eyes. She was standing at the mirror in a pale-green shift, her bare arms upraised, brushing rhythmically.

I watched her with simple, mindless pleasure. "Is that what they're wearing in the Air Force these days?"

And as I said it I realized that I could put to rest another one of the San Francisco–based worries that had been nagging at me all day. My hormones were functioning just fine, busily—even eagerly—performing their appointed tasks.

"You bet." Her reflection smiled at me from the mirror. "Standard government issue. Like it?"

"Not too bad," I said. "Why don't you come over here so I can see it better?"

CHAPTER 20

One more piece from Max. With it, unless I was way off track, I'd be able to fit most of the rest of it together. I'd have a *why* and I'd have a *who*. I could stop looking over my shoulder. The trouble, I thought, was going to be getting it out of him. But as it turned out, I needn't have worried.

Clearly, he was well on the way to mending. With his bed cranked to a sitting position he looked comfortable, even cheerful. His face had lost its pallor and begun to plump out, and his mustache was sprouting again, as exuberant as ever, if a little grayer. The metal contraptions on his legs were still in place, bulky and awkward under the sheet, but the rope-and-pulley arrangement had been removed, so the place didn't look like a torture chamber anymore.

He was reading a magazine, propping it on a tray attached to the bed. He was, I saw with surprise, smoking a small black cigar; somewhat gingerly but with obvious relish. As I pushed the door quietly open he was putting the cigar down on a saucer to take a sip from the spout of a covered plastic cup, all the time continuing to read.

"Hi, Max," I said.

His hand twitched, his head jerked up. The cup dropped onto the floor and bounced into a corner. The cap popped off. Orange liquid spurted over the linoleum. Max's eyes bugged out at me. "*Chris!*" He gagged, coughed. "I thought you were—I thought—"

And the last major piece dropped firmly into place. "What did you think I was, Max?"

"I—" He got his voice going again. "I thought you were still in Sicily." He managed a flabby smile. "Hey, I'm glad to see you, buddy. When did you get back?"

I shook my head. "You dropped that cup because you thought I was still in Sicily? You practically choked because you thought I was still in Sicily?"

"Well, you gave me a start, partner. I thought—"

"You thought I was dead, Max."

As of course he had. That was what I'd come to find out, what I'd expected to find out, and what I'd been hoping I wouldn't find out. The story Antuono had put out to the press had said simply that a taxi on its way to the airport had been blown up, resulting in the killing of an unidentified passenger. Why should Max or anyone else assume it was I—unless they'd had a hand in it? "I think it might be helpful," Antuono had said, "if the person who tried to kill you were to believe he succeeded."

And so it had been. It had helped me find my would-be killer: none other than my old friend Max. Signor Massimiliano Caboto—lively companion, drinking crony, jolly descendant of the illustrious Giovanni Caboto.

As moments of triumph go, I thought sourly, this was far from a winner. I didn't feel like exulting, and I wasn't even consumed with satisfyingly righteous wrath at Max's perfidy. On the other hand, I wasn't wallowing in the Slough of

Despond, either. Vexed, that's what I was. I'd wanted it to be Croce, or maybe Salvatorelli, or best of all, the evil, faceless Mob; I certainly hadn't wanted it to be Max, and the fact that it was made me damn irritated with him.

"Wait a second now," he said, rubbing his forehead with his fingertips. "My mind's about as sharp as a doorknob with all the pills I pop. You know, now that I think of it, I think somebody did mention you were dead."

"Oh, sure. Who would that have been, Max?"

"Well, let's see now . . ." He picked up the cigar and took a couple of puffs, temporizing like mad. But who was there to name that I couldn't easily enough talk with later?

"No, it was you, Max," I said. "You're the one who had that bomb put in my bag."

He had gained back his wits by now, and decided the way he wanted to play this. He blinked at me through the cigar smoke, his expression humorous and wry, a man who didn't quite get the joke yet, but was willing to go along with it. "All right, I'll bite. Tell me, why would I want to put a bomb in your bag?"

"To keep me from finding out that you'd cut away the back of Ugo's Uytewael and replaced it with a phony back."

"Ah, I see. Of course." A flick of ash into the saucer. "And just how the hell would I manage that? I've never even had it in my shop. Check with Ugo."

"I did check with Ugo. He said you're the one who worked with the shippers to have his collection sent down to Sicily. Obviously, you'd have had plenty of opportunity."

Or maybe not so obviously. It had taken long enough to occur to me.

"Opportunity?" Max said. "What does that have to do with anything? Amedeo had it in his museum for a week. Benedetto Luca could have gotten his hands on it there, too. So could the whole damn staff. Clara Gozzi's the one who brought it back from London, for Christ's sake. Or are you accusing her, too?"

"Nope, just you, buddy."

"Look—would you mind sitting down? You're making me nervous." The jokey good humor was wearing thin. He was no longer smiling. The cigar lay in its saucer.

"I'll stand. I'm not staying long."

"Fine, suit yourself. Okay, let's say for the sake of argument I could have done it. What would be the point? What would I want with the back of an old panel?"

"You could forge a Terbrugghen on it and then you and Mike Blusher could use it in a swindle."

"The guy with the Rubens? I don't even know him."

I shook my head. "You're slipping. You told me you'd done business with him."

"I said—?"

"At dinner last week with Amedeo and Benedetto." Another fragment that had meant nothing at the time.

Max frowned, licked his lips, made a partial recovery. "Oh—well—*business* with him, sure, but I don't *know* him. I mean—"

"Max, there's no point in this. I'm going now."

"Chris, wait—"

I hesitated. There were loose ends. If he wanted to talk, I would stay a while longer.

"Let me ask you this," he said. "Can you really believe I'd try to kill you over something like this? To cover up some stupid little swindle?"

"It's pretty hard to believe, all right."

"Well, there you are."

"But I believe you'd kill me to cover up a murder."

"A mur—"

"You're the one who stole Clara's Rubens." It occurred to me that I was beginning to enjoy this. One more thing never to tell Louis.

"*What?* Out of my own shop? Jesus Christ, who's the one on the pills, you or me?"

"Your watchman caught you and you wound up killing him. Right?"

"I don't believe I'm hearing this. I mean, Giampietro, he was an old friend."

"So was I an old friend."

He swallowed and raised his hands, palms out; a placating gesture. "Chris, do me a favor and give this some thought before you do anything stupid. You *know* this doesn't add up."

"Oh, it adds up. Amedeo told me he called you right after the Pinacoteca break-in. He wanted to warn you there might be more thefts. It took me a long time to see what that meant."

He tried to laugh, not successfully. "All right, don't keep me in suspense. What does it mean?"

"It gave you a chance to jump on the bandwagon. You hopped out of bed, went downtown, and took Clara's painting from your own shop, figuring everybody would assume the same gang was involved. Which is exactly what everybody did."

I took a deep breath. I was positive I was right, but all the same I was somewhat in advance of the available facts here. And I wanted to get more information from him, not give it to him. "That list of names you had was just so much camouflage, wasn't it?"

"The hell it was," he said hotly. "Amedeo was on it, the two guys who installed the security system were on it—"

"I'm not saying you couldn't name five people, Max. I'm saying it was a smoke screen all the same."

"Smoke screen!" He gestured angrily at his legs. "You think those bastards did this to me because of some stupid smoke screen?"

I didn't have an answer for that yet.

My silence encouraged him. He pushed the bed tray roughly aside. The saucer clattered to the floor with the cigar. Ashes mingled with orange juice. "This gets nuttier by the second. First you walk in here and tell me I tried to kill you. Five minutes later you tell me I screwed around with one of Ugo's paintings and then forged this Terborch—"

"Terbrugghen, Max," I said. "Terbrugghen."

He shook his head impatiently. "Terborch, Terbrugghen. Then I'm supposed to be in some kind of scam with Mike Blusher, for God's sake. Five minutes after that you tell me I robbed a painting in my own shop and killed an old man who was like a father to me."

He licked his lips again and pulled himself a little higher on the bed. "Look, you said—I *think* you said—I tried to kill you to keep you from finding out about Ugo's picture. Only you also said the *real* reason was to keep you from finding out I stole the Rubens and killed Giampietro. Well, which is it? Am I missing something, or what? Is there supposed to be some connection there?"

"I don't know the connection yet," I said.

"Well, what *do* you know, for Christ's sake?" he asked, spilling over with righteous anger of his own. "That Amedeo called me to tell me about the break-in? He called every god-dam gallery-owner in Bologna! What the hell are you picking on *me* for?"

But I'd thought that through before I'd come. Sure, a lot of people could have piggybacked on the museum robbery and stolen the Rubens. For that matter, a lot of other people had access to Ugo's Uytewael before it was shipped to Sicily. And sure, Max wasn't the only person in Italy who knew Mike Blusher. And true, there were even other people—not very many, though—with the skill to forge the Terbrugghen, the van Eyck, the panel itself.

But who else was there to whom *all* these things applied? No one; only Max.

"Look, you're not seeing this right," he said when I ticked these points off to him. "Why—"

"Added to which, your ears almost fell off when I walked in here. That was enough all by itself."

He opened his mouth to argue some more, but gave up at last, sinking back against the pillows. "All right, Chris. What are you going to do?"

"I'm going to call Antuono. So long, Max." I headed for the door.

"Chris, wait."

I stopped.

"We go back a long way, Chris."

I said nothing. I preferred not to think about that.

"You have to believe I never wanted to hurt you," he said. "I tried like hell to keep you from going to Sicily, remember that? But you just wouldn't listen. . . . I just didn't know what else to do." His eyes gleamed. "I swear to God, Chris—I told him I didn't want you killed, not even hurt."

"Who'd you get to do it?" I asked. "Who put the bomb in my bag?"

215

He gave me a wry smile. "Bologna's like anyplace else. If you have the money and you know the right people, you can get anything done."

"Well, you sure seem to know the right people, Max."

"But the thing I want you to know—the important thing— is that I just wanted you scared off, just a loud noise, basically. At least tell me you believe that."

"I don't." I started for the door again

"Wait—will you at least let me explain? Then go ahead and do whatever you think is right. I won't try to stop you."

I hung back.

"Come on, Chris, what is there to lose? I won't lie to you, I promise."

"All right, Max." But first I pulled the door open. I had seen too many movies, read too many books, where someone confronts the villain, announces that he is on his way to the police, and then hangs around to chat, with uniformly unfortunate results. I couldn't imagine Max doing me any harm in the condition he was in, but I was taking no chances.

"Sit down, will you?" he said. "I don't want to talk up at you."

I sat a good six feet away from him. "Go ahead."

It was a rambling, teary, self-justifying story that took almost half an hour. His difficulties had begun, he said, when his wife developed ovarian cancer. Bills had piled up, first from unsuccessful medical treatments, then from prodigiously expensive alternative therapies. In a year he was $150,000 in debt. His business was on the edge of failure, the creditors already squabbling over the proceeds. And more money was needed for a new course of ozone therapy and immunostimulants in Venezuela.

Then had come Amedeo Di Vecchio's lifesaving call in the middle of the night. There were art thieves afoot! Who knew who their next victim might be? As I'd surmised, Max had jumped at the unexpected chance, making off with Clara's Rubens and killing—accidentally killing, he said—the old watchman who'd come upon him in the act. Nine days later, while he was still trying to find a receiver for the picture, Giulia died. His crushing need for money abated. The painting

216

was put in a bank vault in Genoa while he thought about what to do with it.

Max had a problem. Not the police, but the Mafia. They found it not at all amusing that someone had horned in on their meticulously executed robberies, to make a clumsy and amateurish heist of his own. They didn't like being exploited, and they'd let it be known that whoever was responsible might surely expect a word or two of reproach from them. When they found him.

So Max sat nervously on his secret for over a year, and then another opportunity presented itself, a way out. Ugo Scoccimarro, moving back to Sicily from Milan, asked Max to oversee the shipping of his collection to his new home. Among the paintings was one that Ugo himself had never seen: a Joachim Uytewael that Clara Gozzi had bought for him in London and that was now at the Pinacoteca being authenticated. As Ugo's agent, Max had no difficulty in picking up the picture at the museum for hand delivery to the Milanese shippers.

But he did it by way of a two-day stop at his workshop, where he cut the face of the painting from the panel. The sawed-off back was replaced with a copy, the exposed edges were hidden with a thick layer of bogus *cañamograss*, and the piece was reframed. If there were differences from the original, as no doubt there were, Ugo would never notice. How could he? He'd never seen the original. The Uytewael was then shipped off to Sicily with the rest of the collection, while the multitalented Max used the old panel itself as the base for a painstakingly forged Terbrugghen *Lute Player*. The "van Eyck" that he then painted over it was an added subtlety.

"What's all this got to do with the Rubens?" I asked.

"Everything." I had the impression he was disappointed in me for not having seen it for myself. "It was my way of getting rid of that damn Rubens without the Mafia finding out I had anything to do with it. I got it into one of Salvatorelli's shipments to Blusher, along with the fake Terbrugghen—"

"So Salvatorelli was part of this, too?"

Max shook his head. "I do a lot of business with them. I'm always around the warehouse. It was nothing to slip the pictures into one of those big shipments to Seattle. And I figured

Seattle was far enough away so the Mafia'd never connect me with it when the picture turned up."

"But they did."

His hand went to his knees. "Yeah."

"I don't get it, Max. What was the point? You never tried to collect any money on the Rubens. Blusher donated it to the museum."

"Ah, that was the beauty part," he said with every appearance of pride.

He'd given up the idea of getting money for the Rubens almost from the start. Selling it to a crooked receiver or turning it in for the insurance reward, even through a third party, would very likely have led the Mafia to him, a prospect he didn't care to think about.

So he had conceived the idea of using it, through Blusher, as a come-on. Its appearance in the Seattle warehouse would create plenty of preliminary media attention. Then, when the reward was later donated to the museum, there would be even more, and any lingering skepticism about Blusher's motives and honesty would vanish. This would be especially helpful when the second unexplained item in the shipment, ostensibly a skillful van Eyck forgery, turned out to have a "genuine" Terbrugghen under it.

"And that's the story," Max said. "I won't go into the sordid business details."

He didn't have to. It was an old scam. The newly famous, long-lost Terbrugghen could now be sold to a wide-eyed collector who had heard and read all about it. Making a few extra copies of the painting (something Max had neglected to mention) and also selling them as the original was nothing new, either. The trick was to make sure the buyers were: (a) naive; (b) out of the international art mainstream; and (c) from widely separated parts of the world—say, Oman, South Korea, and Uruguay.

If Max and Blusher managed to sell all four copies at roughly $400,000 each, the total would come to $1,600,000, against which the donation of the Rubens reward was no more than a modest investment. But of course Blusher had been too eager, too obvious, too out-and-out dumb. Max didn't know that part of it yet, but I thought I'd leave it to someone else to tell him.

"And now," he said wistfully, "I've got what I deserve, Chris. I'm a cripple for life. I'm still $100,000 in debt. I'll never have a single day free from pain. And most terrible of all, Chris"—his voice trembled, cracked; the implication was of feelings too profound for speech—"most terrible of all, I have to live with Giampietro's death . . . and what I almost did to you."

He dropped his chin to his chest and spoke in a monotone. "Isn't that punishment enough, Chris?"

I sighed and stood up.

His head lifted. "What are you going to do?"

"I'm going to call Colonel Antuono," I said.

CHAPTER 21

I would have, too, but as I walked through the lobby of the hotel on my way up to our room, one of the morning-coated men behind it answered a telephone and signaled me with a raised forefinger.

"For you, *dottore*. He says important." The forefinger described an elegant arc, directing me to a house telephone where I could take the call.

"Do you want to recover the paintings?" was the startling greeting. The words were in Italian, rushed and indistinct, tumbling frantically over each other. This, I thought, was the "somewhat agitated gentleman" who had tried to reach me earlier.

I suppose I ought to say that I responded with a thrill of

220

excitement and anticipation, but the truth is, I was annoyed. I wanted to go upstairs and tell Anne about Max. I wanted to call Antuono. Then I wanted to get on the train and go to Lake Maggiore with Anne. I didn't want to talk to some raving Italian about some harebrained scheme to get back the stolen paintings.

"What paintings?" I said querulously. "Who is this?"

"What paintings? Do you think I'm playing a game with you? Are you testing how far you can go? I'm telling you, I'll destroy them!"

His voice was unsettling. He seemed to be shouting, but muffling the sound with a cloth over the mouthpiece. The result was a disembodied croak, a breathless, disturbing combination of bellicosity and trepidation. The skin on the back of my neck prickled. Was it conceivable he actually had the paintings?

"Now look," I said, trying to sound reasonable, reassuring, "if you really have the paintings, there's no need—"

"Shut up. Leave the hotel. Walk quickly to the corner of Via Nazario, by the back of the fruit market. Wait there. Do it at once. Hang up and go outside."

"Wait, I don't know where it is—"

"Outside, then to your left one block. There won't be another chance, you understand?"

"All right, give me five minutes. I have to—"

"You think I'm insane? No. No telephone calls to your carabinieri friends, no running upstairs to your girlfriend. I warn you—"

He knew about Antuono, about Anne. That meant he knew me. He was disguising his voice. That meant I knew him. I searched in my pocket for a pen and tried to catch the attention of the man behind the desk. If I could scribble a note to Anne—

"Stop!" the voice yawped in my ear. "I can see you."

I stopped dead. I was standing in a glassed-in vestibule at the entrance to the lobby, separated from Via Montegrappa by a row of four clear-glass doors. Across the narrow street was a row of three-story buildings with shops on the ground floor and shuttered windows above. I scanned the upper stories without being able to see anything. Was he really watching me? The situation's comic-opera aspects, marked until then, vanished. A lone shiver crawled down the center of my back. I had the unpleasant feeling that things were about to get away from me; had already gotten away from me.

"Oh, yes," he said triumphantly, "that's right, I can see. I have binoculars. Put your pen back in your pocket." When I did, he said: "There, that's better," and laughed, but there were brittle shards of panic in it. "I've had enough," he told me. "This is it, things are getting too difficult for me. I warn you, I'll burn them!" Possibly he was faking, trying to make me believe he was on the edge of hysteria. If so, he was doing a good job.

"It's too risky," he babbled on. "It's not worth it. If you don't want to do it, fine, excellent, to hell with them. I'll just—"

"All right, take it easy. But what do you have in mind? You have to tell me—"

"I have to tell you nothing! I'm finished arguing with you! Go now, this instant, otherwise it's all off. I mean what I say. The pictures are on your conscience!" And the connection was broken.

"Wait!" I said. "Are you there?" I jiggled the telephone. "Hello?"

I was stalling, of course, trying to buy time for thought, but there was only a rush of questions, jumbled and chaotic. Did this lunatic really have the paintings? What was it he wanted me to do? And why me? And was it really someone I knew? Croce? Salvatorelli? Di Vecchio, even, or Benedetto Luca? Surely not Ugo? Clara?

And of course the critical question: Was the object not restitution but something else? Max had tried to kill me once. Was this another attempt, before I got to Antuono? No, impossible. I'd left him a mere ten minutes before; besides, how could he know I'd go to the hotel and not to Antuono's office? Someone else, then? Had I made it onto the Mafia's hit list, too? If so, what better way to lure me than to tell me that the retrieval—in fact the continued existence—of a Bellini, a Perugino, a Giorgione, a Correggio . . . all depended on my cooperation?

But by the time I replaced the receiver, I'd made up my mind to go. I pushed out through the doors and turned left, as directed. I'd like to say that I was being courageous, but the truth is that I wasn't being anything. I didn't make a conscious choice, I just started walking. I couldn't think of anything else to do.

The Mercato Ugo Bassi was a vast farmers' market under a single roof. Walking to Via Nazario took me to the alley at the rear of it, where the delivery dock was. The back of an Italian farmers' market isn't much different from the back of an American one, except that the cheeses smell better, or at least riper. There were sweating men unloading vegetables from decrepit trucks; piles of empty crates; lettuce leaves and spoiled fruit on the ground; puddles of rancid water everywhere. The day was overcast and muggy, the fresh smells slightly tainted with rot.

I stood in the center of the alley where I could be seen easily, and in a few seconds a small blue car—hadn't I seen it somewhere before?—threaded its slow way through the trucks and workmen, and stopped in front of me, leaving its engine running. The door was pushed open. I got in. The one coherent thought I remember having was: If I get killed, how is Anne ever going to find out what happened to me?

As soon as I pulled the door closed, the car continued slowly down Via Montegrappa, rocking over the alley's uneven cobblestones. I recognized the driver the moment I looked at him: Pietro, the gorillalike thug who had smashed in Max's face and tossed me with such ease into the street, just a block from where we were now. Somehow I wasn't surprised. And I recognized the car now. The last time I'd seen it, it had bounced me around, too; only then I'd been on the outside of it, scudding painfully over the top.

When we stopped at Via dell'Indipendenza, Pietro turned to study me. It was the first time I'd gotten a good look at him: shaven, compact head on a muscular cylinder of a neck, dull, sleepy eyes in a stolid face with an immense, underslung jaw. Fred Flintstone without the hair. Bulky arms bulged inside a blue leather jacket like sausages about to burst their casings. Through the jacket's open front I could see the strap of a shoulder holster. I returned his look as steadily as I could, fighting down the impulse to fling open the door and bolt. As we pulled onto the main street he grunted something.

"What?" I said nervously. "I didn't hear you."

He looked at me again. The heavy eyelids went slowly down, then up. He had long, thick eyelashes. "*Ciao,*" he said.

"Oh. *Ciao.*"

I settled back a little more easily. Nice to know there weren't any hard feelings.

CHAPTER 22

At the end of Via dell'Indipendenza he swung around the Piazza Medaglia d'Oro and into the parking lot of the railroad station. It was 11:00 A.M. There were people milling around in comforting numbers. He pointed at a public telephone. "Go there and wait for a call."

I walked to the telephone much reassured. If they'd been planning to kill me, I'd be speeding along an untraveled country road by now, not walking unaccompanied through a public place. With that all-absorbing worry removed, I began to get excited. Was it possible that the paintings were really about to be recovered? That I was going to be the instrument? There were all kinds of possible reasons for the recovery being handled in this peculiar way. Maybe the person with the paintings was hoping to collect an insurance company reward, but was fearful of dealing directly with the company or the police. I would be a perfect intermediary: uninvolved, knowledgeable—

The telephone rang. I snatched it up.

"Norgren?" The same voice as before.

"Yes."

"Listen. There is a buyer for the paintings. But he insists that an expert confirm they are what we say they are. He wanted to bring his own consultant to do this, but he was told no."

"Why?" I asked, as much to slow him down as anything. He was difficult to understand, and I wanted time to think through what he was saying. And although his voice was still muffled, I was beginning to hear something familiar in the cadence. If I could get him to keep talking . . .

"Why?" he repeated. "Because I don't trust him and I don't trust his expert, all right? He was told a reliable expert would be provided, a respected museum curator."

"And that's me?"

"That's you."

"Does he know it's me?"

"When you get there, he'll find out."

"And he agreed?"

"No more questions," he said irritably. "What's the difference to you? Now, you will be taken—"

"Why should I do this?" I demanded. "Do you actually think I'm going to help you get rid of those paintings?"

I wasn't being particularly brave. The area around the station entrance was filled with people. Pietro was thirty feet away, watching me without interest, placid and sleepy-looking, chewing on something (his cud?). All I had to do if I wanted to get away was duck into the station.

"You told me I could help recover those paintings," I said. "You didn't say—"

"And so you can. After you authenticate them and leave, you're free to notify your carabinieri friends as to the buyer's identity. Thus," he said almost affably, "a felonious receiver will be apprehended, the paintings will be recovered for their

226

rightful owners, and you'll have the gratitude of the Italian nation."

And you'll have your five hundred million lire or whatever it is, I thought. "How am I supposed to know the identity of the buyer?" I asked him. "I don't imagine he's going to introduce himself."

"You'll know, don't worry."

"Why are you doing this to him?"

"I told you, I don't trust him, I don't like him. What do I care—" he stopped abruptly. "Enough questions. There's no more time. Go back to the automobile."

"Look, I need time to get ready for this," I said brilliantly. "It'll have to wait until tomorrow. I can't just go in and authenticate these things without preparation. I need—"

"You need nothing! It's now or never, do you understand?" His agitation level had shot up again. "I'm sorry I got involved with this in the first place. It's not worth it—one problem after another . . ."

I knew who it was. There had been one too many familiar phrases sputtered in that familiar, frazzled manner. Bruno Salvatorelli. I glanced again at the bustling, inviting entrance, and at the bovine Pietro chewing away, staring into the middle distance. What if I dashed into the station now? I could get away with ease and tell Antuono what I knew.

But what did I know? Antuono already suspected Salvatorelli. And I still didn't know where the pictures were. We'd get nowhere, and Salvatorelli would find some other way of disposing of the paintings, perhaps for good.

". . . if you don't want to do it," he was ranting, "just say so, you understand me? I'll throw the damned things in the Reno and be done with them!"

That I doubted, but I couldn't chance it. "All right, I'll do it," I said. "But first I have to know—"

"You have to know shit," he said, and hung up.

Pietro drove a few blocks beyond the station to a neighborhood of nondescript apartment buildings. With featureless exteriors of raw concrete, they might have been built ten years ago or ten weeks ago. The ground floors were mostly occupied by small light-manufacturing operations—electrical switches, cardboard containers—or various kinds of wholesalers. All very functional and commonplace. It was hard to believe we were a five-minute walk from the colonnaded Renaissance streets of the city center.

We parked in front of a ten- or twelve-story building that looked like every other building on the block, and entered a marble lobby devoid of ornament or furniture. I tucked the address away in my mind: Via dell'Abbate 18. We took the elevator to the seventh story and walked to the end of a musty corridor that hadn't seen much recent use; it certainly hadn't seen much care. Pietro knocked on an unnumbered door.

"Who's there?" someone called from the other side.

"Pietro" was the mumbled reply.

What, no secret knock, no coded greeting? What kind of way was this to run a big-time heist?

The door was opened, first a crack and then all the way. Behind it—no surprise—was Ettore, Pietro's scarred, tough partner with the chewed-up ear and the mashed-down nose. Unlike his more easygoing associate, Ettore apparently hadn't forgiven me for inconveniencing him the previous week. There was no friendly "Ciao," only a malignant narrowing of his eyes and a peremptory jerk of the head to motion me in.

The moment I was inside, the hairs on the back of my neck lifted. The pictures were here, all right; I could smell the acrid, leathery odor of old paint and ancient canvas. But all I could see, aside from some scattered, littered pieces of office furniture, was a nervous, buglike man with a polka-dot bow tie, who was standing near the single dirty window and watching us.

Again with no sense of surprise, I saw that it was Filippo Croce. If anything, I felt a little let down. "Is this the buyer?" I asked.

"Let's get to work," Ettore said. "Come on, *dottore*, earn your money. The sooner we start, the sooner we finish."

He's assuming I'm one of them, I realized. They think I'm being paid for this. Salvatorelli hasn't told them what's going on.

It had taken a few seconds for Croce to recognize me.

"*You're* their expert?" he asked, advancing. "*You're* going to authenticate them?" His tone was part incredulity, part glee.

What was he so happy about? "Why not?" I responded gruffly. "You don't trust my judgment?" I saw no reason to disabuse anyone there of the notion that I was one of the crowd; just another crook. And I now understood why Croce, as buyer, had agreed to meet with, and be seen by, an unknown third party like me. He'd been told I was "their" expert, a bought, bent consultant.

"No, no, I trust it implicitly," Croce said. "It's just that I'm quite surprised. Delighted, really. I hope this is the first of many—"

"Let's get on with it," Ettore growled. "They're over here."

I went to the dusty table he'd gestured at, and involuntarily let out my breath. What I'd mistaken for an untidy pile of rubbish—rolled-up old blueprints or mechanical drawings—was, it appeared, an untidy pile of rolled-up Old Masters worth approximately $100,000,000. Not that Croce would be paying anything near that. There were also two painted panels, each about two feet by a foot-and-a-half.

I recognized the panels immediately. Two Madonnas Enthroned, one by Fra Filippo Lippi that had been taken from Clara's collection, and one by Giovanni Bellini from the Pinacoteca. They were a joy to see, their authenticity fairly jumping out at me. All the same, I thought that a little theater wouldn't hurt. I picked them up gingerly, peered at them from a couple of inches away, turned them over, muttered a little, and laid them carefully back on the table.

"Well?" Croce asked.

"They're the real thing."

"Ah!" he exclaimed. "I knew it the minute I saw them."

He sidled up to me, prattling away. "I saw them and I knew. I had faith, I had conviction. Basically, one appraises from the soul, from the innate, spiritual perception an art lover humbly brings to a timeless work of art. Don't you agree, *dottore?*"

I wondered if that was the way he appraised his Comic Abstractionists, too. "Maybe," I said. "But what do you need me for, then?"

229

"Faith," he said, "has its limits. This is a business matter."

"Come on, let's go, let's go," Ettore said. "We're in a hurry." He pointed at the rolled-up paintings. "Get on with it."

"That's, uh, not going to be possible," I said.

Croce looked shocked. "Not possible?"

"Huh?" Pietro said.

Ettore's battered face hardened in a way that made me back up a step. "What's the problem?" he asked.

The problem was the condition of the canvases. From the look of them they'd been rolled up two years ago and never unrolled since. Probably they'd been bound with string or rubber bands until today. The rolling-up had been done with care, thank God, but no matter how careful you are, you can't take a thick, stiff piece of fabric that's been stretched out flat for centuries and curl it up into a cylinder without doing harm. The canvas buckles, and the old paint and varnish, friable as a coat of nail polish, splits and loosens. If you then try to unroll it two years later without proper preparation, you multiply the destruction tremendously.

Add this to the mutilation suffered when they'd been cut from their frames—whatever had been overhung by the lip of the frame had necessarily been sliced through—and the result was twenty-one irreplaceable masterpieces gravely damaged. Sure, they could always be repaired with modern techniques and materials that simulated the old ones, but that magic, indefinable beauty—what it was that had made them masterpieces in the first place—was beyond the reach of twentieth-century formulas and recipes.

"I can't unroll them," I said, and briefly explained.

Croce's foxy face clenched with suspicion. "I'm not paying for anything I haven't seen."

Ettore shrugged. "*I'll* unroll them." He reached for the nearest one.

I grabbed his arm. He looked down at it, then up at me. "Don't do that, *dottore*."

I let go. I was sure he wouldn't need much of an excuse to take up where he'd left off on Via Ugo Bassi. A question of restoring honor, I supposed. He'd been on the pavement when Pietro came along and chucked me into the street.

"You unroll them," I said, "and they'll crack in a thousand places. They won't be worth anything to anybody."

The three of them looked at each other, not so sure anymore that I was one of the boys.

"I won't pay for anything that's damaged," Croce said. He nervously patted his gleaming hair, wiped his hands, and fingered the edge of one of the canvas cylinders, delicately bending up a small corner. It was as stiff as dried leather.

He bit his lip. "He's right," he said. "But you must understand I can't accept these without authentication. My instructions are clear."

We were at an impasse. Unrolling them was out of the question—I would have fought off Ettore and Pietro to prevent it—but I didn't want to see the deal fall through, because that would mean the pictures might go back underground for years, maybe even into the river, as Salvatorelli had threatened. I couldn't think of what to do. We all eyed each other uncertainly. Oddly enough, it was Pietro, surfacing briefly from his torpor, who resolved it.

"Well, can't you tell without unrolling them?" he asked. He picked one up in his big hand—I flinched, but he was gentle—and held it up to his eye like a telescope. "You can see inside a little," he reported hopefully, and handed it to me. "Maybe with a flashlight?"

"Oh, well, yes, of course," I said quickly, taking it. "All I said was I wouldn't unroll them. I never said I couldn't tell if they were genuine or not." At least I hoped not. No one contradicted me, so I suppose I hadn't. "But signor Croce here said he had to see them for himself, that he couldn't take my word for it."

Now, as hoped, Pietro and Ettore swung their persuasive glowers in Croce's direction. He cleared his throat, rubbed his temples, tugged on his bow tie. "I'll have to speak with my client about it."

Ettore jerked a thumb at a telephone sitting in a corner, on the dusty floor. "Call him."

"No, no, that's impossible. I'll see him tomorrow."

Ettore shook his head. "No deal. We either do it now, or not at all. You don't trust the great *dottore*?"

"Ah, you can trust him," Pietro said reassuringly. "Come on."

The sides had shifted again. Now it was Ettore, Pietro, and me against the irresolute Croce.

"All right," he said at last. "I'm at your mercy, *dottore*."

So he was; more than he knew. "Don't worry," I told him, "I won't lead you astray."

I was a little disturbed—but only a little—at my previously unsuspected capacity for duplicity. Tony Whitehead, I'm sure, would have been astounded. And probably delighted. Without giving Croce time to reconsider, I got down to work. I don't remember exactly how I got through the next thirty minutes, but it was a virtuoso performance. I went from one rolled canvas to the next, peering keenly into them (without benefit of flashlight, no less), pointing them toward the window and minutely rotating them—a degree this way, two degrees that way—like big kaleidoscopes. After an appreciative murmur or two, I would make my pronouncement.

"Aha, Correggio, without a doubt; the soft, painterly, almost antilinear style, the luscious flesh tones. . . . And this, this with its icy elegance of line can be nothing but a Bronzino. . . . And this? Let me see— Ah! Tintoretto, no question about it. The masterly use of *repoussoir*, the receding diagonals . . .

It was sheer mummery, of course. I couldn't see a thing. But luckily for me, they had a list of the paintings to refer to, and I somehow managed to bring it off. In a sense I wasn't lying, because I was sure they were authentic, even if I didn't happen to know a few trivial details, such as which was which. I knew it from their smell, their feel, their condition, a hundred little clues. Maybe even by way of a little innately spiritual perception.

"All right," Ettore said the instant Croce hesitantly nodded his acceptance of the last one. "Where's the money?"

"I'll drive you there," Croce said, darting his tongue over his lips. His protuberant eyes glistened. He was looking extremely shifty. More so than usual.

"That wasn't the arrangement," Ettore said. His face had stiffened, darkened, as if a shutter had clanked down over it.

"Of course it was. You're trying to change things now."
Croce's voice was on the rise. "What do—"

"The money was to be left in two packages, wrapped in
paper. Somewhere nearby."

"It is, it is! Only fifteen minutes from here. Come, I'll
take you."

"No, you'll tell us," Ettore said stonily.

"But—" Croce's forehead shone with perspiration. He
looked at all three of us, but help wasn't coming from anywhere. "All right, then," he said. "It's in the Giardini
Margherita, near the tennis courts. Just to the east of them,
in the shrubbery, next to a stone wall, there's a—a concrete
pedestal, a vent of some sort with metal grills in the sides. The
grill on the east side, away from the courts, toward the wall,
it comes off. The packages are inside, taped to the back of it.
All right, are you satisfied? Now, if it's all the same to you,
I'll take these and leave."

He said it as if he didn't think he'd get away with it, and
he didn't.

Ettore ignored him. "Pietro, I'll drive out there and see if
it's all right."

"I assure you—" Croce said.

"If it's all right I'll call, and you can let him have the paintings. Then drive back to where we started from. You
understand?"

Pietro frowned while he absorbed this. "What if you don't
find it?"

"He'll find it, he'll find it," Croce bleated.

"Well, I guess I'll go now," I put in. "I've done what I came
for." Croce was lying, and I didn't want to be there when
they found out. I wanted to get the hell out of there and get
on the telephone to Antuono.

I didn't get away with it, either. "You stay, too," Ettore
said.

"What for? I've done what I was paid for. I—"

"If I don't call in half an hour," Ettore told Pietro, "take
the paintings and get out of here."

"Now you'd better listen to me—" Croce began.

"What about these two?" Pietro asked.

"Take them with you. If they don't want to go, beat the shit out of them. If they give you too much trouble, just shoot them and leave them."

Pietro nodded and patted his jacket, over the holster.

This exchange effectively silenced Croce. I wasn't making much noise, either. But a few minutes after Ettore left I probed for a little more information from Croce.

"Who's your buyer?" I asked offhandedly.

He frowned at me. His eyes swelled with affront. No stratum of society is without its code of ethics.

"Shut up," Pietro said. He sounded edgy. "I don't want any more talking. Sit down."

We sat. So did Pietro, first meaningfully unzipping the front of his jacket. It had begun to rain. For a long time the only sounds were the water thrumming against the window, the traffic noises, and the occasional whine of a jet.

Pietro looked at his watch frequently. After the ninth or tenth time he spoke: "Ten more minutes."

"Don't worry," Croce said with an unconvincing laugh, "he'll call. That vent isn't so easy to find."

Fifteen minutes later the increasingly uneasy Pietro looked at his watch a final time, chewed his lip, and came to a decision. He stood up, shoved a big leather suitcase across the floor with his foot, and pointed at Croce. "You."

"Me?"

"Put those wooden ones in there." The more nervous he got the more he slid into a kind of slow motion.

"These?" Croce said. "The panels?"

Pietro's heavy eyelids drooped. The big muscles in his heavy jaw moved. He took a ponderous step forward.

"All right," Croce said hurriedly. "Very well. They'll have to be wrapped first. I can—"

"No wrapping," Pietro said. "Just put them in."

"But he's right," I said. "You can't just toss them into a suitcase without protection. They'll be—"

The gun came out: stubby, nickel-plated, toylike in the big hand. It waved me quiet, then leveled at Croce. "Do what I say."

"Certainly, at once." Croce knelt, opened the suitcase, and lay the two Madonnas side by side in it, handling them with more reverence than I imagined him capable of.

He glanced up from his knees. "At least let me—"

"Now you," Pietro said. The shiny little gun jerked in my direction to indicate which *you* he was talking to. "Put the rest of them in there, too, quick."

I didn't see much room for argument. I picked up the first rolled cylinder, placed it in the suitcase as carefully as I could, and reached for the next one.

It was too methodical to suit him. "Come on, come on, just throw the damn things in."

"Look—" I said.

Pietro gestured for silence again, then stood motionless, head tipped, sleepy eyes suddenly alert. He was listening intently. All I could hear was the rain. He edged up to the window, his back against the wall, and scanned the street, shielding his body behind the casing. I was reminded of a hundred old movies. This was the scene just before the final barrage of bullets from the cops killed all the bad guys. Or maybe it was Indians, arrows, and ranchers.

Pietro turned back to us. "That's it. We're going right now. You, close the suitcase and pick it up," he told Croce. "You"—me again—"grab the rest of them and let's go."

"What do you mean, grab them?"

"Just scoop them up. Hurry up."

"Scoop them up?" I echoed. "You mean just—just—"

With his left hand Pietro reached around the side of the gun's barrel. There was a click that I recognized (those old movies again) as the safety being released. I gulped, bent to the table, and, as carefully as I could, gathered them up in my arms, all twenty-two of those precious, irreplaceable masterpieces, like so many old window shades to be taken down to the dump.

"Now," Pietro said, "out the door."

But at that moment the door, about four feet to Pietro's right, exploded from the wall with a window-rattling crash. Even before it hit the floor a stream of men in heavy vests and blue police uniforms burst into the room, shouting incomprehensible orders and brandishing handguns and rifles. Croce was swept out of the way. Pietro was still blinking with surprise, waiting for his brontosauruslike nerve impulses to make it to his brain and tell him what was going on, when the gun was deftly plucked from his hand. Two burly officers spun him roughly around and shoved him face-first against the wall. More men crowded in; there were brown carabinieri uniforms along with the blue ones. The room was all dust and pandemonium.

I couldn't believe it. I was so relieved I wanted to cheer. I think I did cheer. I know I laughed. "Your timing's great!" I shouted over the racket. "We—"

"*Alto!*" several of them screamed. "*Zitti!*" I didn't have to be told that these amounted to the Italian equivalent of "Freeze!" At the same time three pistols—heavy, malevolent black weapons, nothing like Pietro's shiny little toy—were thrust out at me, trained on the bridge of my nose. All were held by palpably overstrung men in the classic shooter's posture: tautly crouched, gun hand stiffly extended and supported at the wrist by the opposite hand. All three of the weapons were quivering.

Me too. It took me a moment to find my voice. "Gentlemen," I said in my softest manner and without moving a finger, "I . . ."

I what? I wasn't really heading for the door with $100,000,000 worth of stolen art in my arms? It only looks that way? I shrugged and closed my mouth. Things would work themselves out. The worst was over.

Almost. A slight figure approached from the side and peered at me. There was a long-suffering sigh.

"Weren't you supposed to be in America?" asked the Eagle of Lombardy.

"I can explain," I said, staring straight ahead. "Really."

"If you will put those paintings down over there," he said quietly, "I will do my utmost to see that these gentlemen don't shoot you."

At his nod and a few murmured words, they lowered their weapons—rather reluctantly, it seemed to me—and turned away. Antuono, in his black undertaker's suit, looked down his fleshless nose at me as I placed the rolled-up canvases back on the table.

"Colonel—"

"You could have been killed," he said. "Worse, you might have ruined the entire operation."

His prioritizing of possible outcomes did not escape me. "Colonel—"

"Do you know," he said musingly, "if you hadn't turned up blundering about in the midst of things—with the best of intentions, of course—I think I would have felt a sense of disappointment . . . of incompleteness."

He hadn't wasted any time getting under my skin again. I faced him angrily. "I didn't *have* to be here, you know—"

"Indeed."

"I put my life on the line for those paintings. If you'd let me, I could have been helping you all along."

"No doubt."

"Damn it, I told you *days* ago that Croce was involved, didn't I? But no, you—"

His attention had wandered. He was looking over my shoulder, a slow smile actually lighting up his pale eyes. "Wonderful work, Major," he said. "A year's effort—congratulations!" He reached around me to shake hands. "I believe you already know *dottor* Norgren?"

I turned.

"Sure, we're old friends," said Filippo Croce.

CHAPTER 23

Yes, that wonderful facility of mine to make razor-sharp character judgments had done me in again. The odious, transparently disreputable Filippo Croce was in reality Major Abele Foscolo of the *Comando Caribinieri Tutela Patrimonio Artistico*; one of Antuono's most trusted undercover agents. Antuono, in what I now recognized as one of his little jokes, had practically described him to me at our first meeting, specially grown mustache and all.

For almost a year Foscolo-Croce had been working meticulously to establish his credibility as a shady dealer, first building a suspect reputation in Sicily to provide "credentials" that could be checked when he appeared on the scene here. Antuono and Foscolo had quickly zeroed in on the Salvatorellis, but as

238

Antuono kept telling me, it was the paintings he was after, not the people. The important thing was to get the pictures safely back.

And so, just about the time I got to Bologna, Foscolo had begun working his oily charms on Bruno (Paolo had just been killed). The two *Pittura Metafisica* paintings "discovered" in the Trasporti Salvatorelli warehouse had of course (in retrospect, "of course") been planted by the police. Salvatorelli had truly known nothing about them. The raid had been staged to give him convincing proof that Foscolo was indeed the crook he appeared to be, and that he had art-world connections. More important, he was shown to be a "trustworthy criminal"—the phrase was Antuono's, delivered with a straight face. What he meant was that, inasmuch as no arrests were made, "Croce" demonstrated his reliability at keeping names to himself when required.

In a way, this had all been explained to me days ago by Antuono himself, on our drive back to town from Trasporti Salvatorelli. He'd neglected to mention only a couple of trifling particulars: It was fact, not surmise, and Croce happened to be working for *him*.

And all this time I'd gone along thinking he didn't have much of a sense of humor.

"You must see, *dottore*," he said now, leaning over the table and clasping his hands, "that I couldn't very well let you in on our plans. I had to mislead you just a little. I hope you accept my apology."

We were in the Palazzo d'Accursio, not in Antuono's makeshift warren of an office, but in a big, handsome upstairs chamber that he had commandeered, with thick, wall-to-wall red carpeting, red-flocked wallpaper, and massive old furniture. I had been making statements and signing depositions in one part of the palazzo or another for the last three hours, except for a twenty-minute break I'd insisted on to call Anne and tell her what had happened to me.

"I was starting to wonder," she'd said dryly when I reached her. "You hear these stories . . . 'Yes, well, the last time I saw him he said he was going down to the corner for cigarettes. That was back in '54, of course.' . . ."

But I'd heard the breathy tremble in her voice, and it had warmed me. And now for the last half hour I'd been basking in a different kind of warmth, one not experienced before: the freely given gratitude of a relaxed and expansive Eagle of Lombardy. Antuono had been openly impressed with the information I'd provided on Max and Blusher. He had immediately arranged to have Max placed under arrest for murder and attempted murder, and since then he'd been—well, friendly. And unless I'd misheard him, he'd actually offered an apology a moment ago.

"I accept it," I said, "but you misled me more than just a little. You also told me Salvatorelli wasn't a suspect."

He nodded. "We were very near to moving, as you now know. Your . . . explorations were threatening the sensitive balance we had achieved. I wanted you out of our hair." He smiled, pleased with himself. "I believe that's the American expression."

"Well," I admitted, "Salvatorelli had me fooled all by himself, even without your help. I thought he was just another harried businessman." I uncapped one of the small green bottles of mineral water an aide had brought, and poured it into a glass. "And what do you know, he's tied up with the Sicilian Mafia." I drank down the water thirstily, my third bottle.

Antuono smiled. "Well, I wouldn't say that. The *Milanese* Mafia, yes, but that's all. I doubt that the Sicilian Mafia had any direct part in this."

I put down the glass and stared at him. "But you told me— twice you told me—no, *three* times, you said the Sicilian Mafia was—" Laughing, I sank back against the chair. "You just made it up, right? Also to keep me out of your hair."

"I'm afraid so, *dottore*. It was regrettable but necessary."

"No wonder they had no idea who the hell I was down there."

"They . . . ?" Antuono's eyebrows went up, but then he thought better of it, probably out of fatigue, and decided not to pursue it, which was fine with me.

Something else had occurred to me. "And is that why you told me you didn't want me ferreting information out for you—"

"Correct."

"—even though you'd already told the FBI you wanted some help?"

He nodded. "By the time you arrived in Bologna, we no longer needed help. We were sure Salvatorelli had the paintings."

So what Tony had told me about Antuono's asking for my assistance was true, which meant I owed Tony an apology. I grimaced. I hate it when I owe Tony an apology.

I stretched somewhat stiffly, realizing for the first time just how spent and grubby I was. I'd done a lot of sweating that morning and I needed a shower. And I wanted to be with Anne. "Am I free to leave now?"

"Yes, but tell the clerk where we may get in touch with you."

I stood up. Antuono, watching me with his head tipped against the highbacked old chair, suddenly barked with amusement.

"Did I say something funny?" I asked.

"I was thinking of all your warnings to me about the infamous Filippo Croce. It was hard not to laugh at the time, *dottore*. What do you think of him now? Foscolo's good, no?"

I laughed back. "I still don't trust the guy."

We had been on the train for almost two hours. Anne had a paperback mystery open on her lap and I was leafing through the skimpy European edition of *Time*. Both of us were doing more dozing than reading.

It had been a grueling day. By the time I'd gotten back to the hotel and showered, it was after four. Anne got the idea of seeing whether there was a train that would get us to Lake Maggiore that evening, instead of waiting until the next morning. There was; the Rome–Geneva Express would make a two-minute stop in Bologna at 5:04 P.M. We took a taxi to the station, stopping at a grocery store for sliced mortadella, rolls, fruit, and a liter of cheap red wine with a twist-off cap. By the time the train cleared the northern outskirts of Bologna we were happily gorging ourselves in our seats, and since then, dopey with food and wine, we'd been drowsily watching the countryside glide by.

Now we were in the darkening Po Valley south of Milan; flat, rice-growing country with great, rectangular tracts of flooded land separated by long rows of poplars and willows. Power lines alongside the track bed zoomed and swooped. My eyelids started coming down. The magazine folded into my chest.

"Chris?"

"Mm?"

"That agreement of ours—to pick up where we were and just let things take their course. Does it mean we don't see other people, or doesn't it?"

"Go to bed with other people, you mean?" That was my aversion to ambiguity asserting itself again.

"Well, yes."

I lowered the magazine. "What's this? Do I detect a need to put things into nice little black-and-white boxes?"

"Come on, I'm serious."

"Tell me how you feel about it," I said, treading carefully.

She looked out the window. We were whizzing through the only crossing of a tiny village. Bells clanged faintly. "I suppose we shouldn't lay down any rules," she said slowly. "We're adults. We'll be thousands of miles apart. If we feel like seeing other people, we should."

"And if we don't feel like it, we shouldn't."

"Definitely."

"Well," I said, "I don't think I feel like it."

"Good," she said with a sigh, "I'm glad that's settled." She stuffed the book into the pocket on the seatback in front of her, folded up the chair arm that was between us, and settled her head against my shoulder. "I'm going to see if I can get some more sleep."

"Hold it," I said, pushing her off. "What about you?"

"What *about* me? Are you saying that just because you made a commitment, you think I'm obligated to make one, too? Is that the sort of relationship you picture us having?"

"Damn right."

"Chris, that kind of controlling relationship went out in the sixties. You're being manipulative."

"Damn right. Well?"

She looked at me, head tilted, lips pursed, then forcefully pulled my arm against her, patted my shoulder down like a pillow, and settled in again.

"Well, you're lucky," she said against my chest. "As it happens I don't think I feel like it, either."